For Lesley – love you all the muches -
and to Caro Ramsay for polishing my work into
something shinier.

Chapter 1

The wind drops. Silence. The sliver of a moon provides little light and the cold is a living thing. Creeping into bones. Chilling skin.

A crack. A frozen twig snaps. The sound smacks off the tree I'm sitting beneath. Crystal clear. Close. Too close. I bury my face in the thin material of my summer top. Trying to hide the cloud of breath. Hiding it from my hunters.

I want to run. To move. The immobility is uncomfortable but that's nothing compared to my desire to escape. *Craig, sit still.*

I wait for any more sound and wrap my arms around my body to retain heat. The snow on the ground is frozen and my pants are wet - conducting warmth away from me. Every second I'm leaking life.

A small flurry of ice crystals fall. Above me? I look up. The dark canopy of the Norwegian Pine hides all. I slow my breathing. Holding the air. Minimizing my aural signature. It's time to be quiet.

More ice drifts down and a small puff of air touches my cheek. I let my breath go. Just some wind. No one above me.

I wish myself back to the warmth of the cabin that lies less than a mile away. A log fire ripping heat through the building.

A second sound. Faint. Right on the edge of not existing. A crunch? A light touch of a foot to snow? A shuffle of a hand on the forest floor? Same direction. To my left.

MELTDOWN

Putting me in view. I press into the tree. Merging into the bark. Breathing sap.

It's useless. I will be in plain view. They have night vision.

Time to run? Time to stay? I can't sit much longer anyway. I'll freeze to death. I move my head to the right. Slowly. Trees. Nothing but trees. A blessing and a curse. Even if they have night goggles the trees will provide some cover but, in the dark, I can't move with any speed. I've already head butted two trees on my way to where I'm sitting. They, on the other hand, can run flat out. And even if I lose them my footprints are a trail of breadcrumbs.

Click. A soft click. Metal setting metal. Bullet time.

I'm up. Pushing hard against the tree. Throwing myself forward as the sound of a gunshot shatters the silence. Bark explodes around me. A winging shot if I hadn't moved. I roll to the left and try to overcome my cold-sapped muscles. I am running before I'm fully upright. Away from the sound. I grab the first tree and feel the cool texture, rough to my hands and swing behind it. I gather speed. My feet compressing snow with a hollow munch.

There are no shouts from behind. They're too smart to let me know how many. I pray there's only one but I suspect there are more. Wind rushes in my ears as I duck round the next tree and cut hard right. A second bullet creates a whistle as the air is parted at speed.

Trees flash by. Branches whipping me. Iron hard rods. I don't bother with zig-zagging. Distance is key. I will take a right in fifteen trees. I count as I run. Fourteen, fifteen – a hard right and keep running. Thirty trees now. Then another right. Circle back. Don't do the obvious. Thirty and a right. Now for a long run.

I drop to a jog. The cold is leaving me as the run heats me up. It's a false heat. Draining me. Using up calories that I need. I have no food. No method to replace the energy.

I try to orientate myself. Working my head to retrace my steps and turning rights into lefts – backtrack to the cabin and try to figure my direction. This is a deep, dense forest. Millions of acres spread across northern Canada. The moon sits on my left shoulder and the stars are thick when the trees clear. I keep up the jog and skirt a small clearing. I look up and spot the Big Dipper. I follow the stars to find the Pole Star, turn my back on it, leave the clearing and take up the run again. Civilization is south. North is nothing.

Picking up a rhythm as the forest slides passed I want to stop and front up the pursuers but they're an unknown. I have no body count. One on one might work out. One on many won't. Head down and keep pounding. It's the way of things.

I jig right and hit a slope. The wind in my ears and the pumping of blood take the edge off my hearing but there's something. I stop, grab a breath, hold it and listen. Water.

Somewhere close by there's running water. I turn to the sound and let my Doc Martins find traction and push on. I run at right angles to the small slope and stop again to check for sounds behind. Nothing.

MELTDOWN

I stumble on a rock and catch myself before I go flying. Beneath me a spray of water is bouncing off ice. A small waterfall in a stream has kept up enough speed to stave off freezing. Above and below this spot the stream is frozen but there must be flowing water under the ice feeding the waterfall. The stream slides away into the trees. A silver path, free of snow, gleaming in the half-light.

'*Don't use water as an escape.*' My army instructor's voice debunking a movie myth. '*Wet is cold and weight. Wet is bad.*'

I look at the snow-free ice and imagine plunging through to the water below. I leap the waterfall and run into the forest, sprint downstream for a hundred yards, emerge from the trees and leap over, back into the forest to run down a further hundred. Another leap and another hundred. Fifty and a leap. Fifty and a leap. Twenty and a leap. Tiring. A hundred and a leap. It won't fool them but it'll slow them down.

I cut once more and leave the water behind and run up the slope.

Then I'm airborne.

Chapter 2

For an instant I am above the forest canopy. Beneath me a million white Christmas trees point to the sky. I hit the first tree and throw my hands to my face. I plunge down. Snow and branches whipping me. My shoulder connects with a trunk and I'm flipped onto my back and hit the forest floor – hard.

I lie and take stock of my body. Checking for pain. Moving joints to check for breaks. I let my hands brush away debris and hope there's no blood.

I come up dry. Battered but still holding all my liquid.

This could be a break. The hunters will need to find a way down the precipice I've just fallen over. More time to move. I'll still be leaving a trail but it'll take time for them to pick it up.

Head down. Pump up the volume and move.

Pace is the key. My heart starts to warm to the challenge and the slight down-slope is a blessing. I'm conscious that each step could be into a hole or a stream but walking won't stop that happening.

The air is cold and drawing breath hurts. Burning where it should be freezing. The temperature is still dropping. I can feel my toes. Which is a good sign. But they're starting to numb.

MELTDOWN

I hadn't been dressed for a run in the forest when the hunters had come calling. I should've been. I should've been sleeping in full winter gear. Ready to react. Ready to run. But it had been a week since I had stumbled on the cabin. Dead for the winter. Shut up tight. It had been well stocked and hadn't taken long to heat up once I found the pile of cut logs under a snowdrift. I'd figured that my pursuers were not close. It had been a month since the last encounter. That had been far to the north in the wasteland that borders Ontario and what was once called the Northwest Territories. The road up to the cabin had been three miles and the main road that served the area was a little more than a one-lane blacktop.

My hitch had dropped me at a junction a mile short of the cabin road. The driver of the truck didn't ask where I was going. Only a madman would be dropped off so far from the nearest town – and you don't talk to madmen.

My only concern was that he would talk at his next stop. The fact that I was being chased through the forest was testament to his vocal talents. Short of being tracked by satellite I could think of no way that the hunters had found me. The agency had resources that seemed unlimited. A year of running had taught me that.

The slope tumbles to my left and I follow it. I feel welded to a route that has no destination. My feet plunge in and out of the snow. Ankle deep. Fresh powder. A skier's dream. An opening appears on my left. A wide sweeping gap in the forest. Untouched – even by wildlife. The ground falls away sharply as the gap falls back into the trees – providing a brief glimpse of a vast forest vista. And, for a second, there's something else. Out of place. A small cloud hanging above the trees – too low to be anything but moisture rising from below.

I slow down, back up and take in the view. The moonlight is stronger in the gap. The slit of illumination from the sky pulling up some detail. The cloud is a small column. Rising from the far end of the gap. Dirt colored against the white. We're talking a fire or an engine. In this weather both signal humanity.

A noise rises from behind me. Something screeching. A bird. Moved to voice by a disturbance. Animal or human? I walk out into the gap and pick up a jog.

Out in the open I feel vulnerable. My security blanket ripped from me. Head down I focus on the cloud. I want to look back but if there's a gun pointed my way seeing it won't stop the bullet.

The clearing is deep with snow under foot. I am up to my knees at points and each step is tough and draining. My next step keeps the down button depressed and I fall forward. My head vanishes into the powder and snow fills my world. I reach out to catch the fall and my hands encounter nothing but unforgiving white. I am face down with a good foot of snow above me. I roll my head to grab air and lie still. Cocooned.

I push up and my head crests the snow hollow I've formed. I look back and see no movement. I look forward and the cloud is rising twenty yards away.

I stand up.

MELTDOWN

I shake the snow from my clothes and walk towards the cloud.

A bang sends me back to the ground.

Chapter 3

A voice follows the sound as an engine bursts into life. 'Fucking genius.'

Another voice responds. 'Told you she wasn't dead.'

'Will she last?'

'Don't know. Give her a go.'

The engine note drops and a spray of snow rises into the air. The engine noise pulls to my left, drops in volume for a second and then picks up as it returns.

The first voice sparks up. 'She seems good. Fire up yours and we'll see how far we get.'

A pause before a second engine kicks into life. I need to be nearer. I'm up and striding through the last few feet of snow before the trees starts again. I keep a bead on the cloud. I swing to the left and burst from the cover.

Less than ten feet away two snowmobiles are sitting side by side. A fully wrapped passenger on each. A backpack is strapped to each vehicle. I slew to a halt as the nearest vehicle kicks snow high into the air and moves off. I squat down as it approaches. It's too dark for the driver to see me. The second vehicle starts to move. I keep my eyes fixed on it. The first zips by. I judge the moment and as the second sweeps past I grab at the driver. No casual grasp for cloth. It won't work. The momentum will rip him away. I throw an arm across his throat and let the movement lift me from the snow. I swing a foot at the faring, gain a little purchase and pull the driver off.

We go down in a bundle and I am rolling in the snow, trying to get to my feet. I can't give him time to react. His face is inches from my boot and I lash out – putting as much force as I can into the action. Something gives as my heel takes him on the nose. Then I'm back on my feet.

The safety cord has ground the snow mobile to a halt. I reach down and grab the cord and yank it free from his wrist. The key flies up and I catch it. I jump onto the vehicle, insert the key, tear at the throttle and the beast leaps forward. I've driven motorbikes before but never snowmobiles. There's always a first time for everything.

I use the tracks in front as a guide to find the other snow mobile. I catch up and keep enough distance to stay shy of the snow storm he's creating but close enough that he has to turn right round to check if I'm there. The lack of ski mask and goggles are a giveaway that I'm not his mate but there's enough spray between us for him to miss that unless he stops.

My face is starting to sting from the cold. The man in front is laying on speed and I am at the edge of control. Matching both his speed and direction is a full on job for my concentration gene. We pick up a down slope and plunge through the forest like two diamond cutters slicing through frosted glass. I pull my jacket up over my mouth and tug down my bobble hat. But the snow is cutting skin from my face and I know I can't keep this up. I have to slow down. My eyes are streaming and my vision is closing in.

I pull back on the throttle – opening up some distance and taking refuge in the reducing wind. Twisting the handlebars I lean into a corner and cut through the trees to my left. In seconds I have lost sight of the other snow mobile and I take more speed off. I want to stop but as soon as the other man checks on his mate he'll do a one eighty and start looking for him.

I fumble behind me and feel the backpack strapped to the rear. I'm guessing there will be clothes inside. Even a t-shirt wrapped around my face would make things easier.

Another quarter of mile and I can't take it any more – even though I'm down to the speed of a slow jog. I let go of the throttle and slew to a halt, kicking the snow mobile into neutral. I strip off my gloves and rub my nose but it belongs to someone else. I prod at my cheeks but still nothing registers. Dropping my feet to the ground I dismount and examine the backpack.

It's a full on professional model. No Wal-Mart special. More zips and buckles than make sense and it's stuffed to the limit. It takes me time to unwind the retaining rope and open it up. Even with my ice cube nose the smell of sweat rises from the pack. One by one I pluck clothes from the depths and throw them to the ground. I pick out the least aromatic piece of clothing. A sweat shirt. There's nothing else suitable for the job of keeping out the cold.

The sound of the other snowmobile's engine fires me up. I wrap the cloth around my mouth and nose. Gagging at the smell. Tying it off at the back I pull down my bobble hat and zip up my jacket. I have a two-inch slit across my eyes. I was hoping that there might have been a spare set of ski goggles.

The roar of the other snow mobile emerging from the forest forces me back on the seat and I open the throttle. I pull to the left and send a Hawaii wave of snow into an arc behind me. The wind finds the slit that my eyes sit in, tears rise, freeze and my eye ducts stop working.

I wind the machine right up. Cold and more cold. I press on but I'm losing feeling at the extremities. My toes and fingers are distant things. My control of the throttle is compromised. I haven't the touch to feather it the way that I should. I'm doing little more than screaming through the night, holding onto a hot animal, traveling much faster than I'm competent to deal with. The other snow mobile may be on my tail but I can't take my eyes from the dancing headlight beam thrown out in front of me. A slip and I'll take a pine tree full on.

The trees seem, if anything, to be getting thicker. More to the acre. Less space to work with. The slope is still with me and branches snap at my head with the regularity of a high-speed propeller. Each one trying to wrench me from my seat.

I hunker down. Head low. Forearms in tight against my body. A missile shooting through the dark. A gap opens to my right and I swing the snow mobile into it. I catch sight of a light behind me. The other snow mobile is still in pursuit.

I hit a rise and go airborne. As I land the handles are twisted with a violent tug. I feel the snow mobile begin to tip. I fling myself to the left, fighting the machine, trying to use my weight to keep on an even keel. I ignore the urge to swing the handlebars back and force myself to use the turn to pull them into place. The forest spins as I execute a full on U-turn. A branch catches my shoulder and I'm sent reeling back in my seat. A light washes over me as I flash in front of the other snow mobile. I force my legs to hug metal - it's like trying to ride a wild stallion on steroids. The snow mobile straightens and I feel my biceps strain as I struggle to stay on board. My hands are gripping the handlebars so hard my forearms will hurt for a month.

I take control back and keep the throttle on full. I see another gap and cannonball through the trees – squeezing every ounce out of the engine. I kick to the left and then to the right and start to dance down the hill. A sensible driver would be down to a crawl and I am counting on the fact that my follower is experienced enough to know that what I am doing is suicide. My only way out of this is to use my inexperience to out-bottle his knowledge. Ignorance is bliss and I keep the engine turning the track all the way up to eleven.

The trees vanish and I fizz into open space. A valley lies below. The shape suggests a river but the thick snow, lack of light and sheer speed make it difficult to be sure. I point the vehicle at the valley floor.

Adrenalin is pushing my heart hard and my blood is flowing like hot metal. I daren't risk a look back. At this speed I may not get lucky twice if I start to lose control again. The valley flattens out and I avoid the bottom. If there's a river that's where it'll lie and I ride the last vestiges of the slope instead – keeping the valley floor twenty yards to my left.

Each twist in the valley forces me away from the floor before I can use the curve to bring me back down. This is a crazy rollercoaster. A ride that would fleece you twenty bucks back home.

The lack of trees gives me time to think. A headlong dash is not a long-term option. I'm geographically naïve and I've no idea how much gas this thing has in the tank. Riding the valley seems the best bet. Rivers always flow somewhere. I need to find civilization and take it from there. At least I've shaken off the hunters. If the other snowmobile is still behind me then I'm dealing with a pissed off regular guy. I can handle that.

I drop the pressure on the throttle to look back. The snowmobile bites into the snow as my frozen hand releases the trigger rather than ease it off. The nose drops and I hit a snow bank and slam to a halt. I turn to see where the other bike is but the world is nothing but trees, snow and sky. Somewhere along the way I lost him.

The cold takes precedent again as the adrenalin sours in my blood stream. I want to stop, dig into the snow and create somewhere warm. But it isn't going to happen and I just need to suck it up and get on with the job in hand. I dismount and manhandle the snow mobile from the drift, re mount, adjust my clothes as best I can and set off again.

There's a touch of gray creeping in to the land and dawn can't be far off. The river straightens out but navigating is hard. The snow looks like a skateboarder's dream of white concrete but it's a minefield of hidden rocks, plants and holes. If I drop speed I'll bury the machine. At points the ice coating the river breaks through the snow and it's tempting to swing onto it. It has to be thick. The weather has been in deep freeze long enough. But I remember the waterfall earlier and the thought of breaking through into the icy water below is not a good one.

I drift into a nether world. A place where fires and hot air play with my head while the breaking dawn spits ice cubes into my lungs. I dream of being a degree warmer than I am. Of the joy of a couple of degrees. I ease down on the throttle a little but the nose dips and I lay it on again. My eyes have a permanent cloud floating in front of them. Hands are blocks. Feet are steel. My groin hurts from the constant battering and everything on my little world says stop.

Only if I stop - I won't get going again.

The river slides right and I overcompensate and shoot up the small valley and the tracks lose contact with the snow. The snowmobile flies for a few yards before diving back to earth. I shoot between two buildings. Inches on either side the only clearance. Then I hit a wall.
Hard.

Chapter 4

I leave the snowmobile and do a double somersault before landing in a bank of snow. I roll through the drift and out onto an ice-covered road, sliding to a halt next to the fender of a truck that was built while Kennedy was still interested in Marilyn. The engine of the snowmobile gives in the ghost and the hot engine hisses as snow leaks through the cracked shell.

I lie. I can't do the bone counting thing that I did when I fell through the trees. I've no feeling left to tell if anything is broken. I don't move. A strange warmth blankets my body as the absence of the on rushing wind fools my body.

Light floods around me as a door is opened.

'Joe, what the hell's going on?' A woman's voice.

'No idea, darling. Throw me the flashlight.' A male voice.

A click and light plays around me. It finds my head first and stops.

'Looks like someone is lying under my truck. The man's voice is closer

'Who?'

'How in the hell would I know?'

The light jiggles as the crunch of footsteps moves nearer. I swing my head and a bulldozer of a man blocks out the light from the open door. My eyes are still clouded and I can't make out any detail in the form. The flashlight shines hard into my eyes. He bends down. 'Are you ok?'

I shake my head.

'Where did you come from?'

I try to answer but the cold has reduced my lips to two uncooperative strips of frozen meat. I shake my head again. The form studies me and leans closer. 'Can you stand?'

I have no idea. I try to shift my legs and although they move I'd swear they weren't mine. The man bends and hauls me off the ground. The ease by which this is achieved suggests enormous strength. He grunts as he lifts me. 'Jenny, we got an injured man here. Clear the sofa and call Doc Djukic.'

I want to object but I'm being handled like a rag doll. We leave the cold and enter the hot – I embrace the change. Dropped on the sofa the man leaves and the crackle of a fire fills my world. A heavy blanket is dropped on me.

'Do you recognise him?' The woman's voice.

'Never seen him before.'

The man leaves.

The woman walks over to me. 'Are you ok? Where are you from?'

I shake my head.

The man returns. 'There's a snow mobile mashed into the garden wall. It's a real mess. I reckon we know how he got here. It'll cost a pretty cent to fix that wall though.'

'Should we call the police?' The woman again.

MELTDOWN

'No. Let's see what he has to say for himself. Have you phoned the doc?'

'Give me a chance.'

'Then leave it. I'd like to know a little more before we get the authorities involved.'

The man crosses into my clearing vision.

He's easily two fifty pounds. A grizzly bear of man. Thick beard. Long hair. He's encased in a battered old lumberjack's shirt and jeans. 'Ok. What in the hell are you doing driving a snowmobile into my property?'

My lips are thawing. 'Sorry. I got lost.' It comes out as 'Soddy I'd gort loshed'

'Where are you from?'

'I'm on vacation. I hired the snow mobile for the day.'

'It's seven in the morning!'

'I fancied an early start.'

This isn't a conversation that's going well. It has the air of disbelief floating around every word I say. He shuffles to the left. 'Are you anything to do with the city folk that have been up here?'

'No.'

'Strange that. Tall, thin, wiry, bald as a coot, east coast accent.'

I don't know what to say to that.

'That's what they said when I asked them to describe who they were looking for.'

'Who?'

'Some guys. They left a number to phone. Not local either. Washington. Told me to call them if I saw anyone that matched your description. Told me that there was some money in it for me.'

I stay quiet.

'Things are tough. The credit crunch folded two of my best customers. A handy fistful of dollars wouldn't go amiss.'

'So why not phone?' I say.

'Nope. You don't want me to do that. Does he, Jenny?'

'I don't think so, Joe.' Jenny slumps into an easy chair opposite. She's the polar opposite of her husband. Small, thin with tight bunned gray hair on top.

'No, I don't think you want me to do that,' says Joe. 'Not when their jackets had a bulge where a bulge can only mean one thing. Folks don't carry concealed weapons around here. You keep them out and ready. Bears and cougars don't wait for you to unbutton your clothing. And pistols are a waste. A shotgun, maybe a rifle. Something that will stop an animal in its tracks. Pistols are for killing people, not beasts. Are you ex-army?'

The last question throws me. 'Does it matter?'

'It might. I don't like folks that wreck my property but I'm not a fan of spooks either and your boys have spook written all over them.'

'You can tell?'

'More than you know.'

'Cocky bastards,' says Jenny.

MELTDOWN

'That's it. Nail in the wall, Jenny. Nail in the wall. Cocky. As if shit would slide from them without a mark.'

'Look, I'm sorry about your wall.' I say. Speaking is getting easier. 'I'll pay for the damage and be on my way.'

'Where to?' Joe smiles as he speaks.

'To continue my vacation.'

'Son you ain't on no vacation. There isn't a vacation cabin for a hundred miles open at this time of year. Nobody rents snowmobiles around here so that machine ain't yours. Your clothes are all wrong for a tourist. Functional not showy. Wrong for this weather. You've no ski mask. You can't ride bare faced at speed with the bulb seven notches south of freezing. Your vehicle's now FUBAR. It ain't going anywhere. You could walk but your boots are for shit and it's twenty-five miles to the road that leads to the road that leads to town. So you can tell me what you're doing here or I can start dialing.'

I swing my leg from the chair.

Click.

Metal on metal.

I look back and Jenny has a shotgun pointing at me.

Joe steps back. 'Don't be thinking of trying anything. Jenny's a good shot. Better than me.'

I sink back.

'Good idea son.'

I shift my weight. 'Look, there's no need for you to get involved.'

'Already am son. Already am.'

'You won't get a cent if you phone. You know that?'

'No shit, and if I know anything you've left a trail that a blind man could follow and it leads straight to my door. Those boys are going to be back and I reckon back soon. I need to know what I'm dealing with and you're my insurance.'

'Insurance? They'll kill you.'

'Maybe, but a lot of people have said that over the years and I'm still here. Ain't that right Jenny?'

'Sure is, Joe.'

'So do you want to talk or do we wait for the door to be kicked in?'

Chapter 5

The fire is thawing me out, replacing the anti-freeze in my bloodstream with hot wax. Jenny looks at Joe. 'Coffee?'

Joe nods.

'You?' she adds, looking at me.

'Please.'

She heads off to worry an oversized percolator and soon the smell of fresh ground promises a heavy caffeine kick. I sit up and Joe drops into an overstuffed armchair. 'So what's the story?'

I can see the light growing outside the window but the temperature won't boil ice today. Joe is right when he says I'll have left a trail that a four year old would find easy to follow. Time is short and I consider my options. Joe seems happy to wait for me to speak.

The agents aren't going to give in. I've been the prey for too long to figure they'll get bored. I have something they want and they have the backing of the US government. Clandestine backing but that's the worst sort. No oversight. No restrictions. Joe isn't going to be much protection and for all his brave words my pursuers will put a bullet in his head, then Jenny's, then they'll forget to blink. But Joe could be useful. There must be transport and I need to build up some distance. Gain some time.

I lean forward. 'All you need to know is that the bad guys that are after me have one aim. Me. Everything else is irrelevant. I wasn't kidding when I said they'll kill you.'

Joe is sitting with his hands folded on his lap. He looks relaxed. Like people tell him killers are on the loose all the time.

'Doesn't that bother you?'

He shrugs. 'Maybe. But I haven't got to figurin' if you are on the up or just pullin' my chain. You haven't told me anythin' yet. What did you do that they want you so bad?'

'Nothing.'

'Sure. People have guys with guns on their tails all the time.'

'Look, it isn't important. What's important is that we *all* get the hell out of here as soon as we can.'

Jenny returns with two large mugs of coffee. 'Cream? Sugar?'

'Just black for me.'

She hands me the mug and I sip it. Strong and very tasty. My sort of coffee. 'Nice.'

'Joe only drinks the best.'

Joe smiles at her and I can feel their bond. Soul mates. Best friends. I suppose you have to be this far out. Either that or at each other's throat.

I let the coffee do its thing and wait for Joe to talk.

'Jenny, take a seat.'

She obliges and sits down next to me.

'Ok Mr...' Joe looks at me.

MELTDOWN

I ignore the obvious question.

'No names?'

'It's for your own good.'

'Bullshit.'

'Call me Tom.'

'Ok Tom. So you want us all to take off. And then what?'

'I've no idea. All I know is that sitting here is a shit idea. You have no idea what these guys are capable off.'

'So you keep saying. And still you say nothin'. So here's the deal. Give me somethin' to think on and we can take it from there.'

A distant howl. A wolf? The sound has a loneliness to it. I rub at my defrosting body. 'Government.' I begin. 'Not FBI, CIA or Homeland Security. Not the IRS. Not anyone you will have heard of. I've no idea what they call themselves. They usually dress like they missed the audition for Reservoir Dogs. Black ties, white shirt, black suit. They have extraordinary resources and almost limitless access to personnel. They have a friend in the Senate. Tampoline.'

'The guy from the TT?' he asks.

'Yes.'

'The TT?' asks Jenny.

'Tropicana Terror,' says Joe. "You remember. Down in Florida when all the people in the stadium went crazy and started killing each other.'

'That was terrible. Wasn't the senator blinded?'

'And lost the use of his manhood from what I hear.'

'What the hell got into those people?'

I listen to them and know exactly what got into them.

Me.

'So these people,' Joe pronounces people peooople. 'You have no idea why they want you?'

'I do but you don't need to know. Take it on advice, the less you know the better it is.'

'Still not bitin', son.' He crosses his hands on his lap.

'I can't tell you any more.'

'Course you can, son.'

The son bit's getting weary. Dismissive. A put down. An 'I'm superior than you' statement. I shake my head. 'It's simple. Dead simple. In an hour from now, ten minutes from now, ten seconds from now – you choose – a smoke bomb will come through one of your windows. It's their favorite party piece. After that our chances are slim. We go now – our chances are better, not much, but better. The choices are simple. We go. We stay.'

'Or, son, you go and we stay.'

'Can I borrow a vehicle?'

'No.'

'Then how can I go?'

'Foot.'

I want to be on the move. Away from here. My leg is pumping the floor in frustration and Joe is chilled. I try and stand up. Joe is on his feet. 'Nice and slow.'

'I need to use your bathroom.'

Joe turns to catch Jenny's eye. Something is said in silence between them.

'Down the hall,' he says. 'Third on the right. We'll be waiting.'

The corridor is wood paneled. Long vertical stripes of knotted pine stained a dark brown. The carpet is dark. It's like wandering into an underground tunnel. The bathroom door opens to reveal a room at odds with what I have seen so far. Pristine, clean and white. Just out of the wrapper. No wood. Floor to ceiling tiles. A large round tub dominates the centre of the room. Surrounding it is a double washbowl, a toilet and a shower. Spotlights banish any shadows. A single small window sits above the toilet. I try the handle and the window opens a few inches only to stop against a small jam. Even if I force it I couldn't fit through.

There's no other way out.

I count to twenty and hit the flush. A twist of the faucet and I'm back in the tunnel.

Jenny and Joe are sitting together on the sofa.

'So?'

'So what?' says Joe.

'Are we going?'

'No.'

Shit.

I stop and listen. Trying to catch the distant sound of a gun being cocked or the crunch of a footstep in the snow. The light through the window is strengthening. The cover of night is gone. In the open I'm dead meat without decent transport.

'I'll pay you for a lift.' I say.

'To where, son?'

'Nearest town.'

'Won't they be waiting for you?'

'Probably, but I can't stay here.'

'You got money?'

'Some.'

'A grand.'

'What?'

'A grand and I drop you in town.'

'I don't have that sort of cash.'

'I can always phone a cab.'

'Can you?'

'Sure. Devon Waitlich runs the only cab around here. Mind you he'll be a couple of hours getting here. His old Accord ain't so good in the snow.'

I slump in the chair. 'Who the hell would have an Accord for a cab around here?'

'Devon earns from the tourists during the summer and in the winter he ferries townsfolk to and from the 'Dancing Duck'. No need for an SUV on the main road most times.'

The window smashes and in rolls trouble...

...only it doesn't and it's all in my head. But I know it will. The need for speed has never been greater.

'I'm off then. Thanks for the coffee.'

'Walking?'

'No choice. If I stay here I'm putting you and your good wife in danger. I'll need to take my chances.'

MELTDOWN

I pick up the half frozen sweater from the snow mobile and wrap it around my neck. I'm still south of being warm but it'll need to do.

'Joe, you can't let him walk out like that.' Jenny's voice has surprising steel in it.

'Ain't my problem.'

'Is that the way we treat folks, Joe Kendry? Is it?'

'Jenny, he's trouble.'

They're talking as if I'm a kid caught with my hand in the cookie jar.

'And that makes it ok?' Jenny stands up.

'Come on Jenny. You saw their guns.'

'No, Joe, you saw their guns. What I saw were a couple of suits asking about a lost person. What I now see is a man who needs a little help.'

'He just told us that he's putting us in danger.'

'And if that's true do you think the danger will vanish with him?'

'Christ, Jenny…'

'Don't you blaspheme in this house Joe Kendry. I'll not have it.'

'Sorry.'

I realize that the human mountain that is Joe Kendry is not the kingpin in his own house. He might be built like the side of Hoover Dam but Jenny has his measure.

He sighs. A deep guttural thing. 'So what do you want me to do?'

'Take him to Silver Dollar. He can choose the 599 to the 17 or the 642 from there.'

'Silver Dollar's forty miles away.' Joe's face is reddening.

'And?'

Joe's shoulders drop. He knows when he's beat.

'Give me ten minutes to get ready.'

Jenny watches him go and turns to me. 'Another coffee?'

'Please.'

Chapter 6

The pick-up is not long off the forecourt. The truck I nearly hit must be for shit. The pick-up is not the battered example I had expected. Joe is driving. Jenny is sitting next to him; face forward, eyes on the road ahead. I'm staring out the passenger window. The road leading from the farmhouse is a foot thick with snow and the lack of tracks tell me that Joe and Jenny have been cooped up in the farmhouse for a good few days. Joe is taking it easy. I can see no sign of a road. If it were me in the driver's seat I'd be asking for someone to walk in front with a pole to check we weren't about to go for a three sixty.

The radio is playing gospel music and Jenny is mouthing along to it. Joe is eyes fixed. The trees are thick to either side and the sun is still low enough for the truck to be driving on full beam. There's no wind and the passing truck shakes snow from the nearby branches, leaving its own private snowstorm in its wake.

I slide back to the conversation about the TT. A few years back, nearly thirty thousand people enjoying a rock concert that followed a baseball game in the Tropicana Stadium in St Petersburg simultaneously began to maim and wound their nearest and dearest. The death toll was in the hundreds – the injuries in the thousands. The media had no end of theories as to the cause. None of them were close to the mark. I should know. For I was the cause. The catalyst that leads people to drop their inhibitions. To pull up hidden hatred for others and to act on it.

The TT was the culmination of a series of events. Each one more violent than the last. Me at the centre. Out of control. A lightening rod. Setting off people. Giving them unwritten permission to kill.

I still don't understand it. Not fully. All I really know is that around me people can be pretty unpredictable.

Joe drops the speed a little as we hit a down slope. There's still no discernable road but Joe is showing no signs of stress – just annoyance at having to make the trip.

I close my eyes just as the world explodes in noise. I snap my eyes open and the windscreen is a whiteout. Jenny screams as the car lifts into the air and I'm thrown against the door. The truck heaves over onto its side and for a second I think it might right itself. A branch smashes through the door window and the truck topples over – snow piling through the shattered window next to me. I'm engulfed. The car keeps rolling and lands on its roof. My planet is full of snow and screaming. The car slides for a few feet and stops. My seat belt bites deep and I'm suspended upside down. Next to me Jenny is howling like a wolf at the full moon. The branch missed me but it has impaled Jenny in the upper arm before breaking off from the tree. Blood is pouring from the wound and pooling in the roof space.

I try to move but the belt is solid and I focus on trying to release the buckle.

Joe is lying on the roof. Unlike Jenny and me he chose not to buckle up. He's not moving. My seatbelt won't give.

MELTDOWN

Voices from outside indicate we're not alone and I'm ahead of the curve in guessing who's responsible for our crash. I pull at the belt and push at the release button but nothing happens. Joe stirs.

'Joe,' I say. Trying to keep my voice low. 'Joe, have you got a gun?'

He rolls onto his back and a splash of his wife's blood hits him on the face. He's dazed – trying to figure what is going down.

'Joe – snap out of it. Have you got a gun?'

Joe looks up at me. His nose is mashed from the fall and his eyes are glazed. I want to reach over and slap him. The voices stop. I need action. 'Joe, please. A gun.'

Jenny stops screaming and the voices are closer. Another drop of blood falls on Joe and this seems to revive him a little. 'What the hell?'

'Joe, we need a gun. Now.' My heart is picking up pace. 'Have you got one?' We may have seconds before my hunters appear.

'Gun?' Joe looks confused again.

'Gun, Joe. A fucking gun.'

He looks up at Jenny and registers the branch and the blood. 'Jenny!'

'Joe, forget Jenny. We need a gun. Now.'

'Jenny?' Joe reaches up to her.

I hear the crunch of footsteps in the snow. 'Joe. A gun. Or we're all dead.' My heart hits top gear.

He ignores me. 'Jenny, what happened to you?' Joe touches her head.

She's all but out cold. With the amount of blood she's losing I'll be surprised if she survives.

Then my head explodes. The pain reaches into my core and I scream.

Jenny turns her head towards me and her eyes seem to fade. She reaches for the branch.

Shit.

Through the agony I whisper. 'Jenny. No. Do nothing.'

She turns away and looks at Joe. With the ease that a child would pull a stick from a melting popsicle she grabs the wood in her arm and yanks it free. There's no scream as she does it but it has to hurt. Blood spurts across my face as she lifts the branch across her face. Joe follows the movement and I know what's coming next. 'Jenny! NO!' My head is a supernova of pain.

She points the bloodied jagged end of the branch at Joe's head and while he's still trying to work out what's happening she rams it into his left eye. His scream tops anything Jenny had in her. She pushes hard on the branch and Joe falls back.

Jenny passes out and a hand holding a gun pokes through the snow. 'Don't move.'

Chapter 7

'Get away from the car. Right now.' The voice comes from my left. The gun vanishes. There's a click and canister rolls in through the cracked windshield.

Shit.

***

Dark. Silent. Cold. I'm shivering as I come round. The floor I'm lying on is concrete. I shift to try and help my circulation but I'm sluggish. A hangover from whatever it was that they used to knock me out. I roll onto my back and cough. The sound echoes. I feel awash with pain. Mostly low level. Probably bruises from the crash. No broken bones that I can pinpoint. I draw in some of the cold air - filling my lungs - and the cold sends me into a coughing spasm.

'Mr McIntyre.'

My heart jumps and in the dark I spin my head around looking for the source of the voice.

'Nice to see you again.'

I know the voice. A southern drawl. Confident. I spit words. 'I wouldn't have thought that the phrase 'see you again' was much use to you now.' I hear the click of the microphone being disconnected. Then another click as it's reconnected. 'Funny, Mr McIntyre'.

Pushing my hands down, I sit up. 'Killed any young girls lately?'

'Again, funny. You seem to lack an understanding of your situation. Do you think taunting me will help?'

'Hell, Tampoline. It doesn't make any difference. If you wanted me dead we wouldn't be having this conversation. You want me and you want what I can do.'

'Very observant. You've done remarkably well. How many months since the TT? How long have you been on the run?'

'Not long enough.'

'It takes talent to stay ahead of me.'

'Am I supposed to buy the praise? Because of me you're blind and you're not going to add any small Tampoline's to the world from what I hear.'

'True. But it's only because of what you can do, Mr McIntyre, that you're still breathing.'

'Can you put on the lights?'

'No.'

'Were there many at Lendl's funeral?'

'Not many. It seems that you don't get time for a family and make few friends when you do the job Clive did.'

'It was him that blinded you though.'

'Again, true. But not without your unique help.'

I don't know why we are having this conversation. Clive Lendl had jumped on Tampoline in the Tropicana Stadium in St Petersburg and dug out his eyes with his fingers. It was Clive Lendl who had figured out my 'talent'. My ability to set people off. It was him that had mainlined me on drugs in an attempt to figure out how to control me. Then he killed himself in front of me and, along with hundreds of deaths and thousands of injuries at the stadium, it was all blamed on some mass hysteria. Tampoline knew the truth. Tampoline knew it was all down to me.

'So why am I here?'

'All in good time. Where's your bartender friend?'

'No idea.'

Charlie had helped me escape from Tampoline and had been my sidekick at the stadium.

Another click and I'm on my own.

I stand up and wait until my head clears before exploring the room. Four walls, a door and that's your lot in a twelve by twelve cell. I slump against a wall, curl my arms around my legs and huddle for warmth. Ok, so the agency have their claws into me again. It was always going to happen. You can only run so long. But what now? Last time they tried to turn me into some sort of remote killing machine. Drugs by the gallon.

Same again?

Chapter 8

The lights flick on. The door opens and in walks Tampoline. He looks a little less cock sure than when I first met him. For a start he didn't need the dark glasses and cane. He's also walking with a shorter step. Possibly the result of Lendl's touch down kick in the groin. But he still has swagger. I heard he received a standing ovation from the floor when he returned to the senate. The hero of the TT, some say. Not me. I know what he is. A murderer, and a man with no compassion. I watched him kill a sixteen year old girl in a way that makes me feel sick when I think about it.

He stands a few feet in front of me. His waist is a little thicker than I remember and his hair looks thinner but he has a good Donald Trump going on up top to hide it. His suit's a month's wages for even a good worker. Shoes spit polished to a soft glow. He's a few inches shorter than me and the dark glasses can't hide the spread of wrinkles across his face.

There's no one with him. The door behind is wide open. I step forward. His head swivels in my direction. 'Going somewhere, Mr McIntyre?' There's a click and a suit with a Heckler and Koch MP5 enters my life. 'Before you get any ideas, my minder here is a stranger. I don't know him from Adam. So your little party trick is redundant.' I step back.

MELTDOWN

'Take a seat, Mr McIntyre.'

There are no seats.

'On the floor, Mr McIntyre. You're still a dangerous man to be around.'

I drop to the floor.

'Comfortable?' The pleasure in the word is hard for Tampoline to hide.

'Get on with it. Where's the drugs?'

'No drugs. Not if you behave.'

'Sure.'

The cane cracks the side of my head. The suit steps forward as I react. I sit back down, rubbing my head. 'Thought you were blind.'

'I am. Lucky shot. Coffee?'

I nod and realize my mistake when he doesn't react. 'No drugs?'

'No drugs.'

'Black with one.'

'Make mine black,' he adds.

The suit doesn't move but I hear footsteps recede and figure others are nearby.

'So what is it you want, Tampoline?'

'Slow down, Mr McIntrye. Coffee first.'

We wait. Tampoline rocks on his feet, tapping his cane on the floor. He looks like he's grooving to a tune in his head. I straighten my legs and lean back on my hands. I've no way of knowing the time and wonder how long I was out. I can feel the after effects of canister and something else. A shot of something to keep me out long enough to transport me to wherever I am. The good news is that I'm not dead. After all, the last time I met Tampoline he had decided that my usefulness had run its course and left Lendl to finish me off. Turned on his heels as Lendl had reached down to finish me off. Maybe a little interrogation is in order. Find out what I know about the aftermath of the TT. Then finish the job off. Footsteps announce the arrival of coffee.

The cups are placed on the floor next to the suit with the gun.

'Mr McIntrye, would you be good enough to bring me my coffee?' The word coffee comes out 'coffay' emphasizing Tampoline's southern roots. I stand up and as I approach the coffee the suit with the gun backs off but keeps the weapon pointed at my gut. I sip both cups, spit out the coffee and hand Tampoline the one with sugar. He sips it and screws up his face. 'This is yours.'

'A little sugar won't do you any harm.'

'Do you think we need to spike your coffee?'

'Maybe.'

'Mr McIntrye, I could have you strapped to a gurney and filled with every illegal narcotic I can name and you wouldn't be able to do jack shit about it. So swap the coffees. I hate sugar.'

I do as he asks and drop back to the floor.

'Good,' he says as he sips at the mug. 'So, time for a little chat. Or rather a little story. Questions are welcome. Not that I can promise answers but let's make this as pleasant as possible.' He leans against the wall. His mouth hangs open and a pair of ultra-white teeth frames his lips. I can't tell if they are store bought or a dentist's wet dream. He taps his cane on his leg and stretches out his free hand towards me. 'Have you heard of the Strategic Petrol Reserve?'

I shake my head, realize my mistake again. 'No.'

'You don't listen to the news?'

'Kind of hard when you are on the run. Bits and pieces.'

'Bryan Mound, Big Hill, West Hackberry, Bayou Choctaw?'

'Rock groups?' I try a smile as I say this. A wasted gesture.

'Not quite. Four sites that hold the seven hundred million barrels of oil that we can call on should there ever be a shortage. It would give the President about three months of juice to play with.'

'And?'

'You really have been locked away. Two weeks ago all four were hit by terrorists. Bombs! Officially the damage was light. After all, they are some of the most secure places in the country.'

'And by 'light' you mean bad?'

'You could say that.'

'How bad?'

'Bad.'

'Can't be that bad. Even on the run I'd have heard if seven hundred million barrels of oil had gone up in flames. For one thing it would still be burning.'

'True but the bomb story was a blind. The internet went into overdrive about the attacks and we had to give them something to feed on to avoid too much digging.'

'So there were no bombs?'

Tampoline eases from one leg to the other. 'Oh there were bombs and guns and most anything you can think off. But that was just to get in. Then they got smart. They spiked the oil.'

'Spiked?'

'Introduced a chemical agent. It's got a technical name but they called it IPA. A special formula. Very smart. It breaks down the oil at molecular level. Before we could stop it we had lost over half a billion barrels and have another hundred million that is barely usable.'

'Who are they?'

'They call themselves The Factor. US based. White supremacists on the surface but they're much more. Extremely well funded and very active. They've been around since the early fifties. Formed as a reaction to the growing threat from Communism. McCarthy had connections with them. They have an official side to them called the United States Construct on Future Thinking – USCOFT - based in Atlanta, but we have never been able to link them to any of The Factor's activity. Too smart.'

'And this Factor took out most of this Strategic Petrol Reserve?'

'So we believe?'

'Why?'

'The million dollar question. We have theories to burn, but of course they deny it was them, and to be fair it would seem a strange thing to do for such an ultra-patriotic group.'

Despite myself I was interested. 'So what makes you think it was them?'

'We caught a few. They wouldn't talk but we're not lacking in resourcefulness when it comes to interrogation and they eventually gave up some info - but all of them were drones. No connection to the higher ranks.'

'So we just fill it up again?'

'Great idea. First we need to empty the current reserves and find a place to dump six hundred million barrels of shit. Then we would need a thousand of the worlds' largest tankers to be on hand to deliver the new crude. All the time the world would be racking up the price. A crude estimate is that we could drive the price north of three hundred dollars a barrel. That would give us a bill of one hundred and fifty billion dollars.'

'With our deficit that hardly sounds like a bank breaker. And we could pump it from our own wells. What do we pump a day?'

'Twelve million barrels.'

'There you go.' I do the math. 'You'd be full in two months.'

'Sure. If we stopped using the stuff. We consume a little over nineteen million barrels a day and growing.'

'Do we?'

'It gets worse. We have been reducing our dependency on foreign oil and plans were in place to take the SPR to one billion barrels. But the reduction in foreign dependency has come with a heavy price - blowouts like the Deep Water Horizon rig in 2010 means public opinion is against accelerated production. On top of this we are politically sensitive about where we get our oil from. We don't like all our eggs in too few baskets. Joe Punter thinks we get our oil from the Middle East but forty percent comes from Canada, Mexico and Venezuela, and they are flat out in terms of production.'

'I heard we're heading for becoming an net exporter, what with fracking.'

'True, but not soon enough for the problem we face. To replenish our missing stock we would need to go to some of our less friendly suppliers.'

'Like who?'

'Well Russia for a start. They have massive reserves but you can imagine the deal we would need to strike with them.'

'Saudi, UAE?'

'It's not expedient to take much more from Saudi. The senate have blocked that route before and the UAE haven't got the reserves.'

'Who?'

'Nigeria, Iraq, Angola, Algeria.'

'Nice.'

MELTDOWN

'We do have other choices but no one country could help and none of the combinations we have come up with would be quick enough.'

'So we take our time.'

'And if word gets out the price at the pumps could triple in days. Our manufacturing cost base would rocket. The economy is already battered after the credit crunch - we couldn't take the hit.'

'But the story will get out?'

'True. We have maybe a few days at best.'

'So you're fucked.'

Tampoline moves and taps the cane again. 'Not quite. There's an option.'

'Which is?'

'Iran.'

'Cool?'

'Funny. They have enough reserves to give us half what we need quite quickly.'

'Do we trade with them now?'

'Hardly. Not since the Shah was kicked out.'

'So what makes you think they would play ball?'

'To have power over the evil empire of the world. The new lad in charge seems keen to do business. He's making all the right noises'

I laugh. 'Iran.'

'We've already talked to them.'

'Shit. And what did they say.'

'Surprisingly they didn't say no.'

'What do they want?'

'A lot more than money.'

'I bet.'

'But at least there's a deal to be done. That's a step better than we were.'

'So why tell me all this.'

'Can I get another coffee,' he shouts to the door. 'Do you want another?'

'No.'

We wait while the coffee arrives. I lie on the floor and stretch. This conversation is way passed my pay grade and I can't see where I fit in. If Tampoline's story got out there could be chaos.

More coffee makes an appearance. This time they hand it directly to Tampoline. He sips at it. 'Nice.'

'I'm so pleased for you,' He ignores the taunt.

'Ok, where was I?' Tampoline steps forward. 'Iran. Correct?' I'm not expected to answer. 'So contact is made. Numbers discussed. Negotiations touched on and Iran send a diplomat to meet us. Amin Jamshidi, low-level contact. Ex SAVAK, the Iranian secret police, and the point man for the Iranian government. His job was to get us all to first base and then the big boys would take over. Handshakes, tea and coffee and meet the neighbors type talks. De-risk the start of negotiations. If someone finds out about the chat Amin is a small enough cog to be sacrificed - but of course he comes with some minders. We meet up in a safe house near Sacramento and Amin turns out to be amiable and open. We know the squeeze will come later but as a start we are surprised at the willingness to deal.'

MELTDOWN

'No mention of the Shah?'

Tampoline lets a smile flick across his face. 'None. Amin is well briefed and has been told exactly what to say and what not to say. No promises. No deals, but the door is ajar and we are being invited to walk in. Time is not our friend. The SPR story is not going to stay buried forever.'

'One morning Amin comes to the table with an offer for two of our negotiators to fly to meet the grown-ups from Iran. It would seem that our time had come. We gear up and agree to fly out the following day to meet in a neutral location. Jordan provides a convenient meeting point and our boys on the ground set up a cover and arrange for somewhere to meet. That night four of us are sitting chewing on air in the safe house when the world explodes. I'm knocked cold and when I come round Amin has gone.'

'Someone took him?'

'Yes, but we didn't know who. Although we suspected the Factor. Whoever it was, they were well prepared. The safe house had ten of our best agency men on guard duty and they still got in and out inside ten minutes. The following day I get an email. Untraceable but with a photo of Amin bound to a chair. The message was simple. Cease the negotiations or Amin is killed.'

I shuffle to ease the cold seeping into my legs. 'Why bother? If they want to stop the negotiations a call to the Washington Post would have done the trick.'

'I agree, but for some reason they don't seem to want to go down that route. After all, if it was the Factor they could have let everyone know what they did to the SPR and we would have been in the shit. But they haven't.'

'And if it was them, how are they going to know if you've stopped negotiations?'

'They won't. We could say we have but they know as well as we do that we could start them up again. They also know we need to fix the SPR and if they are half as bright as they appear they will know our options are limited. We've been working on this for two days and no one can figure their end game.'

'So where do I figure in all this?'

'We need your 'talent' to attempt a rescue of Amin.'

'Rescue?'

'The Factor have a track record of killing hostages. We came up with a delaying tactic that gives us seventy two hours before we need to meet with the Iranians.'

'What about Amin's minders?'

'They had flown on ahead to brief their bosses. We had someone do a passable imitation of Amin on the phone to buy us the time. He's supposed to be bedded down in the safe house. We need to get him back before we fly out. otherwise the deal is dead. The Iranians might be talking to us but they are nervous and last night we got word that the Chinese have been in touch with them.'

'The Chinese?'

'They need oil, and with their economy on fire they need a lot of it. It would seem that they did the same sums that we've done and reckon Iran for a good bet on securing a long-term exclusive oil agreement. After all, they signed up a massive gas deal with Russia. The Iranians must think all their Christmases have come at once.'

'They don't celebrate Christmas.'

'If they did every one of them has rolled into town on the same day. Two superpowers courting them and willing to offer them the deal of a lifetime. It's their chance to step up big time onto the world stage.'

'So why wouldn't they just go with the Chinese?'

'They don't trust them. They've had bad dealings in the past. Anyhow, think about the amount of humble pie they'll force us to eat if we have to bend over to get their oil. We're still favorite but losing Amin could swing it to Beijing. If we can't protect a single Iranian in our country they may think that the Chinese are a better bet.'

I stretch out and look up at Tampoline. He's drained the coffee and is twisting the mug around his left thumb. Occasionally he redistributes his weight from one foot to the other. I hate the man. My wife would be alive if it were not for him. And now he wants my help. 'You can count me out.' I say.

'Not an option. This is for America, and if you don't help you can go join that pretty wife of yours.'

With this he swings on his heel and walks out, stick smacking the door as he goes. I shout out but the door is slammed shut and the lights killed.

Chapter 9

'Time to move.' A suit's standing at the door. Six feet, well-toned, square jawed with the trace of a Mohican hair cut going on. 'Here.' He throws me a bag and slams the door as he leaves.

The bag is a battered sports bag with tape holding one of the straps together. I'd left it in the cabin when I had to make a run for it. I open it up and my wash kit and some clothes are packed in. The smell reminds me I haven't been near a laundromat in a while. I pull out the cleanest clothes and change. A scrub with a toothbrush and squirt of Degree and I'm good to go.

I sit down and wait.

Ten minutes later and the door opens. The Last of the Mohicans signals me to follow. I was expecting to be drugged or restrained but I leave the room under my own steam and enter a corridor that is low on lighting. The Last of the Mohicans checks I'm following and sets off at a pace. I drop in behind and keep my eyes open for a way out but the corridor is solid wall either side. Ahead a door is ajar and a second suit's waiting. Before I can reach them the Last of the Mohicans vanishes inside and my new host slams the door.

'Don't I get to say goodbye?' I ask.

MELTDOWN

The new suit's lifted from the same mold as most of the others. Heavy built, clean-shaven, square jawed and short on hair. Silent. He stands at the door and looks at me.

'A dance?' I ask. He steps forward and with expert ease kicks my legs from beneath me. I slide down the wall. 'Sit there and say nothing.' The new suit moves back to the door and stands like a statue.

I spread my legs and give him my best 'fuck off and die' look but he's immune. I settle back and run over Tampoline's story and can't decide if it's a pile of mush or if I'm really being touted as the savior of the United States of America. The sheer complexity of it all suggests a Machiavellian plot of unfathomable reasoning or a set of circumstances that are running away from Tampoline. That I'm the man he would turn to shows desperation. After all, he's blind and impotent and I'm responsible.

What I do recognize is the grip that oil has on the country. Despite years of rising prices and environmental warnings, America is wedded to the stuff. Detroit might be pumping out smaller cars and Mr and Mrs Jones might be switching off the standby at night, but we are a long way from running the planet on sunlight. Even the political landscape is shaped by the black gold. I remember reading that Canada, nice safe Canada, is our number one supplier. Dragged from oil sands it's not the cheapest and not the easiest way to get oil but it keeps us from depending on countries that hate us. The same article said that Saudi Arabia hardly creeps into our top ten suppliers. As to the likes of Iran. Well, since the Ayatollah Khomeini booted out the Shah and screwed over Carter with the hostages and then, to add sugar, we placed them in the Axis of Evil - that was that. The deal that Tampoline was involved in was right up there with Kennedy going to tea with Castro. God alones knows what the real price of the deal is. Whatever bollocks Tampoline fed me, the truth would be that the USA was spreading its buttocks and waiting for the Iranians to pay a visit. And I doubt the words condom or gentle are on their itinerary.

The new suit stretches his neck, sending a click into the quiet hall. He returns his gaze to the door and I shuffle my rear to stop it numbing up.

I'm not sure what the plan is for me. Given that I have little or no control over what I can do it'll be a long shot. Sure, you can place me in a room with two people and they can start to rip each other's throats out. Trouble is that they could just as easily sit and chat about the weather. Whatever it is that I do it's hard to predict. After the TT I'd had a chance to think through what had gone on. How I can set friends against each other. Draw out long buried animosity and let it show itself in the most violent of forms. Supernatural ability? Maybe. Whatever the truth, I was a dangerous person to be around. A dead wife was testament to that.

I'd often thought about seeking help but being on the run made it almost impossible. Also, who could I see that I could trust? Who in the hell would believe that a man could do what I do? And who would be able to help? A shrink? Hospital? Do they have specialists for what I have?

MELTDOWN

Tampoline's interest was based on experiencing what I could do. He saw me as nothing more than a weapon that could be deployed when required. Last time round he had tried to find a cocktail of drugs that could control me. Something to set me off. Something to calm me down. I had become a junkie. A junkie assassin. Two African leaders had nearly torn each other's heads off when they tried to unleash me. The fact that the theater that they were talking in became a boiling soup of hatred as the audience joined in had caused Tampoline's men to rip me from the building. The TT was just the next step up.

The one bit of good news was that whatever Tampoline wanted, it didn't involve me being dead. In the short term this was a good thing. It gave me hope that I could escape. Playing along with Tampoline was the best plan I had; after all, if he wanted the Iranian back then I'd need to be taken along for the ride. And that meant opportunities. I slide a little further onto the floor. Resting my shoulders on the join between the wall and the carpet.

Chapter 10

When the door re opens I'm half way to a snooze. The suit's still rigid. He can probably stand like that for hours. Suit number three in a collection of millions appears. He's not quite from the same mold as the others. For a start he's shorter, a lot shorter. He's also jazzy enough to have his tie loose. His hair is a few inches beyond regulation and he has a stripe running through his suit. All in all, a bit of a rebel in agency world. He talks to the other suit but too low for me to hear. The other suit nods and returns to stone. The Rebel vanishes back in the door and I'm left to play with myself again.

I slide down the wall until I'm lying flat out on the floor. I close my eyes and reckon that sleep is a good idea. My army training, brief as it was, had the 5 S's as mantra – Sleep, Shit, Spray, Shower, Shovel whenever you can. I close my eyes and shuffle my numb butt to ease the pain. Number three on the five S's stops me dropping off. My bladder is full and the last coffee has made its way to the exit. I open my eyes and ease myself onto my side. 'Is there somewhere I can take a private moment?'

The suit holds the pose.

'I'm not kidding here. I need to wet some porcelain.

'

Still nothing from the statue.

MELTDOWN

'Come on. I need to pee. In what way is letting me piss on your nice carpet a good idea?'

The suit looks at me. I tip my head to one side. 'There must be a loo nearby?'

He shakes his head and does the eyes front thing again.

I sit up. 'Come on. You can watch if you want? I'm not going anywhere.'

The door opens and the Rebel reappears. 'Up.'

'I need to pee.'

'So pee.' The Rebel nods to his colleague and he moves towards me. I get up before he can haul me from the ground.

'Through the door.' The Rebel stands back to let me pass. The other suit stays behind and as the Rebel steps through the door he vanishes from my life. The corridor beyond looks the mirror image of the one I've just left. It stretches ahead with no sign of an end or any doors. The Rebel prods me in the back. 'Walk.'

I step forward and he falls in behind me. The corridor reminds me of the tunnels that burrow under Disneyland. The concrete tubes that Mickey and Minnie use to get from A to B without being seen. Only this one is wall to wall carpet with walls painted in eighties beige. 'Where are we going?'

'Just walk.'

A few hundred yards on and the corridor shows signs of life. A door on the left. Non-descript pine with a steel handle. It's the start of a row of them. Each ten paces apart.

They are joined by a row on my right. Each identical. There's nothing to identify what lies behind them. No nameplates. No numbers. Zero identification.

'Stop.' The Rebel slides past me. He grabs the handle of one of the doors and opens it. 'In here.'

I study the door and wonder how he knew which one to open. Maybe it doesn't matter. Maybe they are all for the same use. He steps back to let me in and when I hesitate he flicks his jacket open to reveal a handgun. I shrug my shoulders and walk into the room beyond. The door closes behind me and the lack of internal door handle tells me this is no Holiday Inn Deluxe suite.

The room is a ten by ten square. On wall has a six by three bed against it. A cold grey blanket tucked in at the corners military style. Metal legs bolted to the floor. There's a washbowl next to a toilet on the wall opposite and apart from that the room is empty.

I look around for the expected camera but if it's there, and I'm sure it will be, it's hidden. My first task is to lose the coffee and once I have done that I drop onto the bed and try and make myself comfortable.

A little while later and the lights go out. I think it's a signal to go for a sleep and I try to obey, but my head decides it isn't up for forty winks and wants to go over the whole Tampoline thing again and again.

Chapter 11

'This way.' Light floods from the door as a new suit waves his hand out into the corridor. I wonder where they recruit them from? I wonder if they all sleep in their suits? A special chamber with pods along the walls. Recharge points in each. Glass enclosed. Rows of suited and booted men waiting to be called on. A clone army. Only they, whoever in the hell they are, are smart enough to make them all a bit different. To avoid suspicion. No two the same but close enough for the job. Hair cropped tight. Unless you were one of the rebels. Off the peg Sears suit. Snow white shirt. Pencil thin black tie. All a bit Men in Black. Maybe that's where they got the idea or maybe the film got the idea from them. Who knows?

I stretch and the smell from under my armpits assaults me. A shower is in order but the suit's indicating that it's time to move again. I walk past him and back into the corridor. Same low level light. Same aroma of disinfectant.

He slams the door. 'This way.' Turns on his heel and marches back the way we had come the evening before. We pass four doors and he opens the fifth. 'In.'
I walk in.

The room is another ten by ten but there's no bed this time. A plastic chair sits in front of TV screen that's built into one wall. The rest of the room is beige on beige. I slump into the chair and wait for the movie to begin. The screen flicks and the speaker sparks up. The TV is old school. Cathode ray land. The picture coalesces and I'm looking at another ten by ten. This one has a table in the center; chairs attend it on two sides. I can see bolts on one set of chair legs securing it to the floor. The table is best seventies Formica, curling up at the edges. The limitless funds that the agency seems to work with don't extend to the furnishings.

Out of a camera shot there's the click of a door opening and voices. A head appears in view followed by a second and a young man is encouraged to take a seat while the second head, a suit, drops with his back to me. The young man has a full beard, unkempt and threatening to engulf his face. His hair is long and greasy. He's stick thin and dressed in a white t-shirt, dark chinos and pair of battered sneakers. He looks comfortable with his situation, leaning back in the chair and placing his hands behind his head. He draws a deep breath and closes his eyes. We wait.

I can't see what the suit's doing but he's fiddling with something on the desk. He pushes a folder into view. 'Ok Mr Wheeler, let's try this from the top.' The young man keeps his eyes closed and hands behind his neck. The suit pushes the folder a little closer to the young man. 'Mr Wheeler, or can I call you Martyn?' Martyn doesn't flick a muscle. The suit leans forward. 'Have it your way.' He stands up and blocks out the young man from my view. There's the smack of bone and flesh meeting bone and flesh and Martyn tumbles to the floor. The suit sits down.

MELTDOWN

Martyn lies for a second and rubs his cheek. He pulls himself back on the seat and returns to the eyes closed, hands up pose.

'Now we know that you know where Amin Jamshidi is. We know you know we know. And we know you know that we know you know.'

I had a single by a band called the Kursal Flyers that did lyrics like this.

'One way or the other we need to know where he is, and I ain't got time to dick around.'

Martyn is like Buddha. The suit goes on. 'Tells us what we need to know and we can end this now. No need for any more of the unpleasant stuff. Just a friendly chat. An address maybe, and we're all friends. We're clean out of time so either you start talking or we need to move to plan B, and trust me, you might not like Plan A, but Plan B is a bitch and half. Your choice.'

Martyn doesn't move. It's as if he was in the room on his own.

The suit stands up and this time the punch sends Martyn to the other side of the table and back to the floor. Before Martyn can stand up the suit steps forward and places his foot on his head. 'You know what Martyn? I need a workout. Ain't been to the gym in weeks. A hundred bucks a month and all I'm doing is putting on the flab. I have a half marathon coming up later in the year. Do you know how hard it is to do one of those things?'

He presses the sole of his shoe onto Martyn's ear and twists it. Martyn makes his first noise since entering the room and squeals. The suit lifts his foot. 'I mean I thought about doing the full thing. You know, all twenty six miles and a bit. But I thought I would ease myself in. Hah. Kidded myself there. Shit, even thirteen miles is a bastard.' He stamps his heel down and Martyn gasps. 'I thought, how hard can it be? I could walk it in four hours. But I don't want to. I need to put in a good time. Have a bit of respect for what I'm trying to do. Take a bit of pride.' He drops his foot from Martyn's head and lands a solid foot in Martyn's guts. Martyn grunts.

The suit backs off. 'So I should be out doing laps. You know, knocking the yards off my Nikes. Stacking some muscle. Instead, I'm trying to get your sorry fanny to open up. So I say to myself, why not double up? A little bit of running and a few questions might work a treat.'

The suit hits the blocks. Ready for the 100 yard dash. He squats. Waits for the gun. Snaps into action as the silent report goes off in his head. One hand on the table he circles. Jogging in slow motion. Overdoing the sprinter imitation. Martyn lies on the floor and on the first pass the suit launches a kick into Martyn's thigh. A full blooded sixty yard conversion. Martyn screams. The suit sets off for lap two. Still doing a slow mo Carl Lewis.

Second time round he picks out the same thigh and Martyn tries to roll from the kick. The suit compensates. Martyn doesn't scream but he does vomit. The suit looks down and screws up his face. 'Come on Martyn. It costs us good cash to feed your sorry face. Don't go throwing it back at us.' He sets off for lap three.

MELTDOWN

I look away. I don't needs to see this shit. What kind of people are they?

But I know the answer. After all, they all but killed me last time we met. I'm sure this goes down across the planet. Extraordinary rendition the norm. Waterboarding ain't torture if you listen to ex-President GW. War on terror. Guantanamo Bay. Abhu Grave in Iraq. All in a day's work for some guys. But this lot are on a different planet. Abuse of the rules is one thing, but there are no rules when it comes to the suits. At least none that involve civil liberties or due process.

Dear Sirs, we humbly secede from the United States of America and declare unilateral independence. With our new found freedom we will happily take on the less salacious tasks that your nation wants to undertake. Please pay the invoice but don't ask questions.

I hear a grunt and turn back to the TV to see Martyn trying to scramble to his feet but his left leg is dead from the kicks. He grasps at the table. Looking for purchase. The suit enters the home straight once more and gives Martyn's left thigh the good news for a third time. Martyn collapses to the ground. Landing back in his own mess. The suit throws his hands up as if crossing the finishing line and drops into Martyn's seat. 'And the new world record is set at 9.33. Go me.' He has a sweat on and the sort of grin that suggests this is far from his least favorite job. He's getting off on this big time.

Martyn moans. The suit leans down and taps him on the shoulder. 'Come on Martyn, give it up. I'm just warming up for the second round.' Martyn doesn't respond.

The TV blanks and the door behind me opens. Tampoline walks in. 'You see, Mr McIntyre, what we have to deal with. Non-cooperation is such a pain.'

'So are human rights,' I spit.

'Oh, come now. Human rights? Where are the human rights in destroying a nation's fuel supply? What about the millions that could die if the news gets out? Widespread panic buying. The fuel would be gone in days. Then what? No transport. No food. No heat. No nothing for many people. Anyone out in the boondocks would be dead meat. What about their human rights?'

'Bollocks. Two wrongs don't make a right.'

'Please!' He steps into the room. His stick finding empty space and a suit at his shoulder. 'Get into the real world. This isn't some debating society. If you want to use clichés try 'fighting fire with fire' or 'an eye for an eye'. We haven't got the time to dick around. These guys don't play ball when it comes to the crunch. They want to fuck us over and that's it. No rhyme. No reason. No ten point plan. Job 1 is to convert our life to their life. Their action is our action. Their think is our think. That's what they want.'

'They don't want to sink America. What would that gain them?'

'Who knows? But you don't screw up the US oil supply with a view to improving our way of life. None of it makes sense. No demands. No claims. In a week they put the US on its knees but have said nothing. Kidnapping the Iranian is just another step in making sure we can't fill up the tank. As you saw on the TV, they don't talk much.'

'Maybe he doesn't know anything.'

'For once you have a point. He's too low down the food chain to know much but he can lead us to the Iranian and that's where you come in.'

'How?'

'We need his friends to come rescue him. It's the only way we can track them down quick enough. We've no leads and unless we can present Amin Jamshidi in two days' time, we are in the crapper.'

'So you want to recruit my Sherlock Holmes type investigative skills.'

'No, Mr McIntyre, we want to employ your little anger tool.'

'First, the answer is no. Second, I can't just switch it on. And third, what in the hell good could it do?'

'Fancy a coffee?' He turns to the suit. 'Could you hunt down a couple of black ones for us? Sugar in one.' The suit vanishes and Tampoline turns back to me. 'Mind if I take the weight off.' There's only one chair in the room. He stands and I slide from the chair and hit the floor. He taps the stick up to the chair and sits. 'Thanks.' I don't want to work with the bastard, but last time I learned that a bit of give and take can ease the situation with them.

'So here's Plan A,' he taps his stick on the floor as he speaks. 'Martyn has a friend. He doesn't know that we know. His friend lives a few miles from here. We've had him under observation but the Factor won't go near him. They know we have their man and they've all gone to ground. Since they don't seem up for telling the world what they are up to we assume that they will just stay quiet and let the SH12 hit the fan in due course. We need to engineer a way to get them to show face, and that's where you come in. We want to let Martyn go and hope he runs to his mate. We believe that his friend is a little higher up the pecking order. We thought to bring him in, but that would cut the one tie we have to the rest of the organization. So we need to force them to surface.'

'And I fit in where?'

'We need you to get Martyn here to kill his friend.'

Chapter 12

I'm not sure if silence is the correct response to that statement but it'll do.

'Well, are you up for it?'

'Just like that?'

'Just like that, Mr McIntyre. That simple. No sweat to a man of your talents.'

I laugh. A genuine laugh. Not forced. It bubbles into a full blown fit. I hack as the laugh takes grip and fall to my side. I lose control and howl. The noise is deadened by the soundproofing but it still makes a fist of bouncing around the walls. I embrace the whole thing. Grabbing at the moment of relief. Hoping that even Tampoline would see the funny side. I grasp at air and the laughter begins to subside. Down to a chuckle, I open my eyes. Tampoline has stood up. 'Finished, Mr McIntyre?' I nod but a last laugh leaks out.

'Glad you find it so amusing.'

I sit up and wipe the wet from my sockets. 'Come on, Tampoline. You've got to see the funny side.'

'Frankly no, I don't'

'What? You have the best part of an army at your disposable. Any one of your suited goons are probably trained to kill with a disposable razor and toothpick and the toothpick is only there to remove the Big Mac debris from their teeth. You don't need me for your dirty work.'

'Not true. You are of special regard with what we have in mind. If I wanted a few of our enemies eliminated then there are people far better suited to the task than you.' The word enemies came out with the same tone reserved for something you scrape from shoe leather. 'What we need you for is to give the whole plan a little authenticity.'

'Me! Add authenticity? Come on. When it rains in my world there's fuck all authentic about the look and feel. Hell, I still struggle with it.'

'You may, but I don't. The choice is simple: work with us, or don't.'

'And the 'don't' option doesn't come with sugar and cream.'

'Mr McIntyre, it doesn't even come with a mug.'

'Thanks for the heads up.'

'You're welcome.'

'So what is it you need me to do?'

'Later. Time to get you ready.' He turns and leaves, stick tapping the door frame as he goes. The suit enters with coffee and I'm encouraged back to my cell.

A change of clothes lie on the bed. 'Any chance of a shower?' I say to the retreating suit. The door slamming in my face is my answer. I contemplate a little resistance. Not getting changed. Fighting the inevitable. But the smart thing to do is to co-operate, however crazy the scheme is, and wait my time for an opportunity to run.

MELTDOWN

My brief time in the army had me on patrol in the back end of the Diyala Valley south of Baghdad. We were less than six months into the second invasion and I had less than three months left as a grunt. Only, back then, I didn't know that I'd be sectioned out. I was just happy to get back from each patrol with a full limb count. The patrol had been set up as a sweep for a missing soldier. We didn't hold out much hope. Kidnapping was still a tool for the future for most. The insurgents were more into your old fashioned bullet in the head.

It was early morning daylight when we set out. We had a lead on where the lift might have taken place and our sergeant was bigging up the chances of success. I was new out of the parcel and even I could tell it was bull. Progress was slow – IED's and snipers will do that for you. We sweated in the back of the MRAP until we hit the search area and then we decanted into a straight A sun on the outskirts of a small village. The private had been AWOL for three days and we were all that could be spared to see if he was still breathing. Six of us began the slow walk to the village. With the walls too close together to get the MRAP in we had to cover the last fifty yards on foot. The man behind point, another grunt, carried an aluminum ladder. The rule was never exit from an alley. IED's waited. You got half way along and climbed the wall, checked it was clear and dropped on the other side. A pain in the backside, but better that than being ground beef.

The sweep was a bust. No one was surprised. The village was deserted. Cleaned out as my colleagues had rolled into Saddam's HQ. Fear of us or them – take your pick. At the end things got messy. We were saddling up when there was a shout from the direction of the village. We dropped to the ground and began to scan for the noise. Some of the bastards liked to shoot you in the front and any unexpected loud noise was a signal to drop, not look.

A shape cut between two of the houses and we tracked it. Then a grubby white piece of material emerged from the corner of the last building. Six of us took a bead on it. 'American. Friend,' shouted a voice. No one was fooled. 'Corporal Jack Mizar.' That had our attention. The white fluttered.

'Step into the open,' shouted the sergeant, never taking his eye from his gun sight. A US uniform stepped out and we readied to drop the figure. 'Open your jacket and drop it. Walk towards us. Jones, Craig, get behind us in case the bastards are sneaky.'

Two of our men crawled around to the back of the vehicle. The figure lost his jacket and walked towards us. 'Slowly,' said the sergeant now scanning the surrounding buildings. There were no obvious explosives strapped to the man but this was still far from a done deal. 'Turn round. A full 360.' The man did so and still there was nothing to see but a stained shirt on his torso.'

Sweat began to pool in my back and I had to rub at my eyes to keep them clear. The man closed in on us. If he was being used by the Hajis then they might just place a bullet through his head at the last moment. It's how the psyche game was played.

MELTDOWN

'Stop,' the sergeant barked. The man was twenty yards from us. 'Quick, your name, rank, serial number and a bloody good story.'

'Private Jack Mizar, 325th Airborne Infantry Regiment. Got separated from the unit three days ago. Place was alive with the enemy, sir. Waited for two days until they cleared out. Hid in a basement and was thinking about trying to walk out when you turned up.'

The sergeant signaled for him to walk forward and everyone waited for the bullet. But it never came. It turned out that Jack was one lucky SOB. He had waited and it had come good. That was my motto now. Wait and it'll come good.

So I began the wait.

Chapter 13

The door slams open and one of the suits rolls in. 'Fucking up.' I stare at him from the bed. 'Any chance of a 'please'?' He steps up the edge of the bed and drops a balled fist on my stomach. I gasp.

'I said fucking up.' I raise my arm in surrender. 'Shit, ok.' I roll from the bed and, as I stand, I think about a swift punch to the suit's gut but he looks like he bench presses small elephants for fun and I play the compliant man.

'Out' He points to the door and I wonder why the aggression. Tampoline has me by the balls and I'm no threat to single people. For me two is the magic number. Maybe he just had a domestic with his boyfriend. I walk through the door and into the hall. There's no one else around. Tampoline is taking no chances. My arms are grabbed from behind and a pair of plastic cuffs slid around my wrists. 'To the left'. As he says it he pushes me in the back. 'And no fucking lip.'

'Come on…' the punch to my kidneys stops me speaking mid syllable. 'I told you to keep it fucking shut.'

I decide to keep it fucking shut.

We zig-zag through a maze of halls and doors until we hit a large metal shuttered door. A black box sits next to it at waist level. The suit presses his hand on it and, with a whir, the shutter rises. Beyond is dark and smells of damp.

MELTDOWN

'In' He shoves me forward and somewhere above a sensor flicks lights into action.

The damp is joined by the smell of gasoline.

The suit walks past me. 'Wait here. Right fucking here.' I nod. He marches into the dark and like a model walking the catwalk the roof above him lights up as he moves. Concrete pillars throw out shadows as he vanishes into the distance. It looks like a garage but there are no signs of cars. The receding figure has a fair pace on and there's no far wall to be seen. As garages go this is easily the size of a football field.

The light above me dies and I walk forward and back a few steps to bring it back to life. The lights in front of me go off one by one as if some dark monster is tracking the suit into the garage. The suit hangs a left and in seconds the only light is the one above me and the smallest of glows from the path of the suit.

This place could swallow half a dozen football pitches, not one, and still have room for a few tennis courts.

The shutter behind me closes. A metallic click echoes as my light goes out again. I don't move. In the darkness I can track the movement of the suit. I think about making a run for it but with the motion activated sensors I'd be the easiest prey in the world to follow. I drop to the floor and the light above me comes to life once more.

I sit cross-legged on cold concrete, letting my backside eat up the chill. Back to waiting. An engine fires up. A broken growl that suggests something a bit less environmentally friendly than the compacts that flood the road these days. The distant lights begin to flick on. Faster this time and accompanied by the roar of a vehicle as it heads my way. I lie back and stretch my legs and wonder if the suit will see my move from vertical to horizontal as breaking his 'wait here' rule.

'Up.' The shout is muffled by the misfiring engine of an old Regal. I stand up, but not at the speed the suit wants, and he's out the car and hauling me to my feet. The back door opens and I'm flung in. Before the door is closed the driver guns the engine and we are off.

I slide to the far side and count two in the car – driver and my friendly guard. The car has the smell of long night stakeouts - stale food, sweat and cigarettes. We speed through the underground parking lot and plunge through a short tunnel, up a ramp and slow to a halt. A door in front swings open. We advance a few yards. The door behind closes and another opens. We zip up a second ramp and exit onto a back alley. As we do so my guard pulls a black hood from his pocket and forces it over my head. I'm in a for a mystery ride.

The journey is short, twenty minutes max. The car stops and few seconds later the hood is pulled from my head. We are in another, much smaller garage. Big enough for two cars but stripped of any of the usual mess that garages acquire. The walls are bare and the old strip light above has nothing to cast shadows save the car.

A door to my right is swung open by my guard and I'm pushed through. We enter a laundry room and then through a second door into a hall. The décor is old school and the smell of decay suggests that the occupants are not thick on the ground. I'm pushed forward and into the main room. My guard winds up to give me another shove and I side step it. 'Just ask. I'm not going anywhere. Stop with the macho shit.'

The guard looks at me, shrugs and slams the palm of his hand into my stomach. I double up as my breath vanishes and collapse onto the couch. A cloud of dust welcomes me. I wait for my lungs to start working again and cough as they inhale the settling dust. 'Can I get a drink of water?'

My guard shakes his head and sits on a wooden chair - the only other seat in the room.

'What now?'

He raises his fingers to his lips.

I guess we wait.

***

I doze in fits and starts as the light drops. Outside sodium lighting takes over and my guard has moved once – a brief visit to the bathroom. I asked for the same privilege an hour ago. The bathroom had a metal grill over a two by two window and my guard stood outside while I splashed water on my face. I gulped down as much as I could stand.

There's little traffic outside the house although a distant roar suggests a main highway isn't far away. I'm about to fall asleep again when a car pulls up and I hear it enter the garage. A few seconds later Tampoline arrives. He tells the guard to leave and drops into the chair.

'No coffee?' I say.

'What can I tell you? It's not my house.'

'So where are we?'

'One of the Factors so called safe houses.'

'Not very safe if you know about it?'

'True, but this is where our friend back in the office calls home when he's not down south. We're going to let him go in a few hours and I'm counting on him returning here.'

'And?'

He adjusts his glasses. 'And that's where you come in. As soon as he's free he'll be in touch with his buddies.'

'There not going to be dumb enough to come here.'

'See, Mr McIntyre, that's where you and I differ. I understand people. Of course they'll get in touch with him. How can they resist? They'll want to know what we know. Someone will get in touch.'

'So why do you need me? Aren't you just going to follow who ever arrives?'

'No. They'll suspect that. Whoever they send will have a pre-paid cell. Once he has the info he'll make a call and then be told to take a small vacation. A couple of days in Vegas. Long enough for us to run out of time. Whoever they send won't lead us anywhere useful. I know these guys. We need to be a bit smarter. We're going to let you turn on the charm and then hope they come to the rescue.'

MELTDOWN

I laugh and then start coughing as the dust coats my throat. 'Come on, that's even dumber than the first idea. Why in the hell would they send someone else over?'

'Same reason they will send someone in the first place. They want to know what we know. I've no idea what their end game is but I do know they have one.'

'And won't the new person have orders to take a break in Malibu?'

'Maybe, but this isn't Factor central around here. I'm thinking that there are only a few of them. Maybe three or four – that's how their cells are structured. One boss and two or three grunts. It's the boss we want. He'll lead us where we need to go. If we can get him over then I'm working with something a bit more valuable than a shit sweeper.'

'And your interrogation will be as effective as the guys I saw giving up everything he knows.'

It's Tampoline's turn to laugh. A cold, metallic cackle. 'My dear Mr McIntyre, the grunt you saw had already spilled everything he knew. I put that show on for your benefit. Trust me, if we get the boss we will get the information we need.'

'So you do the killing.'

'No. These guys will smell a trap at a hundred paces. We won't be within a mile of this place. You do your stuff, gives us a call and we wait. When they arrive it'll look legit.'

'This is bollocks. It won't look any different to a set up.'

Tampoline lifts his stick and points it at the ceiling. 'Look up. In the corner, near the window. It's small but if you look hard you'll see a small camera. Looks like a black sugar cube. We've tapped into it. At the moment it's showing re runs of an empty house. They've got them all over. When the show goes live they'll be watching and when things kick off it'll be a Spielberg moment. Solid gold movie action. Authentic to the hilt. That's why we need you.'

I hate these guys.

'So to business.'

'Look, I can't just switch on whatever it is you think I have.'

Tampoline is tapping his stick on the floor. 'Are you sure about that?'

'Yes.'

'Stress seems to work.'

I say nothing.

'So here's the deal. Phone!'

I realize that the last word is an order. My guard reappears with a cell in hand. 'I have someone that wants to talk to you.' My guard throws me the phone. It's a cheap pre-paid. I put it to my ear. 'Hello.'

'Hi, mate.'

'Charlie?'

'The one and only.'

Charlie was the bar tender who mainlined me liquor for a few years when I first left the asylum. He then helped me nail Lendl. After that we had gone on the run until

MELTDOWN

Charlie had to take time out to clear up some domestic stuff. I sigh. He also killed my wife. 'Where are you?'

'No idea. They lifted me two days ago and I haven't seen sunlight since.'

'What do they want?'

'You got me on that one.'

The phone is ripped from my ear by my guard. He hangs up and leaves.

'So here's the deal.' Tampoline says. 'You help us and Charlie gets back to his bar and you get back to whatever's left of your life.'

'Yeah, like I care about Charlie - the guy who killed my wife.'

Tampoline smiles. 'You know it wasn't him.'

'Fuck you.'

'Nice a bit of anger. That's the ticket, Mr McIntyre.'

'So one way or another someone is going to die. Is that what you're saying?'

'Home run. Only it can be a friend of yours or a piece of garbage that wants to screw up the way we live. Doesn't seem like a hard choice to me.'

'I can't switch the thing on. It's not the way it works.'

'That's your problem to solve. All I know is that there will be one less bartender on the planet if you don't perform. We'll let Martyn go shortly and then it's over to you. Let's just makes sure you know the playbook. If you run your friend dies, if you fail he dies, if you try and screw us over he dies. Does that seem clear enough?'

I say nothing.

'I'll take your silence as acquiescence. We've kitted the under stair closet for you. Spyhole to watch what's going on. TV monitor that will let you see all the cameras in the house, and I've even put in a piss pot and coffee in case things get desperate. You lock the door from the inside.'

I look under the stairs. A triangular shaped door sits beneath the treads. 'What if they don't come in here?'

'Your problem. Use the cameras. Now I need to go. I'd say good luck but I'm not sure how much luck is involved in all this.'

'One last question?'

'Sure.'

'If this works out, what's to stop you locking me up and trying to use me?'

'Nothing other than my word as a gentleman.'

'Figures.'

'Last thing. Be in the closet before they arrive. Otherwise you'll be on Candid Camera.'

Chapter 14

Tampoline leaves. I don't move. I need some thinking time. If they release Martyn soon I may have less than an hour before he arrives. Plan A would be to make a run for it. That would also involve Charlie and an early funeral. Plan B isn't quite formed in my head yet. It may never be. I decided to recce the house. Single story, suburban, family home. Kitchen, three bedrooms, lounge, small box room and kitchen. A thin layer of dust covers everything and I avoid touching surfaces. A giveaway to anyone looking for signs of recent activity.

I flip open the closet under the stairs. As Tampoline promised it has been furnished in early stake out. The key is in the lock. I try the space for size. Cramped but bearable. I flick on the TV monitor and after a bit of experimenting find I can pull up six different views. The only room without a camera is the box room. Even the bathroom is online.

The spy hole in the door is tiny. I press my eye to it and can see the chair I was sitting in and most of the room. The camera gives a better view. I pop a piece of paper in my mouth and chew. I stick the chewed paper in the spy hole and feel better. It'll be dark soon and the TV light might be visible through the hole. A couple of old cloths will stop light leaking under the door and the seal around the rest of the door looks good enough to keep my presence unnoticed.

Happy my new abode is fit for purpose I exit and make for the rear to grab some air. The door is locked but a key is hanging on a nail. Security seems a bit thin for a so-called safe house.

The back yard is scrub and weeds. A six-foot fence keeps the neighbors at bay. The hood in the car was designed to keep me guessing where I am but the skyline is pure New York. By my reckoning I'm somewhere out towards Newark airport. A plane circles low down and I can only be a couple of miles from the airport. I was born not far from here. I think about walking to the end of the yard but I've no idea how long it'll be before Martyn arrives and I don't want to be caught outside or on camera.

Closing and locking the door behind me I pee in the bathroom sink and wash round and dry the basin. The toilet water in the bowl has all but evaporated and smart person would know it had been flushed recently. I slide into the closet.

I get comfortable. Flick a few times around the house on the TV to get the feel of the camera positions. Check the coffee flask. I could do with something to eat but there's nothing and a trip to the Seven Eleven isn't on the cards. I'll leave the coffee to later. I may need the caffeine if this turns into a late one. I stretch out my legs and if I angle myself just right I can get a full leg stretch on.

Now for the game plan. Tampoline wants a little action and hopes that the Factor will ride into town and rescue their comrade. I think this is bull. The plan is so tenuous that, even in my world of pain, it has about as much

MELTDOWN

chance of success as a Jay Leno interview being unscripted. I can only conclude that things must be desperate. After all, if the US oil reserve is really up shit creek and the best they can do is put me on the ball park then things are not rosy in Tampoline's patch. He's counting on me being able to set Martyn and whoever appears at each other's throats. I can neither guarantee that will happen or really want it. I can be the catalyst for some bad stuff but it comes at a price. A stunning headache, entry to some bizarre blue world and a need for high level stress or pain to kick it all off. Afterwards I'm for shit. At the TT I had to stab myself in the leg to kick it all off. I nearly died from the loss of blood.

My best guess is that Martyn turns up and he's hung out to dry by his friends and I can do nothing about it. Even if someone does turn up he may not know Martyn, and my shit only works if people know each other. All in all the chances of something going down are thin as my waist.

I settle in for the wait. It gives me time to think. Never a good idea at the moment. My life lacks the basics. Friends, fun, freedom. It revolves around finding a place to hole up and postponing my life. Hotels were the norm after the TT until my cash ran low and Charlie split. From then on in it was any port in storm. The closet is far from the worse place I've stayed this last year. Warm, coffee and six channels on cable isn't bad.

I'm bolt awake as I hear the front door open. Shit. I had dozed off. The TV monitor is in sleep mode and I hit the remote. The old tube takes a few seconds to warm up. A fuzzy picture of the main room materializes and then clears. It's dark and I can only guess that I've been sleeping for a good few hours. The camera sits above the door to my closet and doesn't cover the front door. A bad design flaw. Entrances and exits are essential in surveillance.

Martyn drifts by and I hear his footsteps as he passes me. His long hair and beard are gone and he's now dressed in a Super Dry top and chinos. He's been shopping. I flip to the kitchen camera but he doesn't appear. I pull up the bathroom and he's getting ready for a whizz. I flip back to the kitchen. There's no need for me to get intimate with this guy.

The flush signals he's finished and he enters the kitchen. He pulls open doors and drawers but comes up empty. He fishes out a cell, plays around with it and then talks. The cameras have no sound. I guess we might be in for a bit of fast food. The cell has to be new. It would be a dead giveaway if he used one he had when he was picked up. He opens the back door and vanishes. I use the cameras to dart around the other rooms in case he has a friend in tow but we are a twosome.

I wonder how confident he is that he hasn't been followed. The agency are not short on resources. He has to suspect that they are using him. After all, why let him go? But, then again, losing a tail is far easier than it appears in the movies. If you really want to keep an eye on someone then you need a large head count, plenty of mobility and constant communication. Even then it's a major job to keep track of someone who wants to lose you.

In my short and less than illustrious career in the army we had been given the basics on surveillance. Rule number one was not to let them know you were watching. Once they knew this there was no rule number two that would keep your target in sight. It was just too difficult to cover all eventualities. The visit to the back yard and the call either suggests he feels safe or is playing to the crowd. Only time will tell.

He reappears in the kitchen. I hear him walk past the closet and he goes on a tour, checking the ins and outs of the house. He returns to the main room and I freeze as he tries the door to my closet. He rattles it but the lock holds. I can see him looking round. Maybe for a key. He tries the door once more and then steps into the middle of the room. He's looking at the closet. Something has pricked his radar but short of kicking the door in he hasn't got many options. He keeps looking and I wonder if he can sense me. Maybe dust knocked from the door as I entered. The lack of a key. The suspicion that he has been followed. He takes another look and then flops into the chair I had been in. A cloud of dust floats up and he coughs.

If I thought I was in for more waiting I'm wrong. There's a knock at the door and Martyn gets up and lets someone in. 'Why did they let you go?' The accent is deep New Jersey.

'Not sure.' Martyn's voice is croaky with dust.

'Did you talk?'

'Only what we agreed. They know nothing.'

They both walk into view. Martyn's new mate is a small squat man. Heavy on designer stubble and suited and booted in JC Penney's best. The collar is straining and the polka dotted tie has more of a nineties feel than one off the rack last week. 'Did they follow you?'

'Of course, but once I got on the motorbike they were dust. I dropped it up town, jumped on to the E and then grabbed a cab. I let the cab go in Hoboken. Had a drink and watched the world go by and then another two cabs and the local bus plus a few trips to the washrooms and shops of Springfield. A haircut, a change of clothes and I'm here.

'They could still be on your tail,' says Bad Suit

'Did you check the cameras?'

'Yes. Clean. No one has been in here. I've also got two more people circling. If they're in the area, we'll spot them. They'll phone when they know we're clear, but don't underestimate those bastards. Tampoline has more money than God and he wants his Iranian friend back big time.'

'Is he still safe?'

'How would I know? Need to know.'

'What do we do now?'

'You do nothing. My orders are to find out what you know and then you can go masturbate in public for all I care. Take me through what happened.'

Martyn gives him the low down. He was picked up at his local bar. He doesn't know how they made him but he suspects that he was grassed up. Bad Suit leaps on this and spends ten minutes asking who might have done that but Martyn doesn't have any ideas. This makes Bad Suit unhappy and he isn't slow in letting Martyn know. Martyn puts up a good defense but Bad Suit isn't placated.

Threats of reprisals on Martyn's family and friends are made and Martyn isn't in a good place. The rest of the story is one of suits, fists and a beaten confession. Bad Suit asks to see the bruises and punches a few to check they're genuine. These guys have suspicion as their middle name.

It takes an hour for the debrief. I know that Tampoline will be watching and the lack of any action won't make me his favorite. Bad Suit seems satisfied but there's an edge in the room. Martyn's face is sour and then Bad Suit goes from inquisitor to his best friend. 'You did well, Martyn. Very well. They're still in the dark and you helped us. I'll see you get a reward for this. It's not easy taking a beating, but the organization needs people like you. Hard workers. People who put their life on the line for what they believe in. What we are doing is *so* important. We need to let America see that they can't bend over and take it from every raghead, chink and blackie that wants to own a piece of us. We need to fight and this is the most important step we've ever taken. This will wake them up to what we face.'

Martyn smiles a little but the whole speech feels false. One for the boys just before they go over. Bad Suit moves out of view. 'I think a drink might be in order. What's your poison?'

Martyn looks towards the kitchen. 'A beer would be good.'

'A beer it is. I'll be back in a minute.' Bad Suit exists through the back door. He's gone a good ten minutes and Martyn is soon pulling at the drapes to see if he's outside. Bad Suit walks back into the kitchen, a six pack of Coors Light in one hand. 'A bit warm I'm afraid. But brewed right here in the good old US of A. No foreign shit.'

He hands Martyn a beer. Martyn reaches up to take the bottle opener being offered and Bad Suit reaches into his jacket and, in a well-practiced move, removes a gun and cracks it across Martyn's head. Martyn drops like a wet cloth to the floor.

Bad Suit grabs Martyn under the shoulders and lays him out on the couch. He works through his pockets and removes the cell. He places a piece of paper on the table next to the couch and runs to the kitchen. I switch views and see him reach under the stove. With a massive pull he yanks on something and then returns to the main room. Martyn is stirring and Bad Suit gives him another crack on the head. Martyn slumps back. Bad Suit grabs the beers and takes a last look around before he's out of the front door. I hear the sound of a car starting and I give it a few minutes before I reach for the lock.

I push the door open and stand up. Bones crack. I go for Martyn and check him. Still breathing. Then the smell hits me. Gas. That's what Bad Suit was doing in the kitchen. I head towards the kitchen but the smell is over powering and I cough hard and struggle for breath. Better to get the hell out than try and stop it.

I drop to the carpet and crawl back to Martyn. I pull him onto the floor and slap his face but he's out cold. I stand up to get a grip of him. We need out and we need out now. But as soon as I stand, the gas is in my lungs and I have to hit the floor for air. I try and drag Martyn along the carpet but it's impossible. I can't get any leverage and the hiss of escaping gas suggests that the mains are leaking like a stuck pig.

I change tack and crawl to the front door. If I can get it open it might draw the gas out but when I reach up the handle it's locked.

Shit.

How dumb am I. I race across the floor and pull the kitchen door shut. The fucking obvious is never so obvious when you are in a shit storm. I grab the table that sits next to the couch and hurl it at the front window but the drapes catch it and it falls to the floor. Like a baby on speed I zip over the floor, reach up and yank the drapes from their rails. I pick up the table again and this time, holding firmly to one of its legs, I lash out at the window but the table bounces back.

Even with the door shut the gas seems to be getting thicker and my cough is constant. My eyes are streaming and my throat is on fire. I place both my feet against the wall beneath the window lean back and grab the table, a leg for each hand. I make my old sergeant happy by doing my best ever sit up and smash the chair into the window. This time the window explodes and glass showers down on me. I kneel up and stick my head into the night. Never has air in the city tasted so good. I draw six or seven breaths, wait for a coughing fit to pass and head back for Martyn.

It takes real muscle to move a man, even a small one, and Martyn is easily one hundred and eighty pounds. I get him to the window and throw him over the edge – head outside, the rest of him inside. I check he's still breathing and join him for more fresh air.

I hack my way back to normal breathing and jump outside. I reach back and grab Martyn and try and haul him into the front yard. My muscles feel weak and I'm aware that a spark could lift the house into orbit with the amount of gas that must now fill the kitchen. Martyn is dead weight and the gas and effort are draining me. I heave his shoulders over the edge of the window and pause for a breath.

'Put him back.'

The words are in my right ear. I drop Martyn. He slumps. His head and an arm draped over the edge. A touch of metal on my ear keeps me still. I see the edge of a gun and I can smell smoker's breath. Stale and heavy with Scotch. He coughs. 'I don't know who the fuck you are but stand up slowly.' The voice is familiar. Bad Suit.

My head is starting to pound. A headache building at the base of my skull. I stand up. Bad Suit's an amateur. Holding a gun that close is a crap idea. If he's nervous an itchy trigger finger could wipe me out before he gets a chance to find out what I'm doing. And if I'm quick I can duck and his first bullet will miss. Amateurs are so unpredictable. The good news is that if he was a pro, and wanted me dead, we wouldn't be having this conversation. I cough as the gas escaping the window wraps itself around me. Bad Suit pushes the barrel hard against bone. He forces my head away from him. I step sideways and he reaches over and pushes Martyn's head. Martyn flops back inside the house. He turns to me. 'Now who are you?'

I try to look at him but he uses the gun to keep my face away. 'I was passing by and I saw this guy trying to climb through the window. I'm trying to help him.'

'Is that so? What do we think?'

'Bullshit.' A new voice. To my rear and left. Probably near the sidewalk. 'I saw you climb out the window.'

I nod. ' Yeah. After I saw the window smash.'

The gun raps my head. Hard enough to split the skin. 'Look, we saw you climb out. You were inside.'

'Ok, so I was inside. I saw you leave and I figured that there might be something worth stealing. So I broke in and found the gas on and this guy on the coach. What are you going to do? Phone the police?'

'Why this house?'

'The yard is overgrown but not wild. Suggests that it's tended but not recently. This is an ok neighbor-hood. You had a suit on. I think to myself a businessman who isn't around much. Back for a day and off. No family or the yard would be neater. No clothes on the line. First dry day in a while. Definitely no family. No alarm box. Nice, easy target. Can we get the guy out now?'

'No.'

'You're going to let him die?'

'It's his house. He must have switched on the gas. If he wants to top himself then that's up to him.'

'You can't let the guy die.'

'Watch me.'

'For crying out loud.'

'Is he a friend?'

'Look…'

He cracks the gun on my head again. My headache builds pressure and I can feel the kernel that sits deep inside begin to crack. And that is never good news.

'Enough.' My voice is loud.

'Or what?' Says Bad Suit. 'Can you out-run a bullet?'

'You fire that thing this close to the gas and we all end up jelly.'

Silence. He hadn't figured on that. The metal leaves my head and I duck. The next blow whistles over my head and I twist as I drop. I lash out at his legs but his momentum is against the blow and he grunts as my leg connects with his shin but he doesn't go down.

A shout goes up and I see his friend take a step towards us. Three's a crowd. I roll in the dirt and swing my trailing foot up and uncoil it into Bad Suit's gut. There's no six-pack going on and my foot sinks into flab. Bad Suit gasps and falls back. I land with my back against the house wall just below the window. Bad Suit's friend is six steps away. My new attacker is Bad Suits double. Another squat, ex gym type. A scar across his neck suggests that this is not his first time at this sort of thing. A New York Rangers top hangs over a pair of khaki, cut down denims. The guy is no fashion victim. He swings a kick at me and catches the inside of my thigh. I scream. He steps back for seconds.

I fall to my right and this time he catches me on the hip. I try and roll with the kick and he drops on me. Mistake. I drive my fist up as he comes down and through a stunning headache I see his face crumple as I make contact with his nose. There's no crack of bone but the blow stuns him. He falls to one side, grabbing at his face. Bad Suit's starting to rise. I join him and step away from the gas pouring from the window. Bad Suit rolls his head on his neck and rubs at his gut. He scans the ground. He's looking for the gun.

I could run. It would be the sensible thing to do. Bad Suit hasn't spotted his gun; it's lying behind him and Fashion Victim is still nursing his nose. Time to slip on the old Nikes and put rubber to cement. But I can't leave Martyn. Even though he could be dead by now. My choices are low and the headache's now a screaming jet engine in my head. My thoughts are clouded and Bad Suit has spotted the gun. Fashion Victim is transferring his interest from his nose to me.

I look around, hoping that someone might be witnessing this. But we're in a wilderness of suburban housing and everyone is huddled inside for the evening. Even good weather can't keep the New Jersey workers from their dose of soaps and season finales. We are in a dead end and there are five houses looking on, but light from each is muted through pulled drapes and shutters.

A car engine cuts in above the hum of the freeway but it fades as it passes out of sight. Maybe the agency left someone to watch, but even if they did, would they step in? Not a chance. They now have two suspects to trail should I end my days in the next few seconds. And my murder would give them no end of leverage. *Tell us what you know and we don't feed you to the NJ Police for multiple homicide.*

Bad Suit spots his weapon and picks it up. My headache goes supernova and then the kernel explodes. I drop to the ground as the pain engulfs my head. I lurch forward and vomit and a gun goes off. My headache climbs to new heights and I'm sick again. Then a blue wave washes across my world and I'm dropped in to a cool blue world. The headache vanishes and I stand up.

The planet moves in fits and starts. I see Bad Suit drop the gun, still smoking, in slow motion. Spinning from his hand. The barrel bouncing on the dirt. Flipping end over end and coming to rest with the butt towards me. Then Bad Suit drops to his knees – double quick. A hand cranked movie moment. I turn to see Fashion Victim sprawled on the ground. A deep blue stain spreading across his New York Ranger top. Above him the gas escaping from the house is duck egg blue. Rising in clouds that slowly disperse. In the blue world the night is day.

My vision has built in night goggles. Bad Suit doesn't move and I step into the clouds of gas and reach over the window and in single movement pull Martyn up and out of the building. He lifts as easily as marshmallows from a paper bag. I pull him to the sidewalk. The blue world starts to fade and in seconds the night is back. My headache's gone and time takes up a normal rhythm.

Bad Suit lies still. Fashion Victim is stiller. I scan the area. A car sits across the nearest neighbors drive. I decide that hanging around is not going to end anywhere good and I drag Martyn across the road. The car is unlocked but there are no keys in the ignition. I get Martyn strapped into the passenger side. I'm waiting for the distant sound of a siren. After all, even a re run of The Simpsons can't be more intriguing than the sound of gunfire outside your front door.

I walk back to Bad Suit. I roll him over and I can see that he's trying to figure what the hell just went down. I search his pockets but come up empty. 'Where are the keys?'

He looks up at me and points at Fashion Victim. Shit. I walk over and avoid the worst of the blood and find the keys in his back pocket. I look down at the mess on me as I return to the car. I'm going to be firmly in the fame for this if the police get here. Fingerprints all over the house. Blood on my clothes. And once they find my prints in the closet with the TV it'll all get a bit awkward.

With a last look round I jump in the car and take off – adding Grand Theft Auto to my growing list of misdemeanors.

Chapter 15

Bad Suit and Fashion Victim have a nice choice in cars. A few years old, BMW Five Series. Obviously fucking up your nation is well paid. I check Martyn again and he's still breathing. I should take him to hospital but I've had bad experiences with hospitals before. He'll need to take his chances.

I feel weak. A kitten with ME. The aftermath of the events is getting worse. I slap my face and try to concentrate.

It's been a few years since I've been in the neighborhood but I know enough to get around. I need a bolthole and one that's agency proof. Not easy as they have a way of sniffing me out. It's not about distance; it's about finding somewhere off the grid. Given that my billfold is in Tampoline's office it would need to be Martyn's treat. I reach inside his pants and pull out his wallet. He has a hundred dollars in cash. ATM's are out at the moment. His cards will be red flagged. So we need somewhere easy to get to, not obvious and cheap. A hostel would be good but I need something a little more private. I have an idea but it's a stretch.

Time for a little bad driving. I hit a one way and turn up it the wrong way and keep my eyes on the rear view mirror. A black Regal follows me. Figures. I exit onto the next road and U turn across the traffic to a concerto of horns. I flash past the Regal. I spot an alley and fly down it, cross two streets and crash another one way the wrong way. A few blocks further and I enter another alley, park at the rear of some shops and wait.

Ten minutes crawl by and the Regal doesn't appear. I scan the area for any cameras and it's clear. 'Ok, Martyn, time to wake up.' I slap him but his head just rolls with the blow. I slap him once more and his head rocks the other way.

I look around the car for inspiration but come up blank. I start to think that I should dump Martyn and go solo but I have a plan forming and Martyn sits centre stage in it. I drop the windows and sit back to wait. I need the rest.

The car is history. I might have twenty minutes max. They will be cruising the back alleys looking for me. I breathe and relax. Counting the minutes. I reach fifteen and I clip Martyn once more and this time he responds. 'Wakey, wakey.'

He opens his eyes and confusion is the order of the day. I try on my best smile but that could just make things worse. 'Martyn, I know you feel crap but we have to move.'

'Where am I? Who are you?'

'Later.'

He throws up in my lap. Wonderful.

He closes his eyes and I slap him. I need him to respond. He opens his eyes 'What the fuck?'

'Sorry, no time for introductions. Your agency friends are on our tail. I'm sure they're keen to finish you off.'

He shakes his head. I haven't time for this. I keep glancing at the alley expecting a Regal to appear. 'Look, I was in the house when the guy with the Bad Suit hit you with his gun. He turned on the gas and left you to die. I pulled you free.' I open my palms and shrug my shoulders. Trying to look like his mate. He looks at me as if I have just stepped off a spaceship. I sigh. 'Seriously Martyn, we have no more time for discussion.'

'I have no idea who you are.' He spits out some of the vomit as he speaks. Nice.

'I know, but your name is Martyn Wheeler. You belong to something called the Factor. You were lifted by a black ops agency and given a grilling. Some guy gave you a kicking. You said nothing that time. You were let go and did a great impression of James Bond in losing your tail. At the house the guy in the Bad Suit sweated news out of you. He got real friendly at the end, praised you before he slugged you with his gun, switched on the gas and then for good measure hit you again. I pulled you free.'

'Who are you?'

'Fuck. You can come with me or sit here and wait for whoever comes round the corner. For your sake I hope it's the police because the agency and your friends don't seem to have long-term future for you planned. I didn't need to pull your ass from the fire and I sure as hell ain't hanging around to find who's coming for dinner. I'm counting to ten then you are on your own.'

I open the car door and stagger out. I don't bother with the counting, I just start to walk. I reach the first door and try it. Locked. I try the next and as I reach the third I hear Martyn get out. The handle of the door turns and I pull the door open. I step in.

'Wait.' Martyn catches up with me. 'I need some time to figure this out.'

'Sure, but not here.' I enter a small corridor lit by a single watt bulb. The walls haven't seen paint in an eon. I push on and the next door leads into a small office.

Furnished in late grime it has a single wooden chair and there might be a table but the pile of paper above it hides it well. Another door and we are in shop full of smells. In contrast to the dire back shop, the front is a riot of color. Candles fill the place. Glass shelves groan under the weight of wax and wick. A candle a full three feet tall stands at my feet. Joss sticks are alight on one shelf and on my right a trio of bright green candles are burning. The shop is narrow. Maybe ten feet wide. A young woman sits at a till with her back to a floor-to-ceiling window that looks out onto the street. I'm surprised the shop is open this late. I walk up to her. She's reading and when I cough she jumps. 'Oh my. I didn't hear the bell go.'

'Good book is it?'

She smiles. 'Passes the hours. The boss likes us to stay open 'till midnight. Can I help?'

I try and peer past her and take in the scene beyond but it tells me nothing. 'I was looking for a present for my sister.' She looks at Martyn and registers the bruises and the half-baked look in his eyes but says nothing.

I step to the side to try and get a better view of the street. 'She likes candles that smell of the sea.'

The young woman smiles again. She's more than a little attractive. Tall, short bob black hair and a figure that could be good if the mohair jumper was a little more revealing. Her leggings suggest I'm right.

'I have just the thing.' She steps from the till and heads for one of the shelves. I take the chance to step in and through the window.

'Sir?'

I step back out. 'Sorry I'm... I mean we're due to meet someone and I don't want to be late.'

The young woman brings over a white candle shot through with blue veins. 'Ocean Fresh. One of our better sellers.'

'Could be good. How much?'

'Twenty dollars.'

'Sorry?'

'They are some of the best on the market. Very popular with the celebs. Last up to 150 hours.'

'I was looking for something a little cheaper.'

'Oh.' *For your sister – cheap skate,* I can hear her thinking. She returns the candle and brings another. 'Five dollars?' I pretend to examine it and nod. She wraps it and I hand over too much of my current wealth. All the time I keep an eye on the window but unless the agency suits are wearing orange baseball caps with 'Here I am' they could be anywhere.

MELTDOWN

Whatever the case, we have to move. The candle shop owner is paying way too much attention to Martyn. I thank her and turn to Martyn. 'Say thank you to the nice lady, Paul?' He looks at me with a look that had *Fuck Off* written all over it. But he plays dumb and thanks her with a polite smile.

Once outside I stop looking around and head down the street. You just draw attention if your head is copying the girl from The Exorcist. I have a destination in mind and I spot a bar on the corner and drag Martyn in. He's still playing the subservient role well. I don't want beer; I just need another exit that keeps any followers on the jump. The bar is industrial drinking territory and although it's midweek a lot of patrons are head down. Lifetime achievement awards for alcohol are the norm.

I walk past the barman and look for the washroom. It's at the end of the bar and a fire door sits on the left. I walk up to it and push it open. A shout goes up from the barman as I drag Martyn through and into the street beyond. Head down I walk away from the bar and at the next alley slip in and wait. I count to a hundred and then exit. Martyn trails behind. Four blocks later I'm sure we're not being followed. Unless…

Shit.

I push Martyn into another alley. 'I need to search you.'

'What!'

'You might be bugged.'

'Are you serious?'

'Yes.'

'I'll do it.'

'Do you know what you are looking for?'

'Do you?'

'Yes.' It's a lie. I had some training in the army but not on surveillance and monitoring equipment. Steel Trap Security – my last employer had given me a book on the subject but I'd never opened it. 'Give me your top.'

'I haven't got anything underneath.'

'It'll take me ten seconds to check it.'

He strips it off and throws it at me. Martyn is a regular at the gym – who would have known. I run my hands over the material but find nothing. I give him it back. 'Your shoes.'

'Look, I'm not sure about this…'

I slap him in the face and he reels back. 'I don't care.' I need control. This isn't time for debate. Slapping him might not work. He seemed to take the beating from the suit in his stride. He glares at me. I glare back. 'Shoes?' He reaches down and pulls them off. I play with them for a bit but come up blank. 'Pants.'

'Fuck off.' He says it out of reach. I lift my left foot to walk forward and he backs off. I throw my hands up. 'Martyn, you might not believe this but I'm trying to help you.'

'Sure. And slapping me is your way of showing it.'

'No, it's my way of saying we don't have time to dick around.'

'Check them while I still have them on.'

'No.'

'Yes.' He moves away. I turn to look at the road. Clear. 'OK. Come here.' There's reluctance in his steps. I pat him down but I've no idea what I'm looking for. 'Ok, I think you're clear.'

'And you?'

'I'm clean.'

'You certain?'

I wasn't. I had been out cold. They could have planted anything on me and given Tampoline's plan it would make sense. I throw my jacket at Martyn. 'See if you can find anything that shouldn't be there.'

'I thought you were the expert.'

'I am. I'll check it as well.' I work through the rest of my clothes and Martyn gives me the jacket back. I check it. If they have bugged us it's too small to find on a casual search. I need to be sure. If we are bugged then there's no way out. I look up the alley and see a row of dumpsters. 'Stay here.' Martyn shrugs his shoulders. 'Where else am I going to go?'

Dumpster diving is not a great sport and by the third one I've not found any clothes that might be useable. I hear two voices coming up the alley from the opposite end. I freeze and turn. I try and signal Martyn but he's slumped against the wall and not looking at me.

The voices are slurred. Two down and outs emerge. I jump out of the dumpster and they freeze. They're both five feet ten or so. Both have full, matted beards and both are wearing heavy overcoats. One has an old beret on his head and the other has a bobble hat. The neck of a bottle is sticking out a brown paper bag in the hand of Bobble Hat.

'Good evening gentlemen.'

Neither speaks. Their eyes are hidden in the dark and the way they're swaying back and forth suggests there may have been other bottles before the one they are on.

'I have a deal for you.'

Still silence.

'I need to swap clothes. You can keep the overcoat but I need your shoes, pants and tops. In return you can have mine and my friend's.'

No words.

'A fair swap.'

'Why?' Bobble Hat's voice is thick with drink.

'Does it matter?'

'Maybe.'

'I can sweeten the deal. A ten spot on top.'

'Tops, pants and shoes?'

'Yes.'

'For everything you're wearing?'

'Everything. You can have my boxers if you want.'

Beret whispers into Bobble Hat's ear but it's so loud Martyn could probably hear it. 'Wants to get us naked and play with us.'

I can't blame him. I'd be suspicious as hell. 'Look here's how we do this. My friend and I strip off and put our clothes on the ground and we walk up to the street. You change one at a time and if we come back down before you're finished you can high tail it.'

MELTDOWN

'I'm not stupid,' says Beret. 'I'm fried and couldn't run a yard.'

'Your loss.'

'Another way.'

'Sorry?'

'I have another way.'

'Fire away.'

'We walk to the end of the alley and you strip. You then piss off back here and we get changed out in the street. Once we're done you can come and get the clothes.'

Smart. 'Deal.'

'And it's twenty dollars.'

'Ten.'

'Fuck mister, you look like you could afford a hundred.' Beret is nowhere near as drunk as Bobble Hat.

'Twenty.'

'Up front.'

I hand him twenty. Seventy-five left and I'm a candle up and the promise of an alcoholic's stained clothes. They sway up the alley and I follow. I want them to move quicker. If we are bugged then the agency should be here. The fact there not suggests that we are bug free but I can't take the chance.

When we reach Martyn I explain the deal. 'Are you nuts? I'm not putting on pants someone has pissed or shit in.'

Beret turns to him. 'Who said we had pissed or shit in them? I'm not a fucking heathen. I take a pride. I may be living out of a bottle but you have no idea who the fuck I am. As far as I can see you are the ones in the shit. Why else would you be trading clothes in a back alley with a couple of derelicts?'

I don't interrupt and let Martyn take the verbal beating.

'Now do you want our clothes?' Beret turns to me as he speaks.

'Yes.'

'Well strip.'

I look at Martyn and he shakes his head. I nod. We remove everything but our boxers.

'Everything,' says Beret.

'No way,' says Martyn.

'Look son. If you're naked then you ain't gonna chase us.'

The urgency to get this shit over is overpowering. 'Just do it', I shout. Martyn drops his boxers and so do I. Beret picks them up 'Down the alley.'

We retreat. When we reach the dumpster we wait as they strip and change. They are quick and when they've got their coats on they walk off. 'Time to try on our new wardrobe.' I say. Martyn doesn't smile.

We're halfway back to the road when a couple, out for a late night stroll, pass the alley. The girl looks down and she stops dead. Her partner is dragged to a stop. She pulls at his hand and he looks round. Martyn and I stop walking. Our hands drop to cover our manhood. The man yanks at the girl and pulls her out of site. I break into a run. 'Quick, if they see a police officer she could talk.'

MELTDOWN

Beret was half way to the truth. The clothes could be worse. But they could have been better. For a start I'm five inches too tall for them and although Martyn's seem to fit he's still retching. 'This is gross.' The shoes don't fit and there are no socks.

'Back down the alley. Now.' I pull at him and we break in to a run. We are both bare foot and the stone alley is cold and littered with debris. We slow down as we reach the street. Martyn turns to me 'Where are we going?'

'A few blocks.' I'm lying. I think it's probably nearer ten or twelve.

'My feet are bleeding.'

Across the road there are a pile of plastic bags filled with garbage. I cross over and empty them out. I choose the cleanest bags and call Martyn over. I wrap a bag round each of his feet and tie them off with a strip from the shirtsleeve I'm wearing. I do the same to myself. It's not much protection, but it'll have to do.

We set off again. Me in a set of battered Levis and a pinstripe shirt of indeterminate origin and Martyn in Lee Coopers and a hoodie. 'Keep your head down. Play the part and look out for trouble. Beating up on bums is a national sport in some towns.'

Chapter 16

Five blocks on and the rain starts. It's a mixed blessing. The smell of the clothes starts to wash away but heat begins to seep with it. We stand under a fire escape in the next alley - the pair of us are pressed up against the wall in a doorway. The rain winds up and our shelter is next to useless. Martyn jabs me in the ribs. 'I thought you said a couple of blocks?'

'I've not been here for years.'

'Where are we going?'

'A safe place.'

'In this gear?'

'It won't matter.' At least it wouldn't have mattered twenty years ago. My plan is counting on someone still being where I left them two decades past. The rain shows no sign of easing and I couldn't get any wetter if I went for a swim. 'Come on. The sooner we get there the better.'

Head down and walk. Plastic bags flapping around our feet. Each time we cross a street I take point and look out and check it's safe to cross. Each time Martyn just leans on a wall and sighs. The rain eases off but a chill wind nips in behind it and I'm shivering. It can't be more than a few more blocks. I recognize an old mission on the next street and I know I'm heading the right way.

Two more blocks and I stop. I look out and the street has frozen in time. Old townhouses line one side. The other is a row of boarded up shops. They were boarded up last time I was here. The stoop to each house is bordered with metal rails and I know that further down 'Coin's in the Pocket' will still be manned by Tight Sean and the beer will come with free added water. I'm certain that the 'CM loves LT' will still be carved into the door of the third cubicle in the restroom. The neon in the window will still say Pabst Blue Ribbon – Sean got it as a freebie from another bar owner.

I scan the doors in the townhouses. I spot my goal. The front door is still canary yellow. Only Linda would see it as a good color for a front door. I indicate to Martyn to cross the road. We walk to the yellow door and this time I keep my head moving. Looking for any signs of the agency. It might be a giveaway when I was dressed in a jacket but now I just look mad.

Clear. I jump up the stairs, swallow hard and knock. A few seconds later the drapes twitch. Then nothing. I wait. Nothing. I ring again and then realize what's wrong. I look nothing like the Craig McIntyre of old. I lean down to the mail slot. 'Linda it's me. Craig McIntyre.'

Back then I was thirty pounds heavier and had a full head of hair. I was also dressed in something a little less arresting and didn't have a battered friend as company. 'Linda, it really is me.' The drapes twitch again. Nothing. 'Linda, the last time I saw you we were standing out here. You had just told me to fuck off because I didn't want to marry you. You told me that, and I think these were the words – *I'm not a drunken slag. I'm in love with you. So put up or fuck off.*'

A light goes on in the hall and a voice echoes down. 'I told you I wasn't a drunken shag you shit.' The door opens and Linda has aged far better than me. She takes in the scene. 'What the hell?'

'I'll explain.' I walk in and Martyn follows.

Linda closes the door. She's lost weight. Probably more than I have. She's just under six feet. I have a thing for tall girls. Her hair is blonde. Maybe a bit more bottle than real nowadays. Her face has few extra wrinkles but the loss of weight has pulled in her cheeks and it's not a great look. She's still a looker but maybe a diet too many. She's wearing skintight jeans and calf length boots with a white blouse. She hasn't changed her style in twenty years. Her face is screwed up. 'What the hell is that smell?'

'Us. I can explain, but can we get out of this stuff?'

'Who's your friend?'

'Can we change first?'

'Into what?'

'You threw all my stuff out?'

'Yeah, about ten minutes after I told you to fuck off.'

'I'm hurt.'

'Upstairs, next to the bathroom. There's a closet. At the bottom is your old suitcase. Try it.'

'That's touching.'

'Fuck off and don't come down the pair of you 'till you're scrubbed and those clothes are lying in my back yard. Throw them out the window and I'll get my flame thrower on them in the morning.'

MELTDOWN

She turns to go. I touch her on the shoulder. 'I'm sorry.'

'So you should be you selfish bastard.'

As she vanishes into the kitchen we head upstairs. I root around the closet and pull out my suitcase. I carry it into the bathroom and open it. I examine the clothes. I had taste back then.

I turn to offer Martyn first choice but he's already naked and jumping in the shower. 'I'm going to be in here for a week.' I strip, exit to let him shower and enter Linda's bedroom. It feels wrong to be here with no clothes and I pull a towel from a pile and wrap myself in it. I sit on the edge of the bed and wait for my turn under the hot water.

I hear Linda downstairs. There's the chink of crockery and food wouldn't go a miss. The shower shows no sign of slowing and I lie back on the bed. I wonder if it's the same one that Linda and I first made love on. Footsteps on the stairs halt my train of thought. Linda walks in. 'Off my bed.'

I slip off and stand, like a schoolboy on his first date. Linda shakes her head. 'How long have you been on the street?'

'A few hours.'

'Sorry?'

I can see confusion. 'I'm not living on the street.'

'So the new you is a natty line of clothing along with the bald look and the slimmed down post drug body shape.'

'Two out of three isn't bad.'

'Honestly Craig. What in the hell?'

'Shower, change of clothes, a cup of coffee and I'll tell you all.'

She turns to leave and I uncross my fingers from behind my back. Telling all is not something that's going to happen.

As she heads back down the stairs the shower is still running up a power bill and maybe Martyn is making good on his promise to spend seven days under the thing. I sit back on the bed and a few minutes later the water stops and it's my turn.

Martyn has to turn up my pants and shirt to fit my clothes and he looks like the star of the 'Disappearing Man'. I squeeze past him to get to the bathroom. 'Linda has coffee on downstairs, but wait on me. Don't go down. I need to do the talking. I don't want you dropping us in the brown stuff.'

The shower is gold. A moment of cleansing. I may have only had the clothes on for a short while but the sense of relief is glorious. I scrub and polish. My liberal use of Linda's expensive looking cleaning agents will no doubt draw some criticism. The only downside is that Martyn seems to have used every towel in sight. I make do with the driest of the bunch and slip into my clothes from another era.

My pants are six inches too much round the waist but my shirt isn't bad. The last year on the run had kept me fit and I'd stuck with a daily routine of sit-ups and what my old sergeant called isometrics to keep up the muscle mass.

MELTDOWN

The sneakers are so out of date that they may just be back in fashion. I search my pockets. An old habit when I pull on pants. I find a piece of paper and pull it out. It's a scrap with my writing on it. Fascinated, I twist it in my fingers before reading it. *'37 Carrington Lane, bell doesn't work.'*

I've no idea what it means. But it has been twenty plus years since I pulled on these pants. I push the scrap back in my pocket and follow the coffee smell to the kitchen. Martyn is sitting talking to Linda. So much for my orders. Linda looks up. 'Better. Not much. But better.'

I sit down on one of the two spare chairs that wrap the small table in the centre of the kitchen. It's not the same room I sat in while we used to chat away the night. At some point Linda has sprung for a new set up. The kitchen used to be all pine and plants. Now it's chrome and black ornaments. The floor is slate and there's a gentle scent of recent paint. All in all a pleasant place to cook, eat and chat.

'Coffee?' Linda is looking at me. I nod.

She pours me a black with two sugars. I don't take sugar anymore but it's nice she remembered. 'Any chance of a bite to eat?' She reaches behind her and pulls out a plate of cheese sandwiches. 'It's all I have. I need to go to the shops.' Cheese is good for me.

We eat in silence. Martyn wolfing down twice as much as me. I ask for another coffee but without the sugar and Linda gives me a refill. She rests her rear on the stove. 'So tell me the sad story that washes you up on my shores? Martyn says that you are old friends down on your luck?'

Martyn is an idiot. I had a far better story to spin. 'Did he now? And what else did he tell you?'

She looks at Martyn. 'That his name is Ringo.' I try to hide the surprise. 'And that you were mugged a few blocks away and a couple of bums took all your clothes and money.'

Not bad Martyn. Ok, so Ringo and old pals is a bit thick, but getting mugged is a better story than mine. It lets me spin a back-story in any shape I fancy.

'Correct. Did Martyn tell you how it happened?'

'No, only that you were caught in alley.'

'Stupid of us really. We were trying to get out of the rain. We had been in the bar and went hunting for a taxi. I thought the alley would keep us dry until we could grab a cab.'

'I take you've not been to the police.'

'No. We weren't far from here and I thought that maybe an old girlfriend might take pity on a couple of muggees.'

'What were you doing in the neighborhood in the first place?'

'Back to see the old haunts. You know how it is.'

'After all this time?'

Martyn is finishing the last sandwich while flicking his eyes between us as our tennis match of a conversation moves along. I push my mug out for another refill. 'Any chance of a bed for the night?'

MELTDOWN

Linda doesn't answer. She picks up my mug and adds to my caffeine intake for the day. She tops up Martyn's for good measure and sits down.

'Ok Craig, let's make this simple. I have no idea what's going on. I have no idea why you are here. I have no idea why you look like a refugee. What I do know is that the smell of bullshit around your story is so strong that you could ladle it up and serve it. I have no idea who this guy is but he isn't Ringo and he's no friend of yours. You've got twenty years on him and the two of you have the look of strangers. You had to ask me what he said before you'd answer my questions. I used to use the same trick on my mum when me and my sister got caught raiding the fridge. It doesn't wash.'

I sit my chin in my hands. 'Go on.'

'You and me were so finished that there isn't a word in the dictionary to describe it.'

'I didn't want to marry.'

'I know, but you strung me along for a long time.'

That wasn't strictly true, but now wasn't the time. 'It was twenty years ago.'

'And it hurt for twenty years. I loved you and you knew it.'

'And I think I loved you but I wasn't sure.'

'First time, Craig McIntyre.'

'First time for what?'

'First time the love word has left your lips since I met you.'

112

'I told you I wasn't sure. You pushed and I pushed back.'

Martyn has stopped the tennis eyes. This is getting personal and he's starting to look uncomfortable.

'Your friend doesn't look too happy about the turn in conversation. Surely you've told him all about me. What with you being good friends and turning up at my door in such a state?'

I look at Martyn. 'This is between Linda and me. Would you give us some space?'

Martyn looks relieved and gets up. Linda points towards the front door. 'Second door on the left. Put on the TV if you feel like it.' We watch him vanish and a minute later we hear the sound of Horatio from CSI Miami telling someone that his time is up.

I sip at the coffee.

Chapter 17

'So the truth?' I'm studying Linda's face as she talks. She reminds me of my wife. They say that men have the image of the perfect woman in their mind and if they lose one they go hunt down someone similar. It may be true - Linda and Lorraine have lot in common. Both tall, green eyes and blonde. But Lorraine was model gorgeous. Linda is a different kind of wonderful.

The thought of Lorraine brings up a knot in my stomach. Guilt. She's dead because of me. Dead because of Tampoline and dead because of Charlie. It's complicated but the wounds are only a year old. There was no funeral. At least not one that I attended. I'd tried to track down her body but that had brought the agency after me and I'd been on the run since.

It's Linda's smile that reminds me of Lorraine. For a second she had let her mind wander and whatever land she was lost in had cracked the smallest of smiles on her face. It's gone in a flash but it promised much. That was Lorraine's smile for you. She could stop a rampaging bull with it. Guys melted around her but somehow she had chosen me to be the main recipient of that promise.

'I'm waiting.' Linda touches my hand as she speaks.

'It's complicated.'

'What isn't?'

'I don't want to drag you into it.'

'So what the hell are you doing at my door? If you don't want me involved in whatever it is you're in, why roll up here?'

'Desperation?'

'Great. Linda the last chance saloon.'

'That's not what I mean.'

'What then?'

'Look, can you do me a favor?'

'I'm out of them. The shower, coffee, clothes and food kind of used them up.'

'I need one night to figure out some stuff. One night. Then I'll square up with you. Ok?'

She stands up. 'What if I say no?'

'We'll go.'

'Just like that?'

'Yes.'

'I should never have let you in.'

'Thanks.'

'And your *friend.*'

'I told you it was complicated.'

'How long have you known him?'

'Truthfully, I don't. Circumstance threw us together but I need him and he needs me.'

'You gay?'

'No. What does that matter?'

'Just trying to size up your relationship status. Married?'

'Yes. Once.'

'Why not turn to her?'

MELTDOWN

'I can't. She's dead.'

'Sorry.'

'Anyway we lived in LA. I needed shelter tonight.'

'So no friends to turn to either?'

'Not here.'

'So where are you going to go in the morning?'

I had a thought on how to give my life a little direction. 'I just need tonight.'

'I want you gone by nine in the morning. Promise.'

I nod.

'You'll have to share with Ringo. Use the guest room. It has a double bed.'

'Thanks. We'll manage. Excuse me while I tell Martyn.'

'Not Ringo.'

'No. Not even John, Paul or George either. Martyn with a 'y'.'

I need to talk to Martyn. A serious one to one, but I'm shattered. I tell him we'll get up and early and to trust me till then. He's as knocked out as I am and agrees, all be it with reservation written across his face in neon and glitter. Linda sits back down and we vanish upstairs. I take the floor and Martyn gets the bed. I'm too tired to argue.

***

A bullet glances off the wall behind me. A splinter of concrete cracks off my helmet. I hunker down. A shout goes up and another bullet finishes its flight. The sniper is somewhere high on my left. He has me pinned down. I wait. One of my fellow grunts is working his way round the back. I pick up a piece of old packing case. Worn by the sand. I count to fifty. I throw it up. A bullet chases it. I start counting again. I root in my day sack and pull out a glove. On fifty it follows the wood. Another bullet. Then a longer burst of fire.

'Craig, clear.'

I stick my head up and Carl is pointing at a window. 'Dead. Right between the eyes.'

I keep watching the window. A kill is only a kill when you see it. Dead men do strange things in war. I walk over to Carl and he offers me a cigarette. I shake my head. 'I'm quitting.'

He laughs. 'Can't say that a smoke decreases your lifespan around here by much.' He lights up. 'We should get going.'

We exit onto the back alley. Me in front on point. Carl at the rear. At the end of the alley I flatten on the wall and Carl walks to the exit. He leans round for a view, gun at the ready, pointing where he's looking. You want to be able to pull the trigger and know the target's going to get it full on. He signals all clear and crosses the street, gun aiming at the windows above me, and I do the same for him.

Over the next hour we work our way across the town. A nothing collection of white concrete shells. No life to be seen now. Evacuated before we got here. No strategic importance. A mop up. So far we had found two snipers. We had also seen a couple more locals. Could have been insurgents, but once they drop their gun, how would you know?

The sun is high and we drop for water and rest. Our Individual Body Armor weighs us down. But IBA's save lives. It might weigh like a sack of bricks but better that than six feet under. I flick at my radio but it has been dead for most of the morning. Carl's is dead as well.

We'd got separated from our unit just after sun up. A firefight and we had been forced into the town. We'd radioed we were ok but couldn't get out and decided to work our way round. That's when the first sniper had appeared. I called for support but my radio was screwed. Carl called up and was told to sit tight.

Then we heard an explosion and still no sign of back up. We waited. The sniper kept us occupied. A grenade saw him off and we headed to the far side of town. Out MRAP was a mess. The IED had been massive or someone was firing tank killers. There were no survivors and we searched for a radio to get the fallen back to base but came up empty. We spent an hour burying. We didn't want hajis crowing over our mates. We would mark the spot and get an aircrew to pick them up later. We made the graves as invisible as possible and headed back to town.

I swig at the water. 'There should be some friends on the far side. The MRAP will have been noted by now and someone will come looking.'

Carl shook his head. 'This place is fucked up. I thought we had taken Baghdad. War over.'

'This shit isn't going to stop that easily.'

Carl stands up and signals for me to do the same. He still has his helmet in his hand. I see the incoming. A brief flash and a trail that couldn't exist. You can't see a bullet coming but I did. For a fraction of a second I saw it cross the street. Dead on Carl. I open my mouth but the bullet enters Carl's head just above his left eye. His head explodes and I hit the deck. More bullets rain in and I crawl into a doorway. I want to scream but I need to act. I pull up my gun, roll over and scan the scene. Carl is down and isn't getting back up. More gun fire but this time from behind me. I swing round and US uniforms are running. I look back at Carl. I scream as I pull the trigger and empty the gun. 'Fucked up. You're right. This place is fucked up.'

A last bullet leaves an insurgents gun and picks me out. It has my name engraved inside. It has my mouth in sight. It splits air with a whine that won't be heard until I stop breathing. I try to duck but it has me. Has me dead to rights.

Chapter 18

I wake up. Sweating. My shout wakes up Martyn. It's still dark outside. He leans over to look down on me. 'Are you ok?'

I only spent six months in that hellhole and the dreams still stay with me. Two dreams. The one with Carl and the one that hurts. 'I'm fine. Nightmare. Just a nightmare.'

'Christ, you were screaming.'

'Nightmare. It happens. I'm fine.'

Martyn doesn't look convinced. 'Must be a hell of a dream. Half the neighborhood must be awake by now.'

My heart is still racing. I wipe sweat from my eyes. 'Want to talk?'

'Yes.'

'Where do you want to start?'

'What the hell are we doing here?'

'Safe house. At least it should be. Linda's a gem. But she's no fool. We'll need to move on. What do you know about the Iranian?'

'Like I'm going to tell you. Those bastards used me as a punch bag and I gave up zero.'

'Is that because you know nothing?'

'I'm not talking about it.'

'Come on. Your friends sold out on you. You were supposed to die in the house. You're dead meat. Walking dead meat. If you knew nothing they would have just left you out to dry. They didn't. They were desperate to know what you had told the agency. Once you convinced them you had said nothing they tried to kill you. My take is that you do have info. Your friends don't want it to leak and, given you is now a busted asset, they want you dead. It's not hard to figure.'

He lies back on the bed. I can no longer see his face but his breathing is loud. I sit up and lean on the edge of the mattress. 'We're in this together. Like it or not. The agency wants me and they want you. Your friends want you and probably want me as well. Now I know what kind of resources the agency have and you know what your friends are capable of. How long do you think we will last on the street? Are you just going to go back home as if things are five by five?'

'And what do you suggest?'

'I have an idea, but it needs both of us.'

'What is it?'

'Simple. We get to the Iranian before the agency.'

'Sure, we just stroll in and walk away with him?'

'Why not? You know where he is and I have a few aces up my sleeve. Well one at least.'

'I don't know where he is.'

'Sure.'

'I don't.'

I shift up on to the bed. 'Look, I'll tell you what I think we should do and then you can decide what you do and don't know.'

He nods and I try and get comfortable on the edge of the bed. 'The agency need the Iranian. They are in the crapper without him. They need the oil and the first thing they do is lose the guy the Iranians have sent to start up the conversation. Embarrassing.'

'And that's about it – embarrassing, but the deal is hardly going to go south because of it.'

'You don't know that and neither do they. Think what we're planning to do here. Since Carter Iran has been on America's hit list. Sponsors of terror. Axis of evil. Developing a nuclear capability. The hill is friendly with Israel and Iran aren't exactly ecstatic at the relationship. And now we are stepping up to their pumps and saying fill her up.'

'And they said yes. Why?'

'Leverage. Prestige. Money. Power. Kudos. To stick one over on us. A million reasons. And what do we do? Lose their representative. We could 'fess up and say we're sorry. Please send someone else over and we promise not to lose them this time. Tampoline will move heaven and earth to get him back but not for long. The shit about the SPR can't stay hidden for long. It's too good a Twitter story. I reckon we have twenty four hours – maybe thirty six before they go to Plan B.'

'And what's Plan B.'

'I've no idea but it's bad news for us. If we can get to your friends and free him we have a hell of a bargaining chip.'

'We could just lie low.'

I sigh. Now I'm awake I want to be on the move. As dawn creeps in time is beginning to crush down. 'We could. But we'd just delay the inevitable. Neither the agency nor your friends are going to give in looking for us. Have you a family?'

The question throws him. 'Eh. Kind of.'

'What do you mean "kind of"?'

'I've got my Ma. That's about it.'

'And you think your friends will leave your Ma alone?'

'They wouldn't touch an old lady.'

'Well, you know them.'

He drops silent. I let him think on it. He rubs his temple with one hand. His other is tapping out a rhythm on the pillow. 'They wouldn't.' He doesn't sound sure.

'Martyn, they will. They need you gone. I have no idea what the hell they are up to but the Iranian is a gift from beyond to them. And I'm betting they have figured out the timescales on all this. They don't want you spoiling their party. Either we act or they will.'

'And what do we do if we get the Iranian?'

'Me, I get the agency off my back and you get protection from them.'

'Protection! As if that will work.'

'It's a better bet than running on your own. Trust me, they're not short on cash or contacts.'

'And we have to do this by when?'

'Twenty four hours. Maybe less.'

'Shit.'

MELTDOWN

My thoughts exactly.

The door swings open and Linda is wrapped in a robe. 'There's someone sneaking around out the back.'

Shit.

Chapter 19

'Stay here.' I say to them both.

Linda's bedroom looks out onto the back yard. I slip in the door and fresh scent hits my nose. Floral. Light. She used to wear Charlie but that's probably gone the way of the cathode ray tube by now.

The drapes are closed and I push the door behind me. I skirt her bed placing my hand on the mattress. Feeling my way round. A vanity table sits at the window. In the gloom I pick out a thousand bottles of lotions and potions. I slide to the side. I don't want to disturb the drapes. The movement might be visible from outside. I drop to the floor. The drapes stop about a foot from the carpet. I look under and there's a gap between the material and the window. If I can slide under I can slip my head up the gap and look out.

A crack. Sharp. Metal on stone? It comes from below. Outside. I wriggle behind the vanity table until I'm parallel with the window. I roll onto my side and raise myself on one arm. This used to be an exercise I did in the army to toughen up my love handles. Not that there's anything to grab nowadays. Slim and trim. That's me.

Another crack. Quieter. More to the left. Whoever is outside isn't very good at this stuff. I'm certain we are in people land. No animal out there. Not unless the local cat has a ball bearing attached to its tail. My head is level with the bottom of the glass. I pause and the pain of holding the position begins to tell. I slide my feet along to better support myself and push up a little further. I've probably got six inches of movement before I can be seen from below.

The street lighting from the next road is shaded by the houses across the yard. There seems to be no other lights. Linda's backyard backs onto a small alley. Not wide enough for a car. It runs the length of the block. We used to sit on the back stoop and if the fancy took us use it to go down to Coin's in the Pocket. I once asked Tight Sean what in the hell the apostrophe was doing in the word Coin's. He laughed and told me his brother had told him that it was the proper way to spell it. I told him it wasn't. He knew, but you'd be amazed how many people came into the bar just to tell him. *'There's nothing like a wiseass punter to order up a few beers before telling me about the name. It's good for business'*

I raise my head slowly. Very slowly. The strain on my arm and side is building. Suck it in is the order of the day. The houses on the far side come into view. Dawn is still to break and there are no lights in any of the windows. I keep pushing. There are no more clicks. Either they have learned or they are holding fast. The wall at the back of the yard inches into my vision. Beneath it's an inky pool of nothing.

The muscles in my side are screaming at me. Another few seconds and I'll not be able to hold the pose. Before I collapse to the floor I raise myself another few inches. I look down on the yard and of all the idiotic things I see the red glow of a cigarette. We are deep in amateur world here. I drop to the floor and let the burn in my arm and side cool.

Ok, so are we talking agency, Factor or local druggie looking for a cheap target and some hot goods to fuel his habit? I can't see how the Factor could know where we are. Unless Martyn had put in a call. Unlikely.

Agency? Could be. The suits that did the grunt work didn't strike me as the cream of the American education system. Most of the ones I had met were muscle on remote control. The guys in Canada, though, were a different class.

Druggie? Maybe, but why wait? In and out was the usual game. Patience isn't big with heavy drug users.

Agency then. But their modus operandi was gas canister in the windows followed by shock and awe. Not agency? I roll from under the drapes and stand up. Whoever is out there's not good news. I go back to the spare bedroom and tell them what I've seen. 'Martyn, it's time to go. Linda, have you got any of my old coats left?'

She smiles. 'A goatskin Parka and a leather flight jacket.'

I hated both of them. 'I'll take my flight jacket. Martyn, you can smell of goat.'

He looks at me. 'Fucking goat?'

'Don't ask.'

Five minutes later the fashion parade is on in the lobby of Linda's house. I stand next to the kitchen door. 'Give me five. Whoever this guy is we need rid of him. I'm not leaving you with some stranger in the backyard.'

Martyn steps forward. 'Two are better than one.'

MELTDOWN

'Can you handle yourself?'

'Angel's Hand for six years.'

My face tells him I have no idea what he's talking about. He grins. 'A gang I ran with back in Brooklyn. Fighting was the only recreation we had.'

'Ok but let me lead. If this is agency there may be more than one.'

I open the door to the kitchen and we both walk in. I keep to the left and away from the window. 'He's to the right. Low down. Near the stoop.' I whisper. I loop the key from the hook and slip into the lock. It turns with a faint snick and I freeze. Nothing. 'On three.'

I twist the handle until the lock is free. I drop my voice as low as I can. 'One. Two. Three.'

I slam the door open. It opens away from the spot where I had seen the cigarette light. As I leap out I flick the light switch. Fuck subtlety.

An old man is lying against the fence. The cigarette is hanging from his mouth and he wakes from a sleep. His eyes are wide open in surprise. Martyn skittles out behind me and I drop on the old man and he yelps.

'Jim?' Linda's voice is coming from the door. I turn to her voice. 'Linda, get the hell out of here.'

She doesn't move. 'Jim, what in the hell are you doing here?' She's talking to the old man. I'm sitting astride him with his hands pinned down. He swallows. 'Linda I'm...'

'Get off him Craig. He's my bloody uncle.'

I let go of my grip. 'Your uncle?'

'Silly old bastard. He lives here when he's down on his luck.' She puts out a hand to him as I get up. 'What in the hell are you doing here at this time?'

'Mary threw me out.'

'But you've only just gone back to her. What did you do?'

He picks a spot in the ground and stares it out. 'Why does it have to be me that does anything?'

'Because it always is.'

'Horses.'

'What?'

'Horses.'

'The money I gave you?'

'Horses.'

'Jim, I fucking give in. That was supposed to keep you going until you got a job.'

'It was a dead cert. Ten to one. On the nose. Insider info. Heavy money was on it. Smart money.'

'And did it win?'

His silence is the answer.

'Two grand. You put two grand on a horse.'

He keeps examining the ground.

'And now you want to come back here?'

I stand on the stoop. 'Linda, much as I'd like to play happy families, Martyn and I need to hit the road.'

'So go.' She's down and proper mad.

'We need some cash.'

She lets go of Jim's hand. 'This old bastard just blew all my savings and now you want to add to my pain?'

'I'll pay you back.'

'That's what this useless sack of crap said.'

Jim hasn't stopped the forensic examination of the ground yet.

I reach out for her hand. 'I'm good for it.'

She shakes her head. 'No you're not. You weren't good for it twenty years ago and nothing has changed.'

Martyn taps me on the shoulder. I spin round. 'What?'

'Do we really want to be doing this in the yard?'

He's right. 'Inside.' They don't move. 'Now.' They move.

Chapter 20

Once inside I lock the door and usher them all to the lobby. 'Linda, we need to be gone. If you've no money then fine.'

Jim is hanging back. A dog that has just shit on the best rug. Linda has the face of someone who can't decide if murder is a justifiable option. 'Fine.' She storms upstairs. We all stand in silence. Jim finds another interesting piece of the ground to study.

Linda is back in less than a minute. 'Three hundred dollars. It's all I have. Now fuck off.'

'Thanks. I…'

'I said fuck off.'

So we do. As she closes the door Linda isn't looking to me for a last goodbye. By the time I've checked out the street I hear the door slam behind me.

'Well that went well.'

'Martyn you can fuck off.'

I hit the sidewalk and Martyn follows in behind. I know he'll follow. He has to. It's that or he's on his own. We reach the corner opposite the 'Coin's in the Pocket'. A new sign but same spelling. 'Ok Martyn, give. Where is he?'

'Who?'

'Don't fuck around.'

'Why should I tell you? I could get him you know.'

'Is that right? And they won't spot you at a thousand yards?'

MELTDOWN

'I can disguise myself.'

'Done a lot of this have you?'

'No, but neither have you.'

'Two tours of duty in Iraq. Search and destroy.' This wasn't strictly true but I had been in Iraq once and there was some of searching and destroying.

'BS.'

'Nope. 1st Infantry Division, 4th Brigade, 2nd Battalion, 16th Infantry regiment. If you want to know.'

'No shit?'

'No shit. So are we together or are we going our separate ways? I'll split the three hundred dollars and you can go back to Ma.'

He steps into the gutter and kicks at some paper. 'I don't know much.'

'Anything will do.'

'Colorado Springs.'

'Is that where he is?'

'I think so.'

'Think or know?'

'That's where he was before I got picked up. They could have moved him.'

'Where in Colorado Springs?'

'That I don't know.'

'Not enough. We have a day. I need more.'

'I know someone who will know, but I don't think he'll talk to me now.'

'Leave that to me. Are you sure about Colorado Springs?'

He nods. I'd been there once. A few years back. While I was recovering from my time in the army's psychology care. There's a big military presence in the area. NORAD sees to that. We had been staying at the Cheyenne Mountain Resort at the army's expense. A swanky hotel geared up for conferences. It had a fantastic view of the mountains from my room. The start of the Rockies, so I was told. The town has an airport - we are too far by car. I'm not sure that three hundred dollars will cover the fair for both of us from Newark. But something will turn up; it usually does.

'Ok Martyn, time for a trip to the Rockies. But we're a bit light on cash.' The silence told me something. 'I know you don't have any on you, but can you get some quick?' More silence. 'Come on, help me out. We're in this together.'

'Ok, I can get some cash. Well, at least a credit card or two.'

'No use, they'll have you number by now.'

'Who said the cards were mine?'

'And?'

'Well there must be a lonely wallet sleeping in some guys pants around here. Always is. A little light fingered work and we are away.'

'Pickpocketing?'

'Borrowing. If you like. We borrow, pay, travel and mail the card back with an IOU. Won't matter anyway, the card company will pick up the tab.'

MELTDOWN

It's strange how your morals work. A friend of mine from way back, a guy called Callum Davidson, was the go-to guy in Iraq for your entire daily needs. From cigarettes to a car, he was one of the many who could 'lay his hands on stuff'. Legit or not he made no distinction. There was always a price and he was always willing to deliver. From cool to furnace hot he supplied the high and mighty to the low and needy. He once sourced a Ferrari F40 for a General who was looking for a little excitement on the empty roads of southern Iraq.

I was into him for a few bottles of whisky of the three decade old variety. Yet, for reasons never fully explained, he refused to deal in cell phones. One of the first things we did in Iraq was set up a cell network in key areas. But Callum wouldn't touch them. He'd get you a sim card. He'd get you a legal phone. He'd even recommend someone else for 'back of a truck' options – but not him. If you asked he would mutter something about it not being right and that was that.

Well I'm standing in the early morning light of another New Jersey day and the world has gone south. I'm holding the rope and trying to keep it from dropping through the sinkhole and my head is saying let Martyn fleece some poor bastard. But my heart says no. It's wrong. Go figure. He's still kicking the gutter. I take a few steps. 'Any other options?'

'Sure. I could go for a loan at First and Mutual. My credit's good. Wouldn't take more than a few weeks. Or I could phone my Ma…' He stops. 'Do you think they'll hurt my Ma?'

'Truthfully, I don't know.' I pause. 'Is she ignorant of you and your friends?'

'Mostly. She asks. You know what mothers are like. I don't like to lie to Ma so I just don't talk much about it. But she's not fresh off the banana boat. She knows the money coming in the house is from no nine to five. But she wouldn't know much more.'

'I'd love to tell you that they'll not touch her but I can't.'

Martyn hangs his head. Hand running through the short crew cut. 'I need to go to my Ma.'

I step onto the road with him. I place a hand on his shoulder. 'Not a good idea soldier. The agency and your friends will have it scoped out.'

He pulls away. 'I'm not worried about any agency but I am worried about the Factor. Would you leave your Ma?'

My Ma is long since dead. Something I don't like to revisit. But I knew he was right. 'Where does she live?'

'Union. Not far. Just near the Garden Sate Parkway. A place called Apple Tree Lane.'

'Sounds nice.'

'Suppose.'

'That's on the way to the airport.'

'Yes.'

I weigh up the options and come up with one answer.

MELTDOWN

'Would your Ma loan us the cash for the plane?'

'Sure.'

'Ok, time for a little Mother's Apple Pie.'

'I thought you said the house would be watched?'

'Yes. But are you going to leave your mother without checking her?'

'No.'

'Will she give us the money?'

'Yes.'

'Seems that I have no choice. I hope she makes good coffee?'

He smiles. 'The best.'

Chapter 21

We jump a cab and burn some of the few dollars we can't afford. Martyn directs the driver and we slide through gray water America. The sun is a pallid dirt cream ball. Thin, weak. Inside the cab the air feels the same. Diluted. Thirty thousand foot air at sea level. My lungs want more and my head tells me not to worry. New Jersey residents don't suffer from altitude sickness.

I try and figure a plan of action for when we get to Martyn's mother but there are too many variables. I don't know the layout of the streets, of the area around her house. I have no idea who is waiting. What numbers? Where? What's their brief? Agency to lift? Factor to kill? All I know is that there are few places I'd rather not be. Insanity is writ large in this action.

Martyn points to a row of shops and tells the cab driver to pull up. I unload a twenty and get out. I walk up to the window of the nearest shop. An electrical repair ship with a neat display full of wires. I turn to Martyn. 'Is the house far?'

'No, but I don't know how close we can get. Where do you think they'll be hiding?'

'Your guess is as good as mine.'

I'd expected a run-down area. Martyn didn't seem the BMW type. But silver stars and four circles on the passing cars tell me otherwise. The houses across the road are detached. Detached and pristine. A couple of kids cycle by. A grand a pop for the bikes. Designer gear for scrubbing around in. Maybe Martyn's mum would have cash. I watch the kids pedal away and turn to Martyn 'So where do we go?'

'We can't go down Ma's street. We need to think like they do.'

'I agree. Sounds good. Go on.' I like this kind of talk.

'When I was at school I used to cut through Mrs Laidlaw's yard. It backs onto some scrub. It'll take us to the back of Ma's house. Unless they have someone in the yard we can use the fence as cover.'

'Sounds like a plan. Lead on.'

Martyn smiles. We aren't best buddies. I barely know him. But in adversity and all that. In another life I'd swallow a few with him. He's a bit young for me. And I don't hold with the Factor shit. But he feels like good kid gone south. He limps away. The suit that punted his groin had left his mark. He hasn't complained. But it had to have done some damage. I drop in behind him, my radar on for suits, cars and strangers. Around here that's the whole landscape.

We drop off the main street, down a small alley, cut through a gap in a fence and over a path. We are back on to a row of homes. Martyn cuts to the left and we work our way along. We are in nail clipper lawn and nose trimmer bush territory. An older lady dressed in this season's must have for the elderly gardener looks up. 'Hi Martyn.'

'Hi Mrs Rubenstein. Where's Mr Rubenstein?'

The lady is five feet minus a few inches. Her face is lined and it sets her mouth at a scowl. Her hair is eleven on the severe scale. 'Where he usually is.'

'Is his handicap getting lower?'

'Nope. It's going up and so is his waist. Too little golf. Too much beer.'

'At least you know where he is.'

'True. Say hi to your Ma.'

'Will do.'

Throughout the conversation she never takes her eyes off me.

Martyn heads off with a wave and I drop in behind. 'A friend of your Ma's?'

Martyn looks back. 'The neighborhood gossip. I'll lay a dollar for ten that my Ma will know I'm coming before we get to the front door.'

I look round and Mrs Rubenstein is already on the way to the phone. I stop. Turn round. Jog back. 'Mrs Rubenstein.'

She turns at my voice. I walk up her fence. 'Could I have a word?'

Her eyes lock on mine. 'Yes.' She doesn't walk back to me.

'You don't know me but I'm a friend of Martyn's'

'Are you!' It's not a question.

'Yes. I wonder if you might be able to help?'

She makes no attempt to close the gap between us. I don't want to shout but she gives me no choice. 'It's private.'

MELTDOWN

Curiosity is building in her. She closes by a couple of yards. 'Yes.'

'Private, Mrs Rubenstein.'

I look at Martyn. He's stopped. Wondering what the hell I'm up to. Mrs Rubenstein walks a few more steps and we can talk. 'Mrs Rubenstein. I know you are a friend of the family. And I know that Martyn is a good lad.'

Silence.

'But maybe he's not kept the best of company.'

She nods.

'And you don't know me.'

Silence.

'And that, maybe, some of Martyn's friends aren't that welcome around here.'

'Where is this going…'

'Craig. The name's Craig.'

'Well.'

'Look, I'm not one of Martyn's usual friends. I'm trying to help him. Now you can take that as true or not, I don't care. But you could be useful to Martyn right now.'

'And how would I do that?'

'Do you know Mrs Wheeler well?'

'Well enough to know that she prefers to be called Miss Singer.'

'I didn't know. I've not known Martyn long.'

Her eyes say 'no shit Sherlock'.

'Anyway Martyn's in a bit of trouble. Hospital visit trouble if you know what I mean.'

'I don't.'

'He might have to make an unscheduled visit to the local emergency clinic if some of his friends get a hold of him.'

Martyn is still standing. Not sure whether to come back. I open my palms. Good body language never goes amiss. 'You keep your eyes on your neighbors?'

Her face hardens. I'm on a full count and swinging like a drunk. 'I mean you strike me as the sort of person that has the interests of the neighborhood at heart. I appreciate that. People don't value good neighbors anymore.'

'Son, what is it you want?'

'Have you seen any strangers around lately?'

'Like you?'

'No. Probably suited up. But maybe casual. SUV. Regal. Black car. That type of thing.' I'm erring on the side of agency. I've no idea what the Factor guys might look like.

'And if I have?'

'It'll help Martyn.'

'Like Martyn helps his Ma. Coleen has had nothing but trouble from that boy. And now he's bringing more.'

Time to go for the kill. 'Look Mrs Rubenstein. This isn't just about Martyn. The hospital pass might be for Coleen. The guys that want Martyn might hurt his Ma.'

'Might?'

'Will. I think.'

'I'll call the police.'

'It'll be too late. And even if they do turn up Martyn's friends will just come back later. These are nasty people. Now I'm running out of time. Either you want to help or you don't.'

The morning air is warming up. A car starts up and the commuter exit's beginning. A dog lets rip at something and is joined by the distant roar of a jet taking off from Liberty. Mrs Rubenstein stares me down. I turn to walk away. She taps the fence with her hand. "Ok, there are four men at the moment. Two in a green Honda Prius sitting opposite Coleen's house. Both are dressed in black suits. The other two are on foot. Baseball caps and sweat pants. One's six feet and a bit. Muscled. The other is five feet six and skinny as a rake. They circle every twenty minutes or so. The men in the car left half an hour ago to get coffee and donuts and just got back. That's all I know.'

This woman should have been in the CIA. 'When did the two on foot last pass?'

'Five minutes ago. I saw them through the gap.' She points to the space between her house and the one next door.

'Thanks, Mrs Rubenstein. You've been a great help.' I walk back to Martyn. 'That's some woman.'

'My Ma says she's psychic.'

'Psychic?'

'Well she can't figure out how else she knows all the shit she knows.'

I laugh. 'Right. I have a plan. There are two suits in a car opposite your Ma's house and two on foot. The two on foot are ten to fifteen minutes out. The suits will have eyes on everyone. I need to distract them and you need to get into your Ma's. Say hello. Get the cash and get out.'

'I'm not leaving her.'

'What?'

'I'm not leaving her. What'll stop them going for her when I'm gone? They'll figure I told her where I'm going.'

'True. Has she got a car?'

'No.'

'Has she got a friend with a car?'

'Not nearby.'

'Do you know the local cab number?'

'No, but Ma will. She uses them to go shopping.'

'Ok, as soon as you get in phone one.'

'To go where?'

'Not for us. For your Ma. Has she got someone she can stay with for a while?'

'Her sister, but won't they figure that out?'

'Maybe. Anyone else? Someone that they might not know about?'

Silence.

'Anyone?'

'Yes. Well maybe.'

'Who?'

'Ma's seeing a man. No one is supposed to know. Not even me. He lives in the Bronx.'

'Perfect. Tell her she needs to go there.'

'She won't go.'

'Shit Martyn. You need to make her. You can't protect her. Tell her the truth. Get her to listen because if you don't I'm going to have to go solo. We can't take her with us.'

He stops walking. 'I need to think.'

'No Martyn, you need to act.'

'Ma's house is a couple down. We need to cut through Charlie Semple's yard. It's that one with the monkey-puzzle tree.'

I need to see the road. 'Who lives in this one?'

'The Singhs, but they won't be in. They're back in India visiting family. Have been for a month.'

'You think on what you need to do and I'm going to recce.'

I have the feeling in the pit of my stomach that time is leaking like a burst downpipe in a storm.

Chapter 22

I jump the fence, leaving Martyn to work his brain. The Singh's yard is neat. Well kept. No lawn, just block work and planters. I skirt the edge of the house and pause at the front corner. I can see to my right but Martyn's house is to the left. No sign of foot soldiers though. I drop to the ground and poke my head round the corner. The green Prius is three houses down. One suit's downing a coffee. The other is eyeballing Martyn's house. I duck back and return to Martyn. 'Well?'

'I'll try and convince her.'

'Good.' I head for the monkey-puzzle tree. 'I'm going to try and distract them.'

'How? Do they have guns?'

'Yes.'

'They'll see you coming.'

'I'm counting on it. I need you to be ready to run when it goes down.'

'What goes down?'

'I'm not sure but it'll go down.' I hope.

I walk five houses down. Check the yard is clear and enter. A small shed sits in one corner of a manicured lawn. I walk up to it and kick in the door. I enter. Look around and grab a box cutter from a well-stocked tool rack. I exit. No one shouts out. I pull the door behind me and flick out the cutting blade. I drop it to my side. The point on my thigh. I keep walking. Straight into view and onto the sidewalk.

I turn right. Heading for the Prius. I get within ten yards when the door flies open. I draw a breath. This is a big risk. The suits know what I can do. If these guys are strangers then I'm fucked. Both are the tall and well-built type. Both are sporting crew cuts. One in red and one in black. One could cut it as a model. So could the other. If they needed models for hockey masks. I dig the point into my pants and gasp.

'McIntyre stop there.' So says Pretty Boy. He has his gun on me.

Ugly also has me in his sights. 'On the ground.'

I press the knife a little harder. Skin splits and blood leaks.

Pretty Boy cocks his head. 'Now. On the ground.'

I go for the slam-dunk and rip the knife down my thigh. I drop to the sidewalk. Screaming. The pain flows. A file scraping through my nerves. Shredding them. I feel the kernel. The cold hard kernel at the back of my head crack. High pressure steam burns through my skull. My head dynamites. I drop the knife and grab at my head. The pain in my leg is kindling to the burning log up top. My vision blurs and I hear Ugly. 'What the fuck is he doing?'

'It's to do with that shit he can pull.'

'You believe that nonsense?'

'He's pissing blood. Why else would he cut himself?'

'This is insane.'

Where in the hell is the reaction from these two? Why are they not tearing lumps out of each other? Doesn't it always work that way? Me - the catalyst. Tearing out old wounds from the past. Exposing them. Amplifying them. Turning the unsaid into the unbelievable. If they have history they should be down and dirty by now. The pain in my head takes my vision away and I wait for the blue world. Pray for the blue world. It'll come. It always does.

Ugly is above me. 'He's drawing attention. We need to get him out of here.'

Hands reach down and I will the two to kill each other. Nothing. I'm dragged along the road. Blood runs. Leaving a trail like a snail. Then a gun goes off and I'm dropped. Ugly kicks me. 'Where's the gunfire coming from?'

'Not gun fire. It's the door. Someone's just taken it off the hinges. Over there.'

Voices are raised. A man and woman's. His in terror. Hers in anger. Metal strikes stone. 'Joan put it down.' I try and turn to see but Ugly has my head in a lock. Then the blue world washes in. A cool wave beaches itself on me. The pain dies. Around me everything has changed color. The grass – azure. The road – deep sea blue. The sky – cobalt. My hand is riven with veins of dark and light blue. In the blue world time leaps and bounds. Seconds can become minutes and minutes seconds. Fast forward and slow motion. Fits and starts. Soon it'll pass and then my *power* - if that's what you can call it - will wane.

Ugly lets go and I see the couple who have piled out of the house next to Martyn's mother's. He's a sweat stained mound of lard squeezed into a dirt gray sports shirt. She's an apron clad whirling dervish with a carving knife. He's on the ground and she's bringing the knife down. Sport action slo-mo. The blade is blunt. No edge, but it'll make no difference. She has her full weight on it. He's frozen.

A second door opens and two girls, barely out of their teens fly onto the lawn. Both have their teeth locked into each other's skin. One on the leg the other on the breast. They are trying to chew to the bone.

Ugly gives me another kick. 'Quick, this is nuts. Get him out of here.'

Hands grab me again and I fight back. We leapfrog a minute and I'm still on the ground. Wriggling. Buying time. The apron-clad woman finishes her down stroke and slices the man's arm. Cutting through the left bicep. He screams like a high school girl. She pulls the knife free for another shot.

The two girls are free from each other. Each one chomping at their prize. A shout from the house next to us and the crash of glass tells me that I'm in good form. The blue world has lost its edge but it's still spraying good news around the neighborhood.

I'm lifted again and then dropped as sirens kick in. Close. The suits leap for the car and burn rubber.

The blue is washing to white. The kernel in my head wraps itself into a ball. Burying into the top of my spine. The knife wielding woman drops the weapon to the ground. The two girls spit out. Gagging. Silence hits the house where the glass shattered. They are coming to terms with the aftermath. They always do. Some will have no recollection. Some will see no wrong. No one will know why.

As the Prius leaves I rip the sleeve from my shirt and tie it around my leg. Time for an exit. I hobble back through the yard where I got the box cutter, falling over the fence and out of sight.

I study my leg and the blood is thick. I rip the other arm from my shirt. It joins its brother around the wound. I look up and down the path. No Martyn. He has to be at his mother's. I feel like dying.

The siren closes in. Stopping. It sounds close to the knife attack scene. A radio crackles in the damp air. Voices. Too quiet to make out. This will take some sorting out. I pray I've become invisible to my victims.

I know their memories will be foggy. Martyn needs to have the sense to stay inside until the police leave. Given what's just gone down this won't be quick. I check my leg. The blood has stopped flowing. It'll need stitched but the after effects of the event empty sour juice into my system. I want to sleep I roll into a bush next to me. Burying myself out of sight, I close my eyes and I'm gone.

***

After the bullet, my helmet saving me, my time was still almost up. One more nightmare and I was dispatched back for treatment. PSD. Or more. My final collapse. The trip home. None of it is clear. Like a foggy night when you've drunk too much.

Hatch Roll, where I was sent to recover after my breakdown, an antiseptic environment. An excess of drugs and a lack of sympathy. I'm back - tied to the bed. For my own good. It's dark. I'm in a ward. Six beds. Snoring and farts. I'd blanked out earlier. A common occurrence. And sometimes a violent one. Hence the restraints. I can feel the heavy duty prescription in my head. But there's no sleep. A man approaches. Suit. Dark tie. White shirt. Agency before I knew who agency were. He looks down on me. He lifts the chart at the end of the bed. Studies it. Another suit appears. This one in white linen. A man I'll meet in a few years in the back end of Basra in Iraq. A friend of Tampoline. Another name for the future. They talk. Whispers. 'Promising.' 'Worth keeping an eye on.' 'Best bet yet.' 'What next.' 'Watch and wait.' 'How long?' 'As long as it takes.' 'Others.' 'In the pipeline.' The conversation means nothing.

They leave. A nurse appears. She checks my pulse. She shines a light in my eyes. She attaches the IV to the waiting connection in my arm. Turns the valve. Sleep.

**

'Craig.'

I snap awake. Martyn is pulling at my shoe. I've moved as I've slept. Exposing my leg. A leg that hurts. I roll out. Keeping the weight off the wound. Martyn has panic on. 'Come on, we need to go.'

I stand up and my leg howls. 'I need a hand.'

He looks at my pants. 'Why in the hell did you stab yourself?'

'You saw that?'

'And the rest. What the hell went down?'

'I told you I'd cause a distraction.'

'You're lucky those nuts started fighting. Mrs Rubenstein was on 911 in a flash otherwise you'd have been long gone.'

'Did you get any cash?

'Yes, and Ma's ordered the cab but I couldn't wait. The police are doing a door to door. Mrs Rubenstein will mention us. We need to be gone.'

'I can't walk.'

'You need to. Only to the next street. I ordered another cab but it won't wait. I used an address I know.'

'Good move.' Batman and Robin were bonding. I'm just not sure who is leading our dynamic duo. Martyn cradles me in his arm and we head away from the nonsense. Kitten weak, I try to help as we cut through an empty back yard and onto the next street. A cab is cooling its engine fifty yards away. We walk up and jump in.

'The airport,' I say.

The cabbie must wonder where we came from. 'Is your name Thomas?'

Martyn nods. 'I phoned ten minutes ago.'

Satisfied, the cabbie swings the car round.

It's time to fly.

Chapter 23

'What terminal?' The cabbies voice cuts in. We are exiting the freeway.

Martyn looks at me. I look at him. The cabbie looks at both of us. 'Where are you flying to?' Before I can stop him Martyn says. 'Colorado Springs.'

The cabbie raises a hand. 'No problem.'

Shit.

I look at Martyn. He's just left a trail. The agency will check all the cabs in the area. Of that I'm sure. That would lead to the airport but then they would have to find us. Martyn just handed them us on a plate.

We pull up outside the terminal. I hobble out and pay up. I walk to the door and it slides open. 'Martyn, I need to treat the wound first. See if you can get some antiseptic, a needle and thread.'

'Why don't we go to a medic?'

'They report knife wounds.' I point to the washroom. 'I'll be in there. First cubicle.'

The first door in the washroom swings open and the cubicle is empty. I close the door. Lock it. Sit down. I peel off my pants. The washroom is busy and I wait. Ten minutes.

'Craig.'

I sit up. 'In here.' I flip the lock. Martyn hands me a plastic bag. I close the door. 'Give me ten.'

The bag has a bobbin of black thread, a pack of needles and a tube of Germoline. This is going to hurt. I thread the needle and bite off a good two feet of cotton. I double it up. I remove the bandage and the blood starts up. I grip the wound. Pinch the skin quickly and stick the needle in. My pain meter jumps and I fear the kernel might crack. I work quickly. My work is shoddy but the blood stops. 'I need a bandage' I hear Martyn leave. I tie off the thread.

Another ten minutes and Martyn lobs a roll of gauze into my lap. I unwrap. Rewrap. I sit back down. 'I need pants.'

'What?'

'I'll never get through security.'

'Where the hell will I get pants?'

'Improvise.'

Twenty minutes this time and a pair of jeans fly in. They're a bit tight but I get them on. I exit.

Once outside I pull on my jacket. 'How do I look?'

Like a fashion reject.'

'Where did you get the pants?'

'I lifted a guy's bag while he was taking a whizz in the washroom down the way. He looked your size. I left the bag in the cubicle next to yours.'

'That'll ring the alarm bells.'

'Probably.'

As he speaks a security guard flies by. Then another. Both heading for the washroom. I pull Martyn to the departure board. 'Time to go.'

MELTDOWN

I scan the board. 'There's a flight to Denver in an hour.'

'Is that near Colorado Springs?'

'A couple of hours. The problem is ID. The agency will have the flights monitored.'

'Are they that good?'

'Better. Time for you to go to work again. And quickly. We need some ID.'

'Where from?'

'Someone's pocket. But someone that won't notice for an hour or so.'

'Man this is a bad place for that.'

'You got the bag easy enough.'

'Yeah but dipping a pocket isn't so easy.'

'I have faith. You need to pick someone who looks a bit like you.'

'Why not you?'

'Well if you can find a six foot three bald man feel free. Just someone close. They never check the picture. I'll meet you over by the phones as soon as you can.' He looks dejected. 'Cheer up. If you get caught the police station might be the safest place you can be.'

Martyn heads into the crowd and I head to the phones. I want to phone Linda but that's a no-no. She could be being monitored. I try and blend with the scene. And fail.

Martyn is back in less than five minutes. I look behind him to see if he's being followed. 'Well?'

'We need to move.' He pulls a billfold from his pocket. 'He was getting into a cab. I made out I wanted it and we tussled a little. I hope he doesn't realize until he gets to his destination.'

I pull out the drivers' license. It's not Martyn but it's good enough. The billfold is rammed with cash.

'Bonus.' Martyn is smiling.

I shake my head. 'Not ours. We hand it in once we have the tickets.'

'But there has to be a grand or more in there,' he bleats.

'And it isn't ours. Tickets first. Drop it next. You need to buy. Two coach to Denver. Double quick.'

He takes one last look at the money and walks. I watch him negotiate our flight and follow him to security. We stand in line and go through the pain of being declared safe to fly.

Things are tight as we hit airside. The line has left us a dash for the plane. We hit the moving sidewalks and crash a few passengers to hit the gate. We are late. But I put my arm out and hold Martyn back.

'Last and final call for Mr Beardmore and Mr Smith,' blares the announcement.

'Smith?' I say.

'Best I could do. We should go.'

'Not yet. I want them to rush us on. No ID check. Hold fire.'

The crew at the gate are scanning the crowd. I grab Martyn's arm and limp at speed. 'Smith and Beardmore.' We flash out passes and we are ushered on. We find our seats and I slump.

Chapter 24

Denver is dry and cold. Dry in the mouth in a way that makes you suck when you breathe. Ten minutes into the terminal and I down a pint of Coke. With no bags to pick up we head to the exit. I enquire at the price of a cab and cough a fit at the price. I'm told there's a bus but not for a few hours. I cross to the other side of the terminal, aiming for the private buses and pick up point. I scan the names and spot a bus with a man holding a card with Cheyenne Mountain Resort, Colorado Springs on one side and Brewster beneath it. Go figure. Maybe it's a sign. I leave Martyn and, a handful of dollars later we're filling empty seats. The wind pierces our summer clothing. Inside the bus the heating is on full but the door is still open.

Two other people join us. The Brewsters. An elderly couple on their way to a conference on philately. I ask about the hobby and we are introduced to the word of stamps as we hit the freeway. I have common ground. We are heading for the same hotel I briefly stayed in. I give them the low down and down a bottle of water before we've gone twenty miles. The driver catches my eye in the mirror. 'Six thousand feet and near zero humidity does that to you.'

I smile and use the interruption to avoid Mr Brewster's description of a Jamaica Ten Cent Pink. At least I think that's what he's talking about. I turn to Martyn. 'Where will they be keeping the Iranian?'

'I've no idea.'

'What about your friend?'

'He might know but he might not be my friend anymore. He's an area commander.'

I ignore the grandiose term. 'Where can we find him?'

He hangs around in a bar called Jack Quinns'

'That's it?'

'Best I have.'

'Are you sure? We have less than a day. If that.'

'It's all I got. He talks about it a lot. He calls it his office. Anyway you've been to town. It should be easy to find.'

'I was confined to the hotel.'

We are close to four o'clock. I tap the driver on the shoulder 'How long to town?'

'An hour.'

I turn to the scenery. Dry, barren. We rattle past a clutch of new builds. Nice looking detached. Probably Denver commuter belt? The land is parched. Brown. Green missing. Waiting for rain and sun. Snow lingers in the shadows and the new builds have an ice thick road coursing through the middle. We are ill equipped for the weather. Martyn's cash will need to survive a trip to the mall.

Mr Brewster is still talking. My absence doesn't seem to bother him. His wife is looking out the window. I have a feeling that their lives run on such rails. I ask the driver about clothing shops. He tells me he'll drop us near some. I ask if it's near the Jack Quinn bar. 'Walkable.'

MELTDOWN

We run in to Colorado Springs and the driver drops us in a stretch of two story shops. Low rise is the norm. He points to a shop called Ollie K's Boutique. It takes us ten minutes to kit up and start hunting down the bar. I'm wrapped in a Berghaus and Martyn is in a North Face. Gloves and hat add to the comfort. My shoes are Timberland, as are Martyn's, and underneath we are triple layer. It stripped us of 600 dollars and Martyn didn't blink. Ma has given him more than a small allowance. I ask him how much we have. He says we have enough.

We cross the road in search of the bar. We walk a few blocks and spot it just passed a Starbucks. We enter. It's late afternoon beer time. The bar is faux Irish. Booths down one side and a high side bar on the other. There are a million others like it. I should know. But it's a nice example of one. I order up two pints of Bass and Martyn scans for his contact and shakes his head. We sit in an empty booth. I swipe the last occupant's glasses to the end of the table. 'Martyn we haven't time to wait. We need to short circuit.'

'How? He isn't here.'

'He's a local. You say this is his office. The bar tender will know him. He'll know how to get in touch. They always do.'

'I thought we were playing this softly?'

'To a point. Once the story on the oil goes public the Iranian is a liability and we've lost our million dollar chip. Speed is all that counts. Ask away.'

Martyn raises himself. Pint untouched. I put mine to my lips. Cold, bitter and refreshing as hell in this climate. I take another swallow and watch Martyn chat. He shakes hands with the bartender and returns. 'He's due in within the hour. We're not the only ones waiting on him.'

'Who else?'

'Over there. By the front door. One in green army fatigues. The other's in a jump suit.'

'Toy soldiers. The Factor?'

'Could be. But low down. I'll be on their radar big time and they don't recognize me. Grunts. Probably here to pass on a message.'

'What's your friend's background?'

'He's not a friend. We trained together for a few weeks in Canada.'

'His name?'

'Why should I tell you?'

'Why not? What in the hell would I do with the info? Steal him from you? He doesn't know me from a hole in the wall. Martyn we're joined at the hip on this. The sooner you realize it the better.'

Martyn sips at the beer. 'Ok. Denholm Rouqe. His ma is from Quebec. His dad was something in the local FBI.'

'Is he high up in the Factor?'

'High enough to know about the Iranian.'

'And he'll know where he's being kept?'

'Maybe.'

'And he would tell you what he knows?'

'No.'

'No?'

'I don't think so. I'm in the litter. He's in the canopy on this.'

The Bass was taking the edge of my anxiousness. 'You said he might help?'

'He might but then again…'

Shit.

'Ok let's deal with things one at a time. We meet him and see where it goes from there. But one way or another he needs to talk. Does he have any vices? Drugs, booze, women, young boys – anything?'

'Not that I know of. Married with a young kid. Wife's a looker. Kid's his life. He doesn't like the Factor anymore. Wants out.'

'Why doesn't he walk?'

'You don't walk away from the Factor. You're in for life. It's what you sign up for. They model themselves on the Mafia. Need to know. Small cells. Lifetime or dead. No loose talk. Honor above all. In their world me telling you this is a death sentence. But then I'm already a Zombie.'

'So Denholm won't be predisposed to a chat.'

'No.'

The door swings open and two overcoats walk in. Martyn looks at them and shakes his head. I polish off the beer. 'Well, Mafia or not he needs to talk.'

'How?'

'I haven't figured it out yet.'

The two overcoats are still standing at the door. Both have one arm inside their coats. Legs apart they are scanning the pub. My head sparks. Trouble? The two Factor grunts are watching them. Barely a yard behind. The overcoats' eyes pass over me and keep going. No sign of recognition. They don't look like agency and the Factor guys aren't welcoming them with open arms. This is hardly the Wild West but they look weaponed up. Their eyes fix on something behind me and I turn. Two men in leather jackets are standing next to the jukebox. It's eyeball to eyeball time. 'Martyn, do you recognize the two guys in the leather jackets back there?'

He looks. 'No. Why?'

'I have the feeling we are in the middle of something.'

'What?'

'Trouble. I think.'

The two overcoats step forward. Each with a hand still buried in their coat. I notice that the buttons are undone. Ready for action. But hardly professional. Getting a gun out from under a coat is inefficient. Too much material. Too easy to get the gun caught. Leave it to the movies. It's also a strange time for any nonsense. Night gives cover for an escape. Near rush hour, it's not yet dark and the roads are dense with traffic. Not good getaway material.

I slide along the seat to the edge and encourage Martyn to do the same. I don't want to be here. Knowing me I could turn what might be a bad situation into a nuclear meltdown. I can feel my heart racing and I drag a deep draft of bar room air to calm myself. I tap Martyn on the wrist. 'When the overcoats walk by we're history.' I expected Martyn to argue but he simply nods.

MELTDOWN

As the overcoats draw level they pause. I look at the leather jackets and they're on the move. They know something is going down. The nearest overcoat pulls his coat open and I see the stock of the shotgun as he pulls it free. A shout goes up from behind me and the second overcoat starts to pull his gun free. The stock of the first gun is inches from my face. When it goes off I'll know all about it.

I think about grabbling it but I'm not the target. If I reach out the other could turn on me. The gun is twenty degrees from horizontal. Overcoat number one has his gaze fixed. Finger wrapped around the trigger. A second shout goes up. Higher pitched. A woman. Maybe she has just seen the gun.

Ten degrees to go. Pressure on the trigger will be high. The end of the barrel will be six inches from my face when it goes off. Martyn is already throwing himself into the booth. Away from the guns. I want to do the same but I don't. The guy next to me has crossed the Rubicon. He is on his way to killing another human being. Maybe it isn't his first. Maybe it's his day job. Anyway he's going to pull that trigger and I can stop it.

Five degrees. Maybe a second before he has it where he wants it. Then a half pound more pressure and one less leather jacket customer in the world. I look at his eyes. They are scared. Wide with it. Sweat beads his forehead. He's young. Too young for this. Maybe late teens. Acne still riddles his face. What in the hell is he up to? The gun is shaking in his hand. A cheap digital watch tells me he's no dollar rich kid.

I make a call.

As the gun hits the point of no return I throw my hand at it. Palm up. Aiming for the barrel. I catch it nearer the end than the stock and push it hard. The explosion takes out my hearing. The shot sprays the ceiling and glass shatters somewhere. The boy looks down at me. He's already pumping a second shell into the chamber. The second overcoat ignores the shot and is priming to fire. I kick out from under the table. Hard into the first boy's shin. I follow up with my left hand to his side. I launch him towards his colleague. He stumbles and clips his friend's gun as it fires. Sending shot into the bar next to them. They go down. In a mess of cloth and guns.

I jump up and land on the nearest. I grab the gun and pull it free. Sending it flying behind the bar. The second gun is lying on the floor. I scramble over the two bodies and grab it. The second overcoat lashes out with his foot and catches me on the wrist. I scream but hold firm on the gun. I try to throw it away but the kick has numbed the bottom of my arm. The shotgun tumbles a mere few feet and slides against the foot rail on the bar. The first overcoat tries to use me as a mat. As his foot comes down on my back I flip over and he loses his balance and falls onto me.

More shouting. Cutting through ringing in my ears. I can feel hot breath on my ear. A love whisper from one of the overcoats. He's reaching out. After the gun. I ball my fist and aim at his head. He leaps past and I catch him on the throat. He collapses across me. Gasping. I try and push him clear. I'm pinned. I wriggle. The second overcoat appears. Going for the shotgun.

I feel the headache coming. I want it now. I need it to happen. The electricity to flow. The kernel starts to crack. The head pain escalates. My vision blurs. I wait for the explosion. And then I'm gone.

Chapter 25

'Craig. Get up.'

The voice is a distant echo in my head. The headache at the back of my head is gone. But no blue world! No stop start universe. Just a voice and noise. 'Now. Get up. Police. We need to move.'

My vision is white on white. Hands pull at me. I fight them.

'Now. We need to go now.'

Sight returns. A snapshot of light. Martyn is above me. 'Now!'

He looks like a ghost.

I roll over. He clutches at my jacket. He tries to heave me into the air. But he couldn't lift cotton candy. My feet find traction. I rise. Stumble. Propel myself forward. I look up. We're heading for the back of the pub. I try and co-ordinate my feet. But they belong to someone else. Martyn wraps his arm round my waist. He's using me for support. We hit a fire door and out. The chill snatches at my throat. I choke. Martyn spins me towards him. 'Craig.' His voice is weak.

I order my feet to move. They respond. We are off.

The pub door empties onto another alley. I'm collecting them. We limp towards a five-lane street. Across from us a six or seven story brick building dominates the area. I scan for a cab. Nothing. We cross the street. The red brick belongs to Morgan Stanley. Figures. Martyn spends an age at the door of a pick-up and then he's in. I stumble to the passenger door and the engine is already running. The boy is resourceful.

Martyn heads into the traffic. He swerves over three lanes. He looks like he's about to pass out. My head is clearing. No aftermath. No come down. Whatever happened back there wasn't an event. My head hurts and I touch it. I turn to Martyn. 'What happened?'

'Let me drive.'

Ten minutes later he pulls into a side street and turns to me. Some color is returning to his face. 'One of the guys with the overcoats got to the gun. Thankfully he chose to brain you with the stock. They got up and ran.'

It explains the headache. I rub my head. Strange, but no wound. I let my head run. 'We need to go back.'

Martyn's foot slips. The pick-up leaps forward. He lifts from the gas. Ramming it into park. 'Are you kidding?'

'No. We need your friend.'

'And the police?'

'Did the guys in the leather jackets run?'

'Yes.'

'So who have they left to interview?'

'Us if we go back.'

'We wait.'

'They'll recognize us'

'Who will?'

'The bar tender.'

'If your friend appears we won't be in long enough for him to call back the police.'

'Craig this is a bad idea. The car's hot.'

'Dump it. By the time we walk back the bar will be cool.'

'They'll have our description.'

I turn to the back seats. Two black puffa jackets are lying in the well. I pull them up. 'We use these. Dump the other jackets. We don't need to be invisible. Just different for a few minutes.'

'And then what?'

'No idea. But running's not a good idea.'

Light is sapping away outside. The rush hour is on the build. There's still a surfeit of SUV's and gas guzzlers out here. All-wheel drive for the snow. Above the carbon monoxide a clear sky promises temperatures that will chill the homeless. The sidewalk is quiet. Wheel trumps foot. A lone figure, hooded and heavy shod, crunches over a snow pile. His breath is a steam train cloud behind him. The warmth of the pickup has its attractions. It's hot in both senses of the word. I leave Martyn to chew on the obvious.

A few minutes drift away. Minutes we probably don't have. He looks at me 'What happened back there?'

'Your guess is as good as any. Turf war? Drugs? School kids with too much juice on?'

'Not that. Wrong place wrong time would normally cover it. I mean just before you went for a nap?'

'Not sure what you mean.'

'Like back at Ma's. When everyone seemed to breathe loopy juice. I got a feeling. Back of my head. A buzz. Like licking a battery. I felt it again in the bar. Just for a second. And I saw something in the boy's eyes. Not the one that hit you. The one on the floor. Blank. Gray as a guy with cancer. He was looking at his friend. Like he wanted to kill him. Blank but with menace. Or focus. Then they flicked back to normal as soon as you were hit. Shook his head. As if clearing it. Then he got up and ran but he never took his eyes from his friend.'

'Strange.'

'You know nothing about it?'

'Like what?'

'Like why all those people went nuts? Like what happened to your leg? Why did you stab yourself?'

'A mistake.'

'That's not what it looked like from Ma's window.'

'I'm clumsy.'

'And the buzz? The blank eyes? Normal service resumed when you checked out? What about that?'

'Imagination. What do you want me to say? I can't explain it. There's nothing to explain.'

Martyn takes in the cooling night. Traffic is slicing through the chill. Bodies aiming for home. Fires and central heating mixed with hot food and something to take the edge off their life. Two streams of white and red lights. Blurred by the ice particles that have been whipped up by a growing wind. A night to be indoors.

'So why you?'

The question catches me by surprise. 'Why me what?'

'Why did the agency pick you? You're not one of them. You're not one of us. Why you?'

'History.'

'What kind?'

'Have you ever been to prison?'

'No. What has that to do with anything?'

'I watched a film on it once. Twelve hundred inmates in Florida State Prison. The only real prison in Florida – all the others are called correctional institutions or facilities. Three to a cell. For others, twenty to a room. Wake at 6. Bed at 10. Three meals a day. The real bad bastards do solitary. A guy called Joe. Young kid. In for the first time. Nineteen. Ripped off a liquor store with a gun. His third offence and three strikes and you are out in Florida.

His mother was interviewed. Tears and tantrums. *My boy – my nice boy. Ain't never done nothing bad.* Except he had. The liquor store assistant can't breathe without electricity. A wife and two kids and no medical insurance. Joe says he's innocent. *Mistaken identity. Fitted up. Circumstantial evidence.* But he called it circumental evidence. Kind of described him. He'd been in juvy six times. Kept cycling round to it. Prison was just the next spin on the carousel. He wasn't bright. Skipped school. No qualifications.

Mother was an alcoholic. Never stopped during pregnancy. Joe had all the signs of FAS.' Martyn looks blank. 'Fetal Alcohol Syndrome. He was a case study. Small head, small eye openings, flattened cheekbones and an indistinct philtrum.' More blank from Martyn. 'The groove between your lip and mouth.' Martyn unconsciously licks his. I go on. 'Learning problems and he doesn't understand simple stuff like money or time. He was an accident in progress.'

Martyn shifts his eyes to the road. 'Why are you telling me this?'

'Live with me. We need to give the police time to finish up at the bar. So Joe is dumped in with twelve others. All are in for ten years plus. Most are season ticket holders. Joe is no looker but a fresh fanny is a fresh fanny. Joe is passed round like a spliff at a Jamaican beach party. They smash his teeth so he can't chew his new boyfriends' cocks off. He spends a week in hospital. Six months in and he's a write off. He's not eating. He was skinny to start with but now he's made of straw. The boys have lost interest in him. Rumor is he's HIV positive. He tries to hang himself with his bedclothes then slit his wrists and finally he drinks bleach. He fails on all three counts. His mother has deserted him. He has no father. He has no one. Every day is a day more than he wants on this planet.'

A police car is inching up the rush hour conga line. I pause as it passes. No siren. No lights. We are still good to go. 'One day Joe is transferred to hospital. The doctors give him no chance. He lies steel still all day. Craps himself. Waits for death. Then a small miracle. He begins to turn round. Eats a little. Gets out of bed to pee. Not big stuff but good stuff. Soon he's up and about. Gets his teeth fixed. Hits the gym. A year later he's sporting some shape. He'll never be Arnie. Too much booze when he was in his mother's womb. But he looks good. He doles out a little pay back on the worst of his rapists. He earns a little respect. But there hangs a question. What turned him?

They interview everyone with the same question. *'Who saved the poor bastard from the grave?'* No one seems to know. But this is TV and good TV never leaves you hanging for long. Up steps Cal Toohey. A lifer. Murdered his next door neighbor when he found him in bed with Mrs Toohey. Cal has the big C. Terminal. More tumor than man. Yet he has just finished writing his first novel. A hundred and twenty thousand word blockbuster about a hunt for a serial killer. Four publishers are fighting over the rights. He knew he was dying when he started it.

He admits he went to see Joe one night. They shared a ward. He simply talked to the boy. Told him that he would swap everything he had to be in Joe's place. That he would take it up the black hole nightly and be grateful if only God would rip out the cancer. He told Joe that throwing away your life was dumb. Class A dumb. Something, over the next few visits, clicked with Joe.'

Martyn sighed. 'Has this got a point?'

'Nearly there. Cal lays out his life story. All save the bit about his wife's love life and the knife that ended his neighbor's days. He just skipped that bit. Joe asks what he did. Cal blanks him. Joe presses. Cajoles. But the old man kept his council. As Joe got better, Cal went the opposite way. He joked with Joe that for every press up Joe knocked out God took the energy from Cal.

At the end they transferred Cal to a hospice. No flight risk. Joe saw him off and told him that someone in the kitchen had finally told him what Cal had done. Cal asked if it made any difference to what he thought of Cal. Joe said no. *So why did you need to know?* Joe told him curiosity. *What if I told you that an hour after offing that bastard I went round to his house and killed his wife and six kids?* Joe was stunned. *Now if I'd told you that at the beginning would you be standing here built and breathing?* Joe mumbled something. *And if I told you that I didn't let them die quickly. What then? What if I did more than just kill them? Kids and all? You see son, it ain't always healthy to know someone's past. If they step up to the plate and help you, you might want to leave well enough alone.*

The old man died the next day.'

Martyn rubbed the wheel and threaded his fingers along the seam of the leather. 'In other words don't look a gift horse in the mouth.'

'Something like that. Why I'm here and what I did won't help you in the slightest. But under it all we've got the same agenda. We need to get the Iranian and bargain our way to a better place.'

The traffic is solid heading out of town but quiet going in and it was time for us to go back in.

'Did the old man in the program really kill the family?'

'Maybe. Time to head back. Let's hope the local police officers are keen to get back to their station on a night like this. Skip the walk. We'll keep the car.'

Chapter 26

'I'll go round to the other side.' Martyn is weaving back to the bar. 'We don't want the owner of his car seeing it coming back.'

I know this is a risk. If the owner has reported the car missing and the police are still around we are walking into a cell for the night. More accurately for life.

Not knowing the roads, it takes Martyn a few attempts to find the alley. I see it on the third pass 'There it is. Reverse it in and hit the flashers.'

'Shouldn't we dump the car?'

'No. It's our back up. We might need it. Now reverse up further. We don't want it seen from the road.'

The back entrance of the bar has a small neon sign flickering Miller Lite and a couple of kegs near it. A few yards short of it Martyn halts the car and we jump out. I try the pub door but it's locked. 'Round the front.'

We head back the way we had come in the car and onto the road, Martyn in step behind me. I reach the corner to the street that the bar lies on and stop. I push my head out and we are police vehicle free. 'All clear. I think. Let's go.'

I step round and after a few steps realize that Martyn isn't in tow. I turn back. He's standing on the corner. The edge of his hand against his forehead. Looking at something further along the sidewalk. I join him. 'What is it?'

'Can you see the small café? In the middle of the block?'

'Yes.'

'Standing outside are two men. See them?'

The two men are standing with their backs to us. Both are entombed in heavy weight winter gear – hoods up. There's quite a height difference between them. One has to be a few inches above five feet and the other the same above six. They are leaning in close. The tall man head down to the small man. 'Who are they?'

'The tall one's Denholm.'

'Great, let's go get him.'

'Not so fast. It's the other one that worries me.'

'Who is he?'

'Have you heard of a man called Gaylord Butterworth?'

'No, but with a name like that I'd sure as hell remember if I'd met him. Who is he?'

'Head of the Factor.'

'Really?'

'If it's him, and it's hard to tell at this distance, I've only seen him once and that was only a little closer than this.'

'And?'

'Well my main question is what in the hell is he doing here?'

'I thought the head office for the Factor was near here?'

MELTDOWN

'It is, but Gaylord isn't one for being out and about. At the moment he's wanted by the FBI, CIA, IRS, local police and then you can add on the enemies he has made over the years. Last I heard he was holed up in Washington State somewhere in the boondocks. He runs the whole organization by remote.'

'So he's had a change of heart. Wanted some air.'

Martyn turns away and faces the pub. 'Turn round.'

I join him.

He starts to shuffle his feet. Nerves. I tap him on the shoulder. 'Is he that bad?'

'A bastard of the first order. He built the Factor from nothing into one of the biggest criminal networks in the US. You don't do that with a pleasant smile and cookies.'

'So why would he be here?'

'Beats me. But it isn't good. If he feels he needs to risk being caught in the open it has to be big.'

'The oil is a big deal. So is the Iranian. They don't come much bigger. Anyway he clearly wants to be spotted by us.'

'How do you figure that?'

'Look at the way they're chatting. Like it was over a coffee in the local Starbucks. It's freezing out here. If he has half the status you suggest there are far more discreet places to hold a conversation. Plus you said Denholm wasn't that high up.'

'Not much higher than me.'

'The help go to the employer not the other way round. Plus there's another give away.'

'What?'

'We're being watched.

Chapter 27

'Where?' Martyn turns and I stop him. 'Back the way we came. A black Acura. It was there when we entered the alley and I saw it sitting four back when we jacked the pick-up. Two of them. One in the back seat. The other the driver.'

'Factor?'

'Not agency anyway. Wrong MO. Anyway they double flashed their lights once we exited the alley. Denholm was watching and went inside. I saw it and now he's out chewing fat. We were meant to see him.'

'What does it mean?'

'Well for one thing our attempt at a clandestine trip is blown. They knew we were coming.'

'How?'

'That's a good question.'

'So they know we're after the Iranian?'

'Why else would the two of us be here? I also think the scene in the bar was for our benefit. All too pat if you ask me. Prime time in the bar is not the time to go on the shoot. No matter how desperate you might be. And those kids weren't desperate. They were scared.'

'What did they hope to achieve?'

I have an idea and if I'm right it isn't a good news day. 'I'm not sure. Flush us out? Scare us? Anyway up we're not in control at the moment and I don't like that.'

I swing round and head for Gaylord and Denholm. They sound like a mystery duo from England in the thirties. I jump the 'Don't Walk' sign and a few horns blasted as I piss off some of the commuters. Gaylord and Denholm don't turn round. More proof we sure as hell are expected. I flick my head to see if Martyn is following. He's ten steps back.

There's one street between us and the targets. I wish I had a gun. I wish I was somewhere else. I cross the street and stop a few yards short. The two are still in conversation. I wait for them to turn. Martyn pulls up behind me. He'll know if it's really them. I lean against the wall. It's cold and the temperature is still trying for penguin friendly. Martyn starts his shuffle. I don't blame him. I promised to look after him and now I'm gift-wrapping him to the organization that tried to kill him. He's on a hiding to nothing and knows it. If they know we are here they could have lifted us at any time and they didn't. What's going to be is going to be. I stretch my neck, rotating my head, losing sight of them as I stretch muscle. I've no fear that they'll run. We've been set up for a reason and they're not going anywhere.

The evening traffic is starting to thin out. Gaps appear between the fenders. The wind is kicking up. Stripping heat. The jackets we lifted from the pick-up are more for show than performance. A more civilized place for our meet would be anywhere but here.

The Acura pulls up next to us and the driver and his pal get out. The two may as well have bodyguards tattooed on their foreheads. Both are thick in the arm and leg.

MELTDOWN

Worked up chests obvious even under the layers of clothes. One has a small scar running out from the left edge of his lip. The other is sporting designer stubble. They're only an inch or two short of me in height.

Scarface nods at me 'Get in the back of the car.'

I don't move. He does. I sense the menace. I still wait.

'Leave him.' The voice is high and southern and emanates from Gaylord. He turns round and I gasp. If Tampoline has a smaller brother then this is him. Same eyes. Same cracked jaw. Thin top lip. I like a coincidence as much as the next man but he's too close not to be related. Whereas Tampoline is thin, almost a rake, Gaylord is rotund. A ball of fat with a basketball for a head. But the eyes are alive. Just like Tampoline before he was blinded at the TT. They dart around. Never still. Even the voice is the same.

'Mr McIntyre isn't going to be any trouble. All I want is a quick chat. So be kind enough to slide into the car. You too, Mr Wheeler. Charles and Jason are walking from here. Denholm can drive. Not my choice of car you know. A little too low rent for me, but anonymity is useful.'

I cross to the door and slip in. Martyn remains outside. Butterworth studies his nails. 'Mr Wheeler, if you don't want to join us I don't mind. Charles and Jason will be delighted to accompany you. Memorial Park is not far from here. Quiet. Secluded. You can tell them all about your time with my brother. Then maybe a refreshing dip in Prospect Lake if we can break the ice for you.'

Martyn looks confused but Butterworth has just confirmed that he and Tampoline are officially from the same mold. Martyn decides an icy swim is not on his bucket list and gets in to the car. Charles hands the keys to Denholm. I get a look at his face for the first time. I would say that the Tampoline/Butterworth dynasty has at least one more generation coming through the ranks. Denholm's eyes never sit still. He gets in the driver's side and Butterworth squeezes a quart into a pint pot and overflows the passenger seat.

Denholm plays tag with the traffic until we hit the 115 and he takes us south. Talk is zero. We swing off. A sign tells me it's called onto Norad Road. Butterworth breaks the silence. 'One of the US's top, top secret bases and they tell you where it is by naming the road leading up to it. Go figure.'

We cruise through low-level scrub. Small trees drift past on both sides, flickering in our lights. A 'Restricted Access Official Government Business' warning sign forces us to swing off to the right. We hit a roundabout and enter a residential area. Large homes and condos hunker under the dark. A few more turns and we roll up a driveway and the garage door opens. We enter.

Butterworth is confident. No blindfolds. I could bring down the local army to his house if I wanted. Not a good sign. For someone who is up there on the Most Wanted list he's acting like Mr Innocent.

Doors are opened and we leave the garage and enter the warmth of the house. The decoration is neutral. Show home neutral. We are encouraged to sit in the kitchen. Four of us around a breakfast island. Denholm switches on the coffee machine and we're all happy families.

'Nice house.' I smile as I say it.

Butterworth smiles back. 'Not my taste. But we won't be here long.'

Coffee is poured.

Martyn stirs. 'What do you…'

Slap. Denholm catches him on the ear with the back of his hand. 'No one said speak.' Martyn's eyes flare.

The wind outside is taking on storm force. With the temperature still on the fall there's little chance of escape. Where in the hell would we run? Denholm tops us all up and we sit.

A clock in the next room chimes out eight. A text arrives for Denholm and he nods at Butterworth. He stands up. 'Time to go.'

'Where?'

Martyn gets another slap for his trouble. 'Down into the cellar.'

Not good.

The cellar is clear of the usual household debris. A boiler sits at one end. Firing hard as it tries to beat the cold. Butterworth points to a wall next to the boiler and Denholm plays with a few blocks and what looks like solid cinder slab reveals itself to be a door. Lights flick on as Denholm steps in and starts down the stairs beyond. Alice down the rabbit hole. Curiouser and curiouser.

Butterworth book ends Martyn and me. We drop down thirty steps and enter a solid concrete tunnel. Butterworth laughs. 'Ironic isn't it. The US military are not the only ones that can build tunnels around here.' We walk on. Lights flick into life as we move.

A door stops our progress and Denholm pulls a key from his pocket and unlocks it. The smell of damp rushes in. Cold damp. Denholm reaches inside and pulls free a flashlight from the wall. He lights it up and sprays it into the doorway. He reveals a cave. As we walk in I have to duck to avoid hitting my head on the roof. The walls are wet and the floor beneath is solid rock.

'We are less than half a mile from the Cheyenne Mountain Air Force Station. That's if you could tunnel through.' Butterworth closes the door as he talks. The ceiling gets lower and I need to bend. Butterworth can walk upright. I count fifty steps and feel a breeze on my face. I hear the sound of an engine. Denholm pushes some bushes to one side and we are into the scrubland.

The wind rips my breath away. A SUV is sitting, lights off. Denholm has killed his flashlight and we need to hold onto each other as we stumble to the car. The door is open but the interior light has been killed. We enter under dashboard light. The driver is sitting with night vision goggles on. Once inside he guns the engine and we drive into the dark.

'Pity.' Butterworth is silhouetted in the blue of the dials. 'That house has served us well but no more. Denholm, seal up the exit and get it on the market.'

MELTDOWN

I'm no structural engineer but the exit we just took could not have been cheap to build and Butterworth was writing it off as if it were chump change.

The ride is like a dark roller coaster. With no light to see by every bump is an adventure. We roll for thirty minutes or more until we hit something a little smoother. Not black top but a track. Lights appear up ahead and the driver sparks up the headlights as a small strip mall flies by. Residential, commercial, gap, highway and we are being buffeted by the wind as the driver ramps up the speed.

'I'd get some shut eye if I were you.' Butterworth settles back. 'We have a few hours to go. Denholm, are we clear?' Denholm flips open a laptop. He waits for it to power up. As it does so he checks his cell. 'No alerts on the cell.' The laptop allows him access as he types in a password. He draws up a web page and studies it. 'All clear. We have no one back at the house.'

'Satellite surveillance?' Butterworth sounds relaxed.

'Unlikely. We'd have a tail by now and the two trail cars have spotted nothing since we hit the high way.'

I lean forward. 'I'm surprised. Cheyenne must be one of the most watched places in the country.'

'Exactly.' Butterworth turns to me. 'But who would try and screw around with a nuclear proof shelter? The car we arrived in will have been noted but it's registered to the house. Only dumb people would place a safe house that near a major military establishment. All the residents are checked and double checked and after that they're left alone. We've had that house for six years. I lived there for two. Best place to hide is in plain sight. I even went for a walk once to look at the base. So many people do it that they don't even bother with you unless you get too close. I have more chance of being spotted in New York. But you, Mr McIntyre, are hot property. Our military neighbors might not be bothered but my brother – he's another matter. Him I worry about.'

'How do you know he didn't have us followed?'

'He did. But we dealt with that. Four of them are cooling their heels in a hotel in downtown Colorado Springs. I had to be sure there were no more before we set off. Hence the wait at the house until we got the all clear. My brother will be pouring resources into the area but we're ahead of him. Even he doesn't have the ability to seal off a highway at such short notice and if we kept clear of his eyes in the sky he'll have no idea where we are going or what to look for. So relax.'

'And what is it you want from us?'

'Later.' Conversation over.

The road is an endless conveyor belt of white light coming towards us. The storm is doing its best to blow us off the highway but our driver, now without night goggles, ignores the road and plays with the radio. AOR enters our life. He's cool with it all.

Why does Butterworth want me? If he knows we are after the Iranian he has no need to kidnap us. Just move the Iranian and we're dead in the water. If we still prove to be a nuisance then he could probably have us killed. He seems as toyed up as his brother. I can't get my head round the situation.

MELTDOWN

I thought I had this figured. Rescue the Iranian. Use him as currency and see if we can cut a deal. But time is of the essence and no matter how good Tampoline's machinery is you can't hide the destruction of America's oil reserves for long. Too many Twitterers, Facebookers, Bloggers. It had to be out soon. After that the game's over. No Iranian. No oil. Panic. Gas prices through the roof. Lines for gas with no end. No economy.

When the UK tanker drivers went on strike in the naughties the UK nearly ground to a halt inside a week. We wouldn't last half that. So why would Butterworth's lot do it? What's to gain? Collapse the country, rise up and take control while the chaos reigns? Not a chance. The military would step in, and unless the Factor have a million in reserve that are ready to roll, there ends any coup. Yet Butterworth has the Iranian. If Tampoline is right he spiked the oil. There has to be a plan to all this. But what?

Martyn has sat like a stone. Denholm is next to him. Fearing another slap. He must be wondering what the upside is in all this. They already tried to kill him once. He hasn't enhanced his chances of surviving by teaming up with me. Now we're with the people he most wanted to avoid.

Despite myself the day starts to catch up and the heat of the car is mugging me. The conveyor belt goes on and I doze.

Chapter 28

I jerk awake as the heat is sucked from the car. The door next to me is open and Denholm is waiting for me to get out. We're off the main highway. There are no lights around. I step onto the side of the road. The storm tries to lift me off my feet. Martyn follows me out and Butterworth rolls into view. The SUV takes off.

I can feel the heat leaking from me. Denholm fires up a walkie-talkie. He fingers the button. The sound is off. He's using the transmit button to alert someone. The green screen flickers in the night and concentration is writ large on his face.

I lean towards Butterworth. 'You do know that if they have eyes on you from above this is a waste of time.'

Butterworth rubs his chin. 'True. And if they do we've been dead men since Colorado. To be more accurate we'd be dead men by now. My brother has access to some fancy technology. Predators are designed to remove people like us.'

I'm not sure this is a conversation for such a night but he's dragging me in. 'Oversight. Butterworth, even Tampoline can't order a strike on US soil.'

Butterworth laughs. A high-pitched giggle that would better suit a five year old. 'Mr McIntyre, in my brother's world he's the oversight committee. Trust me, if he knew where I was I would be on the receiving end of a

MELTDOWN

Hellfire missile. You won't hear it coming. We'll just stop being. And since we are still here then he doesn't know where we are.'

An engine struggles to be heard above the maelstrom. A mini-van appears. The doors open and warmth swims over us. We clamber in and do the hand rub thing as we try and inject the heat into our veins.

We are back on the highway. I see a sign for Denver and then a stream of towns I don't know. As we approach midnight we slip from the three lane onto a single lane. Butterworth makes no attempt to hide the location. We skirt a town and down a back road. A set of imposing gates rear up and we glide through as they open automatically. The house we pull up in front of could swallow Southfork and not need a toothpick.

Inside I expect a sweeping staircase and get two. One to the left and one to the right. Both rise two floors and the carpet could hide a squad of Oompa Loompas. Denholm shows us to a side room. If you can call a basketball court sized room anything beginning with the word 'side'. Overstuffed armchairs are the furniture of choice. That and more antiques. I slump in a button-backed chair and sigh. Martyn does the same but omits the sigh. His nerves are showing again. I lean forward. 'Relax. If they wanted rid of you then you'd be gone.'

'You don't know that.'

'I do know that. They wrung you dry at the house. They tried to kill you. They failed. If they really wanted you dead you wouldn't have made it on the plane. They want you here. Why? No idea. But they do. So chill. Worrying won't help.'

'Coffee?' Denholm is standing at the door.

'Have you anything stronger?'

'Name your poison Mr McIntyre.'

'A Coors Banquet. It's only made down the road. Should be fresh.'

'And you Mr Wheeler?'

'Martyn. It's bloody Martyn. Christ we've know each other for years.'

'What drink Mr Wheeler?'

'Same as him.' He shakes his head as Denholm leaves.

Denholm reappears a few minutes later with two on a tray. No 'I'm sorry but we don't have that brand.' Just there it's. As if the drinks cabinet won't let him down. Must be some drinks cabinet.

I crack the can, take a slug. 'Any chance of a sandwich? Food has been a bit thin on the ground.'

'Type?'

'Anything but fish.'

'Mr Wheeler?'

'Same.'

Ten minutes later we have a pile that a New York deli would be proud of. They are gone in twenty, along with another beer each. I feel a damn site better.

Denholm re-enters. 'Mr Butterworth asks if you would mind staying the night?'

I doubt that no is an answer that will be tolerated.

MELTDOWN

My bedroom is no let down. Four-poster. Wet room. Walk in closet. Dressing room. Full dining table. Chandelier. 60 inch flat screen. Fully stocked bar. Networked hi-fi. All I'm missing is the maid and butler. As Denholm leaves he turns. 'Drop all your clothes in the bag next to your bed and leave it outside. They'll be washed and ironed and in your room before you wake.'

Cool.

A full stomach. A slight buzz from the beer and I'm gone once I've sorted out my laundry.

***

This is the dream that hurts. I'm in Hatch Roll. A place where the PTSD boys are sent. A rambling mansion built by a gold digger in the late 1880's. I'm in the military wing. The dream always starts with a kiss. A pretty young nurse that I'll never see again. She doesn't fancy me. She pities me. She's also scared of me. I'm the eye of a cyclone around here. Trouble firing off. Me at the centre but never affected. It'll be years before I realize I'm the cause. A pretty nurse will. tell me all this one day, while having a beer and watching the sun go down on the Mexican gulf.

My dream nurse smells of roses. Sometimes of cinnamon. Sometimes of nothing. I can't see her face. I try a smile but she's turned and gone. It's night. Always night. I used to be in a ward with others but now I'm alone. Sealed off. I'm my own communicable disease, though I don't know it yet.

I get out of bed. To pee or just for a walk. The door is locked. No surprise. I pick up a chair. Metal with canvas straps to sit on. I lift it by one leg and smash it into the window next to the door. The glass explodes and I wait for nothing. Because nothing ever happens. No one comes running. No alarms. Silence. Then I hear someone moan from the ward at the end of the corridor. I clear the glass from the edges of the frame and jump through.

My feet are bare. I bleed. I should put on shoes but I never do. I crunch glass and head for the ward. I won't make it. It's not in my future. I want to walk through the doors and talk to the other men. To tell them that this isn't real. Lift up your bed and walk. Instead I slide down the stairs on my blood. Slipping and sliding. The slosh of liquid coating the concrete. Too much blood for the cuts on my feet. A stream that should drain me in minutes. But it won't.

I pick up a couple of walking sticks that lie at the bottom of the steps. I take up a skiers pose and use them to push off. I shoot across the floor on a cushion of blood. Taking up the Norwegian way of getting around. Feet showering red behind me as I lift them.

I'm on a down slope where no down slope could be. Indoors. The piste is smooth. White. Doors either side are open. Beds empty. The incline is gentle at first but not for long. I'm soon slaloming to burn off speed. A two prong trail zig-zags in my wake.

A nurse steps out in front. She stands square in the centre. Her arm outstretched. Hand up. Stop. I don't. I treat

191

her as a gate and clip her as I pass. Then there's another. Two becomes three and three doubles.

The nurses get older the further I go. Wrinkles deepen. Faces lose cohesion. The last one I pass is no more than a skin coat on a skeleton. The slope picks up an angle that should throw me into space but the blood that lubricates becomes glue.

I'm aiming at the oncoming ground. My face the first point of contact. I can't scream. I won't scream. I know it's a dream. But it'll still hurt.

A hand reaches out from the wall and grabs at me. My blood coated ankles slip free. A second hand tries to catch me. A wedding ring glints for a second. My Lorraine's ring. When the dream first happened she was alive. Now she's dead. Killed by me. I want her to hold on. She can't. I'm too heavy. Moving too fast. I don't want to leave her again. But she's gone.

A last hand reaches out. Thick set. A body builder's hand. One used to pouring beers. A friend that was never in the original dream but now comes closest to stopping me. The hand grips and for a second I start to slow before the grip breaks. My speed is reduced. Not by much and it won't reduce the pain. The ground is heading for me. An express elevator on its way up. High speed. Designed for the tallest of buildings.

I wish this dream had a better ending.

***

I wake up. A dry scream stuck in my throat. My face creased in agony. My heart at 200. Breathing not far behind. I'm slick with sweat and I throw myself over the edge of the bed and vomit. Every nerve is on fire. I find my voice and howl. Straining my vocal chords to breaking point. Then the kernel in my head explodes. Electricity flies from my fingers. I want to hurt people. I want to maim. I scream to gain control. To stop the hurt flowing from my body.

The door flies open and Denholm is standing with a gun. It has me dead centre. I flop around the bed, wanting the pain to end. Butterworth appears beside Denholm. Denholm's eyes blank out but before he can turn Butterworth swings at him. His hand is holding a statue. It catches Denholm high on the forehead and he drops like a brick. Butterworth drops the statue and turns to me. My head flashes and the world turns blue.

Butterworth dances around. A stop-start mannequin in a cheaply made horror film. The blue fades and leaves with a cool breeze. Denholm is moaning. Which is a good sign. Butterworth is smiling. Which isn't. 'My God, my brother was so right about you.'

I slump back. Spent.

Chapter 29

Butterworth gives me to just after seven o'clock the next morning before he bursts through my door again. 'Good morning Mr McIntyre. And how does one feel after last night's 'exertions'?'

'Fuck off.' It's the best I can think of.

'Not nice. But understandable.' His high pitch whine is grating. 'We've a long day ahead.'

'We?'

'Certainly. I have such plans for you.'

'I'm not in the plans mood. Not for hire. Not a freak show. Nothing to see here. Move along.' I pull the duvet over my head. Childish.

I hear him walk towards the bed. Soft padded footsteps. Thick with weight.

'So we can play this easy or we can play it hard.' He pulls the duvet back.

'You're so like your brother.'

'You think? Most people say we have little in common. A little facial resemblance. Southern accent. Maybe a little too driven for our own good. But beyond that not much else.'

'Isn't that enough?'

'Mr McIntyre, or do you mind if I call you Craig?'

'You can call me Nancy for all I care. I know what you want and it isn't for sale.'

'Everything has its price.'

'Not this.'

'Everything.' The smugness is oozing from his pores. A man used to buying his way to what he wants.

'Born to money, weren't you Butterworth?'

'Sorry?'

'Born to money. You can tell. Never had to earn it. Don't know what it's like to have none. Never had to graft. Fingers dirty – no chance. Nice home. Mom and Dad with a mountain of folding. Ask and you shall receive. Tell me Mr Butterworth, how much is a pint of milk? What does it cost for a large latte in Starbucks? How much is a Trojan? How much does your dentist earn?'

He smiles. Just smiles. 'No idea on the first three. Last one I reckon he clears three hundred k a year. Am I supposed to feel bad about how I was brought up? Are you saying you wouldn't, given the choice, be born into some money? Who wouldn't? Save your cod psychology. You have no idea how I think. No notion of my values. All you see is a fat ball and think greed. And do I look like I give a fuck?' His whine is hitting new highs. His face has a tinge of beetroot. But his eyes are ice cold.

'Scary.' I smile back at him. 'That probably works on most people. Lots of cash. Big boys at your back. A hidden threat of violence.'

'It's not hidden, Mr McIntyre.'

'I thought we were all pals. Craig, not Mr McIntyre.'

MELTDOWN

He rolls back on the balls of his feet. If he falls over he's fat enough to roll three sixty and end up upright. His fist balls. I'm not in a position to fight back.

I raise my hand. 'However little I know about you - and to be fair I don't think I'm that far off – you know squat about me. Throw a punch. See where it gets you.'

'Friends, Craig. You need friends for your little party trick. Two's the magic number. I saw it in Denholm's eyes last night. If I hadn't given him an early night he would have killed me. I know more than you think.'

'You know jack. Neither does your brother. What ever you think it is I do, you know nothing. I'm not interested in what you have to say.'

'Of course you are. You haven't heard me out.' He's down an octave. The speed his anger dissipates marks him as dangerous. He can switch it on and off. Not easy to do. 'Let's talk over breakfast. I guarantee you'll be interested. Very interested.'

With this he leaves, high-end cologne trailing behind him.

I rip the duvet away. I'll shower myself into a better mood. It fails. All I feel is clean and dirty at the same time.

Breakfast is on a patio, despite the freezing conditions. A slicing wind cuts through a morning mist but six heaters are beating the elements. I said this place out-Southforked Southfork. Now we're having breakfast outside in conditions which rival the worst weather they had to endure. But Butterworth is in a good mood. Denholm is nowhere to be seen. More worryingly, neither is Martyn.

Butterworth is treating himself to a deep fried, lard induced future visit to the cardiac unit. I stick with OJ and coffee. Ever since the TT I've been on the right side of getting fit. Eat well. Exercise. I'm even back to self-defense training. I'm pushing north of two hundred press ups and a thousand sit ups when I feel the need. My arms are picking up muscle and my neck size is up and inch or so. I feel good. I run my hand over my head. Bald. I lost it when Tampoline used me as a drug trial. My thick hair days are gone.

The view from the patio is one of green. Augusta National green. An ocean of grass spreads before us. Dull with winter but still cropped tight. A single path winds its way to a hut in the distance. I say hut. I mean house. Trees surround us about a mile out. Screening us from the rest of the world. The wind whips their tops and I huddle closer to my coffee. Butterworth doesn't seem to notice. He chews more cow and licks more grease. A second plate arrives. Borne by a small lady with dark skin. If anything it has more food on it than the one it's replacing. Butterworth says nothing.

I play with my OJ and refill the coffee. Nice stuff. I can wait him out. I stand and walk to one of the heaters. I take a blast full on the back of my legs. The heat rushes up my back. Heating the outdoors. No green credentials around here. I move until the heat is coursing across me in waves. I sip the coffee.

'Well Craig. Are you not hungry?' The second plate has been vacuumed.

'Coffee is good.'

MELTDOWN

'Can't beat a good breakfast.'

'Lot of animals died for that one.'

'Sure did.' He doesn't rise to the bait. Or doesn't care. 'Let's go inside. I love to eat outdoors but it's too cold for much more.'

He rises. Rubbing his vast belly. Burping and dropping a big one from the other end. He grins. 'Better out.' I'm thankful I'm up wind.

He pushes through the French doors. We enter a new planet that benefits from central heating.

'Drink?'

I look at him.

'You know. Alcohol?'

'A bit early for me.' It's a bit early for a hardened alcoholic.

'I like a sharpener in the morning.'

The more I'm around Butterworth, the less he has going for himself. 'Feel free.'

'Thanks. Take a seat.'

He opens an Aladdin's cave of drink and pours a slug measure of Jack Daniels. My favorite. He slumps in an oversized sofa. 'To business.' He downs the drink in one. Licks his lips and speaks. 'I want you to kill my brother.'

Chapter 30

The howling wind outside is audible. Just. Triple glazing does that. Other than that, silence. Butterworth seems happy with this and lifts his bulk from the chair to pour another drink. I know I should say *What?* or *You're joking* or something but I don't. I don't need to. I'm sure he's serious.

He burps again. Second drink down. Third in hand. We are not even at office hours yet. He sips at the drink. 'Well?'

'No.'

'That's it?'

'That's it. No.'

'No questions?'

'No.'

'Curious?'

'No.'

'Don't you want to kill my brother?'

'If you mean would I lie in a darkened room mourning his damned soul, the answer is no. Would I like to see him dead? Only to get him off my back.'

'And the fact I'm his brother doesn't intrigue you?'

'No. You're cut from the same cloth. Nothing would surprise me.'

He looks upset. I've stolen his wind. He was looking for a far bigger reaction. 'And the thought of removing him from your life and earning for the privilege still holds no attraction?' He's trying to recover the high ground. 'A million dollar's worth of attraction?' He's reaching for the very high ground.

'A million would be cool.' I stand up. I feel like playing the psychology game as well. I stand over him. He crashes another finger of bourbon. I'd be on a buzz by now. But he seems millpond calm. Sailing a straight ship. 'But I'm not playing.'

'Tell you what. Let's not rush to decisions. Have a little chew over it. A million – cash. And no more Agency in your life.'

I step as close as I can. The smell of the cologne is overpowering. Does he bathe in it? 'I don't need to think. The answer is no.'

'Pity. But I do so need your help.' The help comes out as 'haiyelp'. The southern drone the richer for the drink. 'I'll ask once more...'

I don't let him finish. 'The answer is no.'

'Denholm.' A few seconds later and his sidekick appears, head lost in white gauze. 'Work the damn TV.'

Denholm isn't a happy person. I'd be in the same place. He crosses the room and hits a button. My bedroom's TV's big brother appears. We get a few seconds of CNN and then Linda is staring at me.

Shit.

'Say hi to your girlfriend.'

She's gagged and sitting on a wooden chair. Her hair is bloodied and matted. Her left eye swollen. Her lip is split. Head lolling.

'She wasn't as co-operative as we would have liked. Has a great vocabulary though. I can't remember being called a 'pus filled bag of vomit' before.'

I turn to him and Denholm pulls a gun from his jacket. Loyalty is a lot deeper than a bang on the head for this boy.

I breathe. Deep. 'Let her go. It has nothing to do with her.'

'Of course. Once you help me.'

'Butterworth I'll kill you.' My tone is flat. No emphasis on any of the words. A simple, old-fashioned threat. Butterworth shows no reaction. Denholm clicks off the safety.

I'd been here before. Only it was my wife I couldn't save. And it was Tampoline to blame. 'I tried to kill him before. In case you haven't noticed he's blind and seedless.'

'Ah, but you failed.'

'Killing Linda won't help you.'

'It might. And if not, we have your bartender friend Charlie and his girlfriend. Martyn and his mum. I'm sure there are others. Everyone has others. It's a little fact that I picked up along the way. No one is alone. No matter how hard they try. All you have to do is dig. Get on a rowboat and dip the oars for a lifetime. There are always the special ones. People who project a grapple into your heart. Snag it in a corner and hang on. We all trail them with us. Time doesn't loosen the grip. Not unless you're psychotic. Maybe an old school friend. Someone who has been a wandering albatross in your mind. Circling but only returning to land once in a while. I could pluck him from his domain. Drop him on his knees in front of you. Flick the safety from my gun. Press it to the temple and ask you to suck me off. I think you would comply. It might not save your friend. You might even enjoy it. I may even take some pleasure from your mouth. But I'll put a rock of gold to one of silver that you unzip my pants. So don't waste my time. Linda or my brother? Tell me that's not Hobson's choice.'

Linda is still. The skin on her neck stretched tight. The angle of her skull too sharp for comfort. A spit of blood leaks from her lips. She's in her nightdress. I can feel the simmering heat of my distress wind up my heart. It flushes out some sweat.

'Denholm.' The word is an order from Butterworth.

Denholm, still half mummy, opens a small black case. Inside lies a bank of syringes. Each one is full. Gold in the light. Butterworth picks one up. 'My brother tried to control you once with drugs. I've no idea what he used. I don't care. This stuff will do the job. An opiate of rare vintage. Addictive as hell. Deep repeat request stuff. I should know. Got a little too friendly with it a while ago. I still dream of the party it throws. I know anger is your trigger. And stress. So this is a little liquid chill pill. So let's calm down. You're in an easy place. Help me and Linda walks. Don't and well… Then we try Martyn's mother next.'

I step away from the TV. I inhale. Hold. Exhale. Again. Time to regain control. A little composure. A ledge on the cliff of anger.

'Release her and we talk.'

'Sure.' Butterworth is heading for the drinks again. Gold for gold I think in his addiction stakes. 'Denholm. See she gets home. Safe and sound. A little cash for her trouble.'

Denholm kills the TV and leaves.

'That easy?' I try and sound calm.

'That easy. We can pick her up anytime. So are you in the saddle for our little excursion?'

'Not without a lot more information.'

'Background I have plenty. But not now. Let's get the ball rolling on this one.'

'You know it didn't work last time. Killing him. What I do doesn't have an on/off switch.'

'So?'

'Well you can put me in a room with your brother and fuck all might be the score at the end of the fourth quarter.'

'Sorry, but maybe you misunderstand what I'm asking. I want you to kill my brother. I don't give a shit about how. Shoot him. Knife him. Whatever it is that you do is irrelevant to how you end his life. If you want a Bugatti Veyron to run him over I'll supply. There's no talent to this. Just murder.'

The floor moves under me. Sand for floorboards. I'm no killer. Six months as a grunt in Iraq doesn't qualify me for a taker of life. 'I can't.'

'Of course you can. Everyone can. It's all about the leverage. It's all about motivation. Twist the right dial. Depress the button marked go. Stand back and watch.'

'But if you don't want what I can do, then why me?'

MELTDOWN

'Because my brother wants you. He wants you badly. There's no one on this planet he would rather meet. You can get closer than anyone I know.'

'And I'm supposed to just go? Forget about why I'm here?'

'Do you mean the Iranian? The oil? The threat to the American way of life?'

'You said it.'

'The Factor's attempt to ruin the US economy? The deal with one of the evil axis? What was the plan? Capture the Iranian and bargain for your life?'

'You seem to know the answers to the questions.'

'A few facts that might enlighten you. Firstly, there's no threat to the Strategic Petroleum Reserve. Never was. I wouldn't know how to spike a billion barrels of oil. No one does. Shit, you can't get near the reserves. And even if you could, it's not one giant lake waiting for a drop of something. It's way more complicated than that.'

I sit down as he winds up. 'Secondly, we might have a bit of a panic on our hands if you could do it. But we're no longer dependent on others for all our oil. Have you heard of fracking? Oil sands? Shit, we'll be exporting the stuff for years to come at this rate. So why the panic? We just divert our own production. Ok so the pump price might spike, but it'll settle. And Iran? Really? Things are changing. Evil axis? Try difficult trading partner. They pissed on Carter but they know which way the oil stained rag will fall. If we did do a deal would the world end? Every enemy we have ever fought has ended up being, if not our friends, at least an acquaintance of mild interest. Iran is no big deal.'

The wind has blown to a new high. Even the triple glazing can't kill the noise. Butterworth raises his voice, though I suspect he would have gone there anyway. He holds his JD up and swirls it. 'And why would we do it anyway? Where the hell is the logic? My brother is tugging your string.'

'So where is this going?'

'My brother has played you for a Charlie. Ok so you might have slipped the leash, but there's no Iranian. All he wanted was me, and you were expendable. But there's an emergency exit and I'm showing it to you. Kill him and you have a chance. If you don't your friends suffer, you suffer and my brother is still waiting for you at the end of the road.'

The latest JD vanishes and he sways. The first sign that the alcohol is kicking in.

I stand up. 'I need to think on this.'

'Fine, do your thinking on the plane. You and Martyn are booked on the early evening flight to New York.'

'Tonight?'

'Business class. At least you'll be comfortable while you figure that my brother's death is the path to freedom.'

'Why New York?'

'He's due to make a speech tomorrow morning at a fundraiser in Stamford. It would seem that my brother has ambitions higher than his station. Presidential ambitions.

Tomorrow he kicks off his bid. And tomorrow it finishes. Now I need some quiet. Please treat my home as your own.'

He heads for more drink. Denholm holds open the door to let me out.

'One last question.' Butterworth turns round. 'Yes?'

'Why does he call himself Tampoline?'

'Adds to the mystique. He's done a wonderful job of hiding his roots. Orphan. Poor kid done well. American dream. Well engineered.'

'His real name?'

'Constantine Butterworth.'

'Constantine and Gaylord?'

'Fine names, don't you think? My father's idea. He was called Joe and hated it. So we were his step into the exotic.'

I leave. I need some space.

Chapter 31

Back on a plane. Back to the east. Back to death. The flight is full and business class isn't helping. Martyn is up to speed with the situation. Why he's with me is a mystery. They tried to kill him once. Why not finish the job? Anyway up at least I have cohort.

I haven't stopped thinking of the task at hand since this morning. I've twisted and turned the problem into a coiled spring. Optioned out the options and come back to killing Tampoline. Any alternative puts Linda in the grinder. Martyn knows his mother is in the firing line, so he's probably along to make sure I don't hit the sidewalk to anywhere but Stamford. I've never been to the place. A little surfing on one of Butterworth's iPads told me it's an hour north of New York by train. Tampoline is speaking at the head office of a star of the Dow Jones. A multi-billion-dollar player in software. Probably a donor he's courting. I've no doubt I'm not on the guest list.

I order up a JD and coke and let my brain chew on nothing.

We land in a storm. The landing is more sideways than text book. The woman behind screams. We are back in Newark. Luckily we have an air bridge. As we exit the rain is a percussion master class.

We head for the bus. I'm in no hurry and the line at the cabs is being scouted by those with cabs a little less yellow than the legitimate ones. Plus it's a hundred dollars by cab and thirty odd by bus. Martyn might have cash but I object to paying when I don't have to.

The bus is full. Backpacks to briefcases fill every spare inch. The driver has a rough time keeping it in the lane. Blasts of water-laden air slam against us with metal bending ferocity. We are crawling in the face of the mayhem. I stop looking forward as I can see nothing out of the front windshield. I just hope the driver has better vision than me.

An hour and half later we pull into the Port Authority. We're booked into a Ramada hotel on Lexington. Cabs are as rare as udders at a rodeo. Walking is no better than jumping in a pool. The subway can't help. I'm hungry and decide that a Starbucks for an hour might see the back of the weather and the decline of cab patronage.

I'm wrong. An hour later we are in the cab line, shuffling along as each cab appears. And they are few and far between.

It's midnight before we check in. Separate rooms on the eleventh floor. Tampoline is due to speak at eleven o'clock the next morning. I'm planning to be there two hours ahead. I need to get a train just before eight o'clock. I also need a plan and I don't have one.

'We'll meet downstairs at seven o'clock. In the breakfast room.' I shut the door on Martyn as I finish speaking.

The room is not too small given this is New York. I flick on the TV and find CNN and fill the tub with water too hot for skin. I'm not on the news so I kill the TV. Silence will do. I wash my boxers, socks and t-shirt and hang them to dry. It takes me five minutes to locate the towels hidden beneath the washbasin. You need to be on your hands and knees to find them.

I slip into the water. A slow process of heat adjustment. Inching my way horizontal. I start to sweat but a strategically placed towel comes to the rescue to wipe it away. I pick a moment in my past and recreate it, clearing my head of everything else. I choose a day I went swimming in the ocean not far from Santa Monica pier. Lorraine lying on the beach. Drawing looks from every passing male. Her model figure belonging to me.

Since her death I have kept her alive in my thoughts. Forcing through the hurt this caused at first. Embracing memories. Her candle still flickering. My soul has a hole like an animal. A Depeche Mode line. Lorraine saw them once at an up close and personal gig off Sunset. She loved it. We had been a foot deep in CDs and DVDs inside 24 hours. All you can eat Dave Gahan and team.

If Tampoline really is running for president, security will be hot. Too hot for me. I slip the gears in my head and try and get back to the beach.

Then there's a knocking at the door. It refuses to go away. I throw a towel around my waist and I'm at the door still dripping. I open it to find Martyn. 'I'm not that way inclined.' I wonder what he means. He sees the confusion. 'You're just not my type.'

'Funny. What is it you want?'

'Would it hurt to dress first?'

'I've nothing to put on. My clothes are just as wet.'

'Ok I'll come in. But at the smallest hint of your penis I'm history.'

I laugh. A first in a while. 'Let me get more towels I'll cover up like a modest monk.'

As I wrap myself in white Martyn talks.

'And that's the plan?' I make like I'm sucking a lemon.

'Yip.'

'So let me get this straight. We set off to kidnap an Iranian that doesn't exist and now you want to kidnap a potential future president?'

'Yes. Think about it. It's our only chance. We trade him. In return we walk.'

'Trade him to who?

'Butterworth.'

'Do you know how successful kidnapping is these days?'

'But we don't want cash.'

'So what?'

'It's the cash that gets you caught. You have to pick it up. We won't be doing that. Once we have Tampoline we have the upper hand.'

'Martyn, we'd be the subject of the biggest manhunt in history. Fuck the Agency. They would be second rate next to the FBI, CIA, Homeland security, state police, local police and any patriot who wants to make a name for themselves.'

'Good.'

'Good – how in the hell is that good?'

'Well if we get that far then we have Tampoline.'

'You think it's possible?'

'Of course it is. He's not expecting it. Especially tomorrow. His head will be in a different place. All thoughts on the oval room. And we'd have an ally.'

'Who?'

'As I said, Butterworth. He wants Tampoline. We hand Tampoline his brother. In return we get an exit.'

'What exit?'

'I haven't thought that far ahead yet. But it beats you trying to kill him. That's a suicide jump.'

'And kidnapping Tampoline isn't?'

'Maybe, but if we pull it off you will still have a heartbeat.'

I tighten a towel that's threatening to unravel. Martyn has a point. Killing Tampoline is a one-way ticket. Kidnapping is at worst the same. But at its best it might work. 'And you'd help?'

'Maybe.'

'What, were you going to skip town before breakfast?'

'The thought had occurred.'

'And Butterworth will leave your Ma alone?'

The wind is still strong but a touch off its zenith. A squall hits the window and Martyn sighs. 'I'm in, but I've no idea how this all goes down.'

'We head to Stamford and see what goes down.'

MELTDOWN

'You do know that the place will be in lock down.'

'Actually, now you've put the idea of kidnap in my head, I'm counting on it.'

Chapter 32

I dream the hurting dream and wake up screaming. A painful alarm call, but I'm washed and at breakfast before six. I make a call before I leave the room. The breakfast room is an L-shaped tribute to minimalism. Self service OJ and bagels. Seats designed to move you on.

Martyn looks tired. I know I look like a ghost. It doesn't seem to impact his diet. He wolfs through most things on the menu. I sip at some OJ and kill the coffee machine.

We exit to a dark and still New York morning. The storm has blown itself out during the night. Flotsam and jetsam are strewn across the roads. Traffic is light. New York might not sleep but it does lie down for a break now and again. We cross onto Park Avenue and head for Grand Central. I look up at the Met Life building. Years ago helicopters used to land on the roof. Then one day a Sikorsky toppled and killed five people – one man at the corner of Madison and 43rd was killed by a flying blade.

Grand Central Terminal (it hasn't been called Grand Central Station since 1913) still impresses me. It feels like no other railway station in the world. For a start, it's not obvious where the trains leave from. We enter from the south and cross to the main concourse. A vast vaulted space that flicks the bird at the lack of space in Manhattan, with a ceiling a hundred and twenty five feet above us. They restored the ceiling in 1998. The night sky that adorns the ceiling was brought back to life by scraping the dirt away. Dirt that turned out to be mostly tar and nicotine. Smokers of the US be proud.

There are more than forty platforms between the upper and lower levels and thankfully the guy selling tickets is quick to direct to us a train about to leave. It's earlier than I planned but the mood I'm in I can do with all the recce time available.

New York slips away. Tunnel at first. High rise. Low rise. Homes. Grass. Water. The train is dotted with passengers. Heads bobbing. Minds generating their own version of reality. Neurons fire. Thoughts. Debates. Memories. The space around me is alive with the unsaid. The kernel at the back of my head is solid. An unbreakable rock. For now.

Martyn has said little since we left the hotel. He picked up a paper at the station and is using it as a barrier. He hasn't turned a page in twenty minutes. The headline is a dud. *'Can The President Avoid Disaster?'* One for boosting circulation. Lazy. The disaster is another round of financial talks. A 'so what' once you've read the detail. False advertising. There's no crisis. Just the need to sell papers.

Melrose, Tremont, Fordham, Botanical Gardens. Port Chester, Greenwich, Cos Cob, Riverside. Other people's territories. Myriads of lives unfolding beyond the window. Too many to comprehend. Too many to track. History being consigned to the trashcan. No records. No need. Most will contain nothing of note. Except, maybe, mine. What I have planned will knock the sloth in charge of the newspaper into a spin. '*Presidential candidate kidnapped!*' The exclamation mark his one concession to indolence.

Stamford appears. It looks no different to the landscape we have ploughed through for an hour. Martyn is still silent as we decant. We drop down stairs following the few people that got off with us. We walk into a concrete tunnel and a small Subway offers up coffee and sandwiches to the needy. I think of asking the assistant where the building I'm looking for is located but I don't. We are already recorded on the CCTV. Whether I'm successful or not I need time to escape. The police will interview everyone in the station. Asking for directions will mark me out as a suspect. I keep walking.

We exit onto a road lined with commercial office space. To our left is a bus terminal. To the right a drop off point for cars. Across the road a small park sits between two steel and glass edifices. I've no idea where we are going from here. I cross to the park. It's really more of a set of concrete paths, some grass and bushes sewn together to make the buildings look more friendly. I perch on a low wall. Martyn does the same.

We are still early, and the commuter rush is in its infancy. I may have to ask after all. Then a man in a blue coverall walks by. The badge on his breast pocket displays the company logo of the place Tampoline is due to talk. I stand up and urge Martyn to follow. I fall about twenty yards back and hope the man is going to work. He takes us back over the road and into the station and I fear he's heading for a train. But he simply uses the station as a cut through.

We enter residential land. A gothic inspired building dominates one side. The Holy Name Parochial School. A red brick monster that is more prison than school. The windows are steel shuttered. Rows of them. Some childhood. It's bordered by a grass verge and the man in the coverall walks on it. I expect a warden to appear with a gun and shoot him dead for the trespass. We pass a church built in the same style.

I keep back. There's no one else to be seen. The last winds of the storm gust. A car cruises into sight. A dog barks. The world is ready for a kidnapping.

The road T Bones and the man in the coverall wheels left out of sight. We follow and the building we are looking for rises from the ground. A major piece of architecture, but somehow understated, as if the owners commissioned it in two minds. Corporate statement v quiet confidence. The result is bland. The chaos unwinding outside is not. Four TV trucks are lined up a few yards from us. Technicians playing worker to the queen bees as the presenters are tidied up by make up girls and boys for the breakfast shows. Beyond them black is the order of the day. FBI, local police, Secret Service, CIA – a cocktail of law enforcement swirling around the main entrance. A few yards further and a small group of spectators are being forced back behind twisting yellow tape.

I turn slowly and walk back out of sight, catching Martyn by the arm before he can be seen. 'Keep walking.'

He obeys and we head back the way we came. A truck loaded with mobile barriers is starting to off-load near the church. 'This way.' I guide Martyn down a side street. A truck is setting up barriers at the far end. 'In here.' I walk up a concrete drive to a clapperboard house. Trying to look as casual as possible I wander up the side and stop. I look back. No-one.

'What now?' Martyn's first words since breakfast.

'We need to lie low. They'll have this placed skintight in moments.'

'They'll check all the houses.'

'Are you sure?'

'Fairly. Tampoline is stepping up to the big time. Did they see you?'

'I don't know. It seemed a bit chaotic. If we'd got the later train we wouldn't have got within a mile.'

I look at the back yard. There's no place to hide. With no car in the drive the house might be our best bet. I try the back door. Locked. The house is quiet. Commuters gone for the day? Someone down at the grocers? Due back soon? Bed full? Out for the count? Or empty? Take your pick. A car's engine sounds. The car stops. Doors slam. Voices. Instructions to check the homes. We need to act. I turn to Martyn. 'Check the window.' I get to work on the lock. I bend down to examine it, trying to keep my heartbeat down to double figures.

The voices stop. Not good. They are on the move. I pick up a stone. I think of putting it through the door window. I put it back down. Too much noise and obvious to anyone that checks the rear. I seek out Martyn in hope. He shakes his head. The window is solid.

The doorbell goes. Whoever is checking at the front door rings again and again. No polite pause. They bang on the door. If they check the rear we are road kill. I scan the yard but there's not even a fence to crouch behind. The nearest cover is a hut two houses down. But we would be seen by anyone on the street.

It feels like fight time.

Chapter 33

There's no sound of footsteps. The driveway is concrete and if there's someone walking towards us they are wearing soft soles. I move to the edge of the house. I try and melt into the wall. Martyn is standing to my left. He seems calm. A bit too calm if you want an opinion. I grab a breath and hold. Tense. Ready to strike. It's the only option. Hit and run. I'd give us one chance in fuck all.

I can hear a distant conversation. Someone being quizzed. My eyes are fixed on the corner of the house. As soon as I see an arm I'll try and grab the initiative. Lock on. Full weight and fall back. Take them with me. Surprise. Down and over. Get them on the ground. Hope Martyn follows up. Silence is the key. No alert. Disable. Then run.

A click. Foot on concrete? I tense.

'Are you finished?' The voice comes from the street.

'Just checking the back yard.' The voice is so close I jump. Feet if not inches away.

'Forget it. Skip did the backs earlier. We need to get a move on. We're behind schedule.'

'Ok.' The voice is receding.

I drop a lump of used air through my lips. Martyn smiles at me. I shrug my shoulders. We still need to move. An engine finds a gear.

'Shit, that was close.' Martyn is still smiling as I speak.

MELTDOWN

'Go figure. Our luck is in.'

'We're not out of this yet. If they check the other street', I point over the yard to the backs of the house opposite, 'they'll see us. Let's make ourselves scarce.'

A couple of hundred yards along there's a gap. It must lead onto the street where the office sits. A small gray cinder block building squats near the far houses. Power company maybe. 'There. We can get cover and keep an eye on the office.'

I walk, no running, across the yard and slip into the neighbors well-tended domain. I don't look left or right. If someone sees us there's nothing I can do. I count down the yards and no one shouts. They could be on the phone dialing 911. But how would I know?

The small building is anonymous. The door is locked and we can't be seen from either road. I slide my back down the door and sit in the dirt. Martyn joins me. His smile is gone. 'Ok Craig what's next?'

'We wait for an opportunity to present itself.'

'What are we looking for?'

'An opportunity to get into the office building.'

'Fat chance.'

'People must still be working. That building holds a good few hundred people. They'll have to get to their desks.'

The alley looks out on the main entrance. If I'm careful I can keep an eye on the comings and goings. But I question my faith in opportunity. I can't see a way to get to the street without being spotted. A thought bounces off my useless brain.

Shit.

'Up.' I'm on my feet and dragging Martyn up. 'Now!' We're not dressed for the part but we'll have to do. 'Follow me.' I head for the office.

'Where are we going? We'll be seen.'

'Exactly. What was I thinking.' I exit the alley and wave at a complete stranger. He waves back. Red tape has been drawn across the road and a steady trickle of employees is being checked. Passes required. The line is five strong but the road has a number of employees walking towards it. If I time it right there'll be a couple of dozen soon.

'Slow down.' We are fifty yards from the tape. 'Let the numbers build.'

A man as thin as a wire brush swings past us. I tap him on the shoulder. 'Sorry to bother you.' His face is an osteologist's wet dream. His skin is drum tight over his skull. His forehead has a pronounced lump and his jaw line is a roller coaster of small bumps. His hands are simply bones with tracing paper for skin. Eyes pop from the sockets. Not from surprise at my question, just another distinctive feature. 'Yes?'

'Sorry, we are new starts.'

He takes in our clothes. 'And?'

'Do you know what's going on? We were told to pick up passes today.'

'There's a senator in town. Some big speech we were told.'

'Do you work here then?'

'Yes.'

MELTDOWN

'Do you know Carl Tannoch?'

'No.'

'He's our contact. What department are you in?'

'Research and development.'

'That's where we are headed.'

'Really?' His eyes are threatening to leave his head.

'We're contractors. Tannoch runs our firm.'

'What are you doing in R and D?'

'We've no idea. We got told to report here this morning. Tannoch said he would meet us but he's a no show and his cell is dead. He gave us another name. Director level. It was a PA to a director. But I didn't pay attention. You know how it is. I thought Tannoch would be here.'

'Our main director is Allan Connaught. Would that be it?'

'Sounds right. Has he got a PA?'

'Jenny Moore.'

'That's her.'

'She won't be in yet. Too early.'

'It's too cold to hang around out here. Is there somewhere to wait?'

'Reception.'

'Sounds good. And your name is?'

'Colin.'

'Hi Colin. I'm Sam and this is Dave.' Sam and Dave were a soul band Lorraine used to love.

'Hi.'

'Well don't let us hold you back.'

We fall in behind him in the line. As we near the front I tap him on the shoulder. 'Could you give these guys the heads up about Jenny?'

A police officer asks for Colin's pass. He shows it. We are up. The officer is a time served face of wrinkles. His nose suggests that he isn't alien to a beer bottle. 'Passes.'

'We're new. Contractors. We've been told to ask for Jenny Moore. She's the PA to...' I stop. 'Colin.' Colin has moved on a few steps. He turns at his name. 'Colin, who's Jenny's boss again? Allan...'

'Connaught.'

'Thanks Colin.' I turn to the officer. 'Connaught. See you inside later Colin.'

Colin waves back.

The officer looks us up and down. 'And you are?'

'I'm Dave and this is Sam. We work for Tannoch R and D. We're working in Colin's department.' Colin is out of earshot. 'We started last week. Colin is our supervisor but there was a fuck up with the passes. We've been tailgating Colin all week. We were told to report to Jenny to get it sorted out this morning. But she won't be in yet.'

'Go to reception and sign in. One of my colleagues will need to check you out.'

'No problem. Thanks.' I smile as I let Martyn walk in front. 'Hell of a cold morning.'

The officer nods. 'And I'm here all morning.'

'If I get a chance I'll drop you a coffee.'

'That wouldn't go a miss.'

One down.

MELTDOWN

'What now?' Martyn speaks without turning.

'We're fifty percent of the way there. Speed up. I want to catch Colin.'

We fly through the revolving door and into heat. Colin is about to slide his pass through a reader.

'Colin.'

He turns.

'Could you tell Jenny we are here?'

'Sure.'

I walk up to the reception desk. A squat, black man is reading the paper. Standing next to him is a man in a suit with bulges in the wrong places. His left ear is full of tech. The dark glasses are just stupid. This could get tricky. I spill my story and the receptionist tells us to take a seat. He picks up the phone and I hope Jenny hasn't decided to start early.

Sunglasses moves round and approaches. 'You said you worked here last week?'

'Yes.'

'And you have no passes?'

'Some bureaucratic screw up. We've been person non-gratis. Can't even go for a piss without someone to hold our hand.'

His face shows that person non-gratis is not in his vocabulary. I'm sure it's not the only words missing from his lexicon. He reaches for the microphone in his right hand. This isn't good.

'Kent?' Martyn looks up from the annual report he had picked up. 'Kent Davies?'

Sunglasses pauses mid mike lift.

'It is. Fuck me. Kent Davies.'

'Do I know you?'

'You should. You were shagging the prettiest girl on my street.'

Sunglasses is confused. He's not the only one.'

'Shelley McLean. Billy's sister.'

Sunglasses lips crack a small smile. 'And you are.'

'Billy's best friend. I used to see you when you hung out with Shelley. You'd be a few years older than me. Don't you remember?'

'I remember Shelley.'

'Who didn't.' Martyn stands up. 'What a girl. What happened to her?'

'Last I heard she married an accountant out west.'

'Money. Figures. Shelley wasn't a cheap date.'

'You've got that nailed. Skinned me.'

'What are you doing here?'

'You know. This and that.'

'Secret Service?'

He smiles. He doesn't look Secret Service to me. Those guys don't hire dumb. And this guy has dumb etched on his eyeballs.

Martyn shakes his hand. 'You've done well.'

Sunglasses smile broadens. Something is off here but I'm not going to rock this boat. 'Hi, I'm Dave's colleague.'

Sunglasses shakes my hand. 'So what are you guys doing here?'

'Boring stuff. To do with R and D. Dull as.' I want to let Martyn do the talking.

MELTDOWN

'Sounds it.'

Employees are starting to stream in. A pretty blonde is amongst them. She waves at the reception and the receptionist beckons her over. I watch her cross the marble floor. Smart suit. Neat hair. A small briefcase under one arm. Manager? PA? Other? I let Martyn and Sunglasses chew on the past and keep my eye on the blonde. If this is Jenny I'm going to have to go for a gold in Walter Mitty-ism.

She's a yard shy of the reception desk. The receptionist vanishes from view and reappears with a package in his hand. I zone out of Martyn and Sunglasses' inane chatter. My ears are tuned to the guard.

'This came early this morning. Said it was urgent.'

The blonde takes the package. 'Thanks Jesse.' She drops a killer smile and leaves. Another lady enters the building. I interrupt the chat. 'Kent I'm bursting for a piss. So's Dave. We've been outside for an age waiting to get in. Can we use the washrooms?'

'Sure, but I'll need to come with you. The washrooms are through the barrier.'

'No problem.'

Sunglasses signals to Jesse. 'Can you let these two in?'

Once through the barrier Sunglasses points us to the washroom. 'It's along there. Third on the right. Don't be long. I need to get back to reception.'

Once inside the washroom I check the cubicles are empty. 'Do you really know that guy?'

'Unbelievable. He was in a local gang.'

'I'm amazed he's in the Secret Service.'

'So am I. He got thrown out of school.'

'We need to get him in here.'

'Why.'

'We're in. We won't get a second chance if we get back to reception. I'm out of ideas. We get him in here and put him beyond use.'

'When they find he's missing the crap will fly.'

'But he isn't going missing. He's going to help us.'

'He is?'

'Does Kent have family?'

'His mum was friends with mine.'

'Does she still live on the same street?'

'As far as I know. She used to live in 422.'

'Call him in. Tell him I'm ill.'

Martyn leaves and returns with Kent. I'm bent over. Moaning.

'What's up with him?'

'He just threw up in the toilet.'

Kent moves towards me. I can see his shoes. I rear up. 'I'm going to be sick.' I make like I'm going to vomit. Kent backs off and I leap forward. I use his rearward motion to slam him into the wall and down. I stand on his right hand and yank the earpiece out. I rip his jacket open and before he can recover pull his gun from the holster under his armpit. I jump back and point the gun at his head, checking the safety is off. If this guy is Secret Service they are scraping the bottom.

MELTDOWN

Kent does a lost puppy dog look. Pathetic. 'Kent, this is easy or this is hard. It's your choice. The easy way is you return to your job. You tell Jesse you found someone to help us and if a Jenny Moore talks to Jesse you head her off. See – easy.'

'And why should I do that?' He's regaining some composure. Never easy sitting on a toilet floor.

'Well I could shoot you.' His eyes widen.

'You'd never get away with it. Half the FBI are in town.'

'Sure, but that would be my problem. You'd be dead.'

'You wouldn't.'

'There's a third way. I use my cell and call a friend. He pops round to number 422 Apple Tree Lane and pays your mother a visit.'

He squirms at the mention of his mother. 'Sure. And I'm to believe this?'

'It's up to you. But do you think we planned this without crawling over every detail? Take the chance.'

He won't. I wouldn't.

'What are you after?'

'You don't need to know. Let's say I have a little unfinished business to attend to. What do you want to do?'

Time is of the essence here. Every second is a second closer to, if not already a second past, Jenny appearing. After that the game is up. I gently kick his foot. 'I'd hurry up and decide. I need you back out there.'

A tiny buzz comes from the earpiece swinging in front of his shirt. I kick his foot again. 'If that's for you tell them you are in the can.' He places the earpiece in and listens. 'Not for me.'

'So what's the answer?'

'What choice do I have?'

'Good man.'

I back off. He stands up. 'My gun.'

'I'm not stupid. I keep the gun.'

His eyes flare. He might not be bright but he's well built and ex gang. I should be able to take him on but I'd rather not. 'Now go. And I'll be watching.'

Martyn opens the door and checks outside. 'All clear.'

With a last glare he leaves.

Martyn shuts the door. 'What now?'

'We hope he plays along.'

'They'll sweep the washrooms.'

'Martyn, you are a font of knowledge. Not only do you know someone in the Secret Service, you know their routine.'

'Kent's as much a surprise to me as you. And the washrooms are obvious. Where else could you hide out and not be spotted?'

'Fair point.'

I open the door. The building feels empty. A few souls are entering but it's a big space. 'Come on. Let's go exploring.'

Chapter 34

'Up a few floors. Let's put some distance between the front door and us.' I point at the escalator. A man in a blue coverall steps on in front of us. I look at my clothing. Time for a change.

The man rises three floors and I keep in step, ten yards back. Martyn is back to being a pet dog at my heels. The man pushes into a space crammed with workstations. Only a few are occupied. No one looks up as we cross the floor. He reaches the far side and keeps going. We follow.

He pushes through a door. Beyond is a storage space. The walls lined with shelving. Before I'm fully in I turn round and Martyn has to slam to a halt to avoid walking into me. 'Back off.' I wheel right and find a water cooler and pour myself a drink. 'Baseball or football?'

Martyn looks confused.

'If someone gets near do you prefer baseball or football?'

'Football.'

The man in coveralls leaves with a mop and a bucket. I drop the cup in the trash. 'Into the closet.'

Once inside I tell Martyn to keep a lookout. The space is rammed with janitorial supplies. At the far end there's a unit piled high with folded coveralls. I size Martyn up and pull one for me and one for him from the pile. I throw it to him 'Put it on.'

They both fit, after a fashion. There are skip caps lying next to the coveralls and I flick Martyn one. My bald pate vanishes under a cap. 'Grab a couple of brooms.' I pick up two long handled dustpans. 'We're now on sweeping duty. Let's see if we can find where Tampoline is speaking.'

The building is built round a large central atrium. The escalator we climbed rises up the edge. At the far side a bank of glass elevators are in motion. The office is sterile. And quiet. It looks like it could hold north of a thousand but I've seen barely fifty people. The clock on the wall shows eight thirty. I need to know three things: where Tampoline will be, when he's speaking, and an escape route.

At one of the pods a young man is bashing a keyboard. I cough. He turns. 'Sorry to bother you, but we're new here and we've been told to report to the room the senator is speaking in. Seems the cleaners last night weren't as thorough as they could have been.'

He adjusts badly chosen glasses on an oversized nose. 'It's in the boardroom. Top floor.'

'Thanks. You don't know when he's due to speak?'

'Eleven I think.'

'Have a nice one.' His reply is the clicking of keys.

'It'll be extra hot up there.' I head for the atrium. So far everyone has passes on show. We have none. Two women are filling up on coffee. Neither have a pass on display. I scan the floor. Two chairs are pushed out. Above them a coatrack holds two coats. Both have badges. I sweep my way to the coats. Keeping an eye on the ladies, I scan the badges. *Jo Swinden and Jane Callum.'* Not great but better than nothing. I pocket both and sweep back to Martyn. 'Put this on.'

Badged up we head for the elevators.

Three floors up and the feeling of a morgue deepens. If this is a vibrant thriving business then where the hell is everyone? As we exit the elevator security is heavy. The far end of the floor is alive with radios and guns. A temporary barrier has been erected and two heavies are standing guard. I nudge Martyn. 'Start sweeping.'

Martyn follows my lead and we work our way along the floor. We make it look like the mess is a foot thick. The floor is dedicated to meeting rooms. On either side of the atrium glass walled rooms dominate. All are empty. I pick one a few short of the barrier and try the door. It swings open. Ten chairs attend a polished table. The carpets are thicker up here. The room looks out onto the street. 'Keep sweeping.'

I look down on the scene below. The line is longer and there are more TV vans. I hope Kent is still a good mummy's boy. I use the broom to brush my way to the glass wall. A few people approach the barrier and their passes are checked. There are no photos on the passes. I might get away with Jo but Martyn won't pass for a Jane. 'Ok I'm going to fly solo.' Martyn is standing next to the table. 'I need you to be ready when Tampoline arrives.'

'What are you going to do?'

'Beyond the barrier there are more rooms. I'm going to be the best cleaner in town. Go back down to the closet and pull up a few buckets and assorted sprays and cloths and come back here.'

Martyn obeys. I keep a watch on the comings and goings. The boardroom is to the right of the barrier. Two more suits stand at the door. Inside seems quiet. Tampoline will want TV. The elevator door slides open and as if by magic a TV crew appears. They hustle up to the barrier. Four of them. Plus gear. A few seconds later another crew are disgorged. Martyn is squeezed in with them. He hustles to the room. I grab a bucket. Fill it with nonsense. 'Stay here. If things go south get out.' I ram Kent's gun in to the back of my pants.

I step out and join the TV crew. The man at the front is arguing with one of the suits over something. I stand, trying to look bored, sweeping at an imaginary cigarette stub. The argument blows over and the crew are allowed through. I'm up next.

'Where are you going?' The suit to my left's breath is a cloud of minty freshness.

'Cleaning the rooms.'

'Not today.'

'No skin off my nose. But I was ordered up. Told to make sure no crap was on view for the senator. Seems he's a bit of a bastard. Blind as a bat but hates mess. Fired the last aid he had. Seems she thought him being blind meant she didn't have to clean up. He stepped on a candy packet and nailed her. I hope the room's clear because I'm not taking any heat. What's your name?'

'What do you need that for?'

MELTDOWN

'So I can tell my boss who stopped me. I'm not getting canned.'

Another TV crew are vomited from the elevator. The suit turns to his colleague. They chat. Low. I can't hear. He turns to me. 'How long will you be?'

'I'll do all the rooms except the boardroom. I'll need to wait until everything is set up in the boardroom and give it one last clean before the senator arrives. I can't see these guys,' I swing a hand at the new TV crew, 'giving a monkeys about being tidy.'

'I need you gone before the speech starts.'

'Sure. Why in the hell would I want to listen to some dipshit politician when I could be grabbing some java in the canteen? I don't envy you your job. You must hear some boring baloney in your game.'

I don't get a smile but he searches the bucket. I'm let through. Another step closer.

I hit one of the far rooms. It's small. One round table and six chairs. Executive chairs though. I empty the bucket and scatter the contents on the floor. I pick up a can of polish and spray it on the table. I rub it clean and check the guards. They now have a queue of radio and press guys to deal with. I'm a historic item.

I work each room slowly. Clean and tidy. I do a good job. There are eight rooms including the boardroom. I estimate twenty minutes per room and Tampoline should be in the building by room seven. I see Martyn entering and exiting beyond the barrier, bucket and broom in hand. So far so good.

The next bit will be the tricky bit. I have two options. Bold or subtle. With Kent's gun I could go balls out and try and hustle Tampoline out at gun point. Brave but foolhardy. I've spotted three snipers on the surrounding roofs already. I might get to the main entrance but these guys can knock the pimple off an ant's fanny at two miles. Subtle is the game. I dig the gun out and transfer it to the coverall pocket.

The escalators are sealed off. Tampoline will be escorted in the main entrance, up the escalators, into the room and back out the same way. If I were the other side of the barrier I'd be shut off from him. I enter room six. There's a buzz of activity and more suits appear. It feels like show time. I cross to the boardroom. The two guards stop me. I go through my routine and point to the suit at the gate. They make eye contact and nods are exchanged. I'm in the inner sanctum.

The room is a Tetris puzzle. Not an inch free. There are sixty people crammed into a space that usually accommodates sixteen. Cables snake across the floor. Five cameras are sited at the back. The board table has been removed and replaced with seats. Every one is full. Standing room only. There is less floor space than a basketball court after the NBA title has been won.

A lectern has been set up at the front. A sign is stuck to the front. It reads 'Time to Climb.' Tampoline's name is emblazoned beneath the slogan. The lectern has a clutch of microphones tied to it, each with a small sign advertising the TV or radio station.

MELTDOWN

Behind the lectern a banner has a picture of a tambourine and the slogan repeated across it. I wouldn't be surprised if he brought one of the things in with him.

Lights spotlight the lectern and a space has been cleared to allow Tampoline to enter. Someone hits a button and 'Mr Tambourine Man' by Bob Dylan blasts out. Didn't that song have drug connections? I squeeze into the back corner. I rub a spot on the glass. A TV cameraman gives me a glare.

Tampoline wheels in with an aid on one arm. Many blind people try and play down their blindness. Not Tampoline. To him it's a war injury. One obtained in the service of his country. The fact he got jumped by a crazed, overweight agency director is irrelevant. He has a white stick with a gold top. He walks with a limp.

This is the man who killed a sixteen year old girl in the most brutal way possible. A man who set up the murder of my wife. A man who drugged me to near death. Someone who thought nothing of throwing that off his back and using me to his own ends. I feel the gun in the small of my back. I could end this here. One bullet and no more presidential ambitions. Butterworth gets what he wants. I probably go down for life but the bastard is gone. I finger the trigger and my heart picks up some pace.

Tampoline is shown to the lectern. His suit's box-cutter sharp. Tie as crisp as fresh ice on a pond. His dark glasses are designer. His hair a quaffed comb over. I slide my finger onto the trigger. Check the safety is off. My fingernail strokes the trigger guard. The metal is cool. Smooth. Inviting. I raise the gun a little, to the lip of my waistband.

Tampoline lets the music fade. Cameras are running. Digital recorders live. The world waits. I edge the gun over my waistband. Does Connecticut have the death sentence? Could I hack life if they don't? I can feel the kernel in the back of my head begin to heat up. I should try and calm down. I should, but I don't want to. Lorraine sits centre stage. Dead because of this man. Her face floats in front of me. Her smile a way to light up the planet. And now she's gone. All because of a experiment to see if I could do their bidding. The thought of never seeing Lorraine's smile again racks up my heartbeat. The gun slides free, the grip now clear of my pants.

Tampoline coughs. 'Ladies and gentlemen, thank you for taking the time to come along this morning. I am delighted to be here in this perfect example of what America can do. A strong, global business that has built itself from the ground up on American values, ingenuity and hard work. Can I thank Tim Maychen for inviting me here? Tim, can you stand up?'

A small, dapper man in a light gray suit stands up in the front row. He looks around, an uncomfortable smile on his face. He sits down when it's clear that there's no round of applause forthcoming.

'Tim is a long-standing friend of mine. I've admired his work ethic and vision for years.'

'And his check book.' The cameraman winks at me as he whispers the comment.

MELTDOWN

'And I think it's time we remembered that it's men like Tim that make America great. Men and women that often put their own lives to one side to drive this country forward. Men and women who have climbed the hardest of mountains to find success. And yet what do they get in return? Layers of red tape. Taxes that cripple their ability to grow. Imports flooding our country and foreign countries with highly restrictive barriers to trade. Instead of making it easier to do business this current administration seem hell bent on making it as difficult as possible. We seem to have lost sight of the simple fact that it's business that will drive this country forward. Hard working businesses that employ hard working people. Hard working businesses that generate hard earned profits. Hard working businesses that do the work that brings us all prosperity.'

Tampoline's voice, high enough, is knocking on the next octave. He scans the audience, as if he can see them all. He uses his stick to beat a tattoo on the floor. I keep the gun behind me. Out of sight. One of the suits is looking at me. I freeze. His face says 'what in the hell are you still doing here?' I shrug my shoulders. I couldn't leave if I wanted to. And I so don't.

'Someone has to take a stand against the erosion of our business community.' Tampoline is winding it up. 'The constant attacks that undermine the very fabric of our society. I have tried. God knows that I have tried to fight this malaise. My record on the floor is second to none when it comes to championing our workers. I voted for the recent tax cut. I voted for the relaxation in red tape. I was one of the few brave enough to vote for the 'Collins Amendment.' Yes it was controversial. Yes it was daring. And now it's a clause that is seen, universally seen, as being a missed opportunity.'

'If you don't give a rat's shit about workers rights it is.' The cameraman feels a need to pepper the speech with his pearls.

I rub the gun against the small of my back. Feeling the solidity. Comforted in the power it seems to exude.

'Ladies and gentlemen, fellow citizens of America. I have sat in the wings to long. I have watched us fall. Seen our status in the world tumble. Viewed us slide towards the pit. And all I can say is, no more. Fellow Americans, it's time to climb. Time to climb into the driving seat. Time to climb the rock face. Time to climb back to where we belong. And to help us do this I am prepared to put my name forward for my party's nomination to stand for the next president of the United States of America. It's time to climb.'

The silence as he stops is disconcerting. His speech wasn't written for this crowd. It was written with the world in mind. In his head thunderous applause is no doubt reverberating.

His aid steps up the microphone. 'We have time for a few questions. Please let us know who you represent when you place your question.'

'John Caple, New York Times.' The journalist is invisible to me. 'Mr Tampoline, as you said, you supported the Collins Amendment. Do you really believe that this is the time to be standing on workers rights?'

'Told you.' The cameraman is a happy bunny.

Tampoline taps his stick. 'Mr Caple, or can I call you John?' He doesn't wait for an answer. 'John, I am supportive of our workers. Of our people. Ok, so there may have been a little loosening of some strings in the amendment, but in the long run it would have given our businesses the ability to compete at the highest level. Freed them of unnecessary bureaucracy. Secured workers' jobs. It seems to me that this would be good for the country.'

I catch movement out of the corner of my eye. The suit's sliding up the wall towards me. I slide the gun back into my pants. Tampoline is handling the Q and A with aplomb. The suit arrives. 'What are you doing here?'

'I got trapped. The senator was in the room before I could move.'

'Well you've got a new friend in me. You stay here until he's well gone. Ok?'

'OK.'

Shit.

Chapter 35

Tampoline works some magic in the room. I hate the bastard but he can handle a crowd. Someone picks him up on his lack of experience in military matters and he brushes it off. 'My dear sir. We have some, if not THE, finest military minds in the world on our payroll. I know nothing about plumbing and wouldn't dream of touching a pipe, but I know a man who can. Being president is about knowing who to trust and who to listen to, and I certainly know a man who can when it comes to our armed forces.'

This gets a laugh. My new friend is uncomfortable. There isn't really space to stand and the cameraman is back to glaring. The suit's shoulder is near the lens. 'The cameraman points to the other side. The suit obliges. He isn't happy but he moves.

'And what makes you the candidate of choice for the party?' The question comes from a man with a beard that could hide gorillas.

Tampoline turns to the voice. 'I think that question is best answered by my colleagues. But I believe in straight talking and action. We have been hog tied for too long by a malaise that has spread its roots through the White House.' I can see the word malaise being Tampoline's favorite. 'And we need strong leadership to root it out and let us climb back to where we belong.' Ok so maybe the word climb will be favorite.

MELTDOWN

The aid steps in. 'Sorry ladies and gentlemen, we have a tight schedule today. A full press pack is available but the Senator has to open a new wing of St Simon's Elementary school and we don't want to keep the children and teachers waiting.'

Tampoline lets himself be guided out. My new friend looks at me. 'Wait.' The cameraman begins to pack up. He pushes me out of the way to get at his box. A man with a stringy haircut cuts in behind me and pushes me forward. I look back and my new friend is trying to catch up.

A lady in an eighties power suit stands up and blocks him. 'Excuse me madam, I need to get through.' Power Suit gives him a look that would freeze-dry coffee. 'And what am I, Swiss cheese? I need to get back to my paper.' She throws her head around to emphasize the conversation is over. Another reporter cuts in behind me and I'm caught in a human stream heading for the door.

As soon as I'm clear of the door I notice the barrier is gone. Tampoline is on his way down the escalator. Everyone else is being sent via the elevator. I spot Martyn and signal him to follow me. I zip past the elevators and head for a fire door. It opens onto stairs and I take them two at a time. I crash through onto the main lobby. Tampoline is being helped through the security gate. A few people are standing to one side to let him through. I join them.

Outside a group of photographers are hanging around to get a shot. Once Tampoline is outside we're allowed to follow. I avoid eye contact with Jesse and cross to the door. Tampoline is near a limo. He has stopped to be photographed with a young woman. No doubt handpicked for her visual contrast to the Senator. She has beauty on her side.

I push the revolving door and some suits make sure I am steered away from the limo.

This is going to hurt. I turn to face a concrete pillar. I pull the gun out. I kneel down in a patch of grass, as if tying my shoes. The gun turns in my hand. Grabbing a clutch of my skin around my thigh I press the barrel into the fold. I push skin and gun into the grass. I pull the trigger.

There's a dull thump and I scream. The bullet rips through the edge of my skin. Embedding itself in the ground. The kernel in my head explodes and I fall to the ground. People will be looking at me. I see nothing but dirt and bright light. My cranium is splitting clean in two. My leg is on fire. I wait for the blue world. No sign. I roll over. All four photographers are on the ground, trying to rip the hearts out of each other. Beyond the tape chaos is the order of the day. I try and stand up. My good leg is weak. I have seconds to get to Tampoline. Where is the blue world? I stagger to my feet. Blood is pouring from the gunshot wound. I stumble towards Tampoline.

Tampoline only has one suit with him. He's looking round in amazement, his eyes on the revolving door. There must be more nonsense going on inside the building. I keep the focus on Tampoline. The suit sees me. He starts to intercept me.

MELTDOWN

Then he's down on the ground. Hitting the concrete like a sack of ball bearings. Martyn appears. He looks worse than I do. His eyes are blood red. His skin is corpse grey. I take a step and the blue world rushes in. My pain vanishes as the blue world washes in. I leap up, grab Tampoline and open the limo door. I throw him inside. He doesn't resist. I jump in. Martyn follows in fits and starts. The stop/start world is in full effect. The driver is looking at us. I pull up the gun and point it at Tampoline's head. 'Move now. Right fucking now.'

I slam the door shut and the limo leaps forward. I see the privacy screen begin to rise. 'Stop that or I shoot.' The screen stops rising. 'Put it down.' He lowers it. I scramble over to the front seat.

The driver is mid forties. Maybe a good early fifties. Clean cut. Good looking. He looks at the gun. 'Eyes on the road.' I tap the gun on Tampoline's shoulder. I look out and we are clear of the melee. 'Left here.' He swings the car out of sight of the building. I need to act quickly. When the blue world goes I'll be spent. Add in the pain from my thigh and I'll be useless. 'Martyn, how are you?' Silence. I look back and he's out cold on the seat next to Tampoline.

'Craig McIntyre.' Tampoline grins. I reach over and club him hard on the head. He rocks and falls on top of Martyn. I hope he's not dead.

We have minutes at the most before people realize what has happened. The limo is too obvious. But we can't decant. 'Turn left again.' The driver obeys. We are on the street with the school. 'Stop.' Large metal gates are half

244

open. 'In there.' He hesitates. I smack him with the gun. Hard enough to draw a grunt. He pushes us through the gates. 'Stop.' I jump out and push the gates shut. I keep the gun on the driver. I climb back in. 'Over there.' In the far corner of the yard are two double doors.

The school looked deserted on the way here. I pray I'm right. We reach the doors and I jump out again. Both are open. I wrench the first set of door open and I look in. Full of garbage bags. The second doors reveal marginally less garbage. I point the gun at the car windshield. 'In.'

The car creeps forward and crushes the bags as it enters. The sound of glass crunching fills the space. I urge the driver to get the limo all the way in. It's a squeeze but as soon as the trunk is over the threshold I close the door. In the blue world all this happens in jumps and slow motion. I check a door at the far end. Locked. I grab a garbage bag and press the gun to the plastic. Aim at the lock and pull.

The garbage bag explodes. The lock disintegrates and I'm showered in shredded paper. The improvised silencer wasn't that good. The gunshot reverberates around me. I look through the door. Stairs lead up.

A side door leads back to the yard. A string of old bicycle locks hang from a rail. They are the type that need a four digit number to lock and unlock. I grab two open ones and squeeze out the door into the yard. The doors are not overlooked. I feed the chains through the doors and lock them. I pick up dirt, spit on it and rub it into both locks. I throw more dirt on. The locks could have been there for years. I check for tire tracks but there are none. I re enter and pull the door behind me and it snaps on the latch.

I go back to the car. I open the door. The driver is trying to leave. I leap over the hood and slam the door shut. His leg is caught and he yells. I give it another kick and something cracks. I rip open the rear door. Martyn is still out cold. As is Tampoline. The driver is crouched in the driver's seat. He's clutching his leg.

I reach in and slap Martyn. 'Martyn wake up.' He moans. I slap him again. His eyes open. The redness has dulled. 'Martyn I need you to wake up.' He looks confused. I dive out and look around. The blue world is fading. I need to be quick.

An old fire extinguisher catches my eye. I retrieve it. Read the instructions. Point. Depress. Martyn's face catches the stream of CO_2 full in the face. He gags as the oxygen vanishes. I keep it on him. He throws up his arms. I stop. He coughs. 'Enough.' I lean in. 'Are you with me?' He nods. I throw the extinguisher to one side. 'Help me get Tampoline out.'

It takes a few minutes to haul the dead weight out of the car. This isn't working. I reach for the extinguisher. Depress. Full in Tampoline's face. He snaps awake. Lungs heaving. I stop. 'Tampoline, if you want to live, stand up.' The last thing I expect is a laugh. 'Craig. Good to hear your voice.' The cackle is painful.

I grab him. Lean into it. Pull. He heads for vertical. I place the gun at his temple. His laugh stops at the feel of metal. 'You're not going to shoot me.'

'Maybe not. Then again a bullet in your leg might be good.' I slide the gun to his thigh. 'Or maybe I finish off what's left of your manhood.' I move the barrel onto his crotch. 'Now stand up.' He finishes standing up.

'Martyn, we're going for the door over there. First we need to disable the driver.'

I open the limo's front door. I can sense the blue world ending. I need to get this done now. 'Out.' My mouth is inches from the driver's ear.

'I think my leg's broken.'

I drive the gun but into the other leg. 'I'll break that one. Up.'

He stands on one leg.

'To the back of the car.' He hops round. I reach in and pop the trunk. 'Martyn, get him in.'

Martyn shoves and slams the lid down. 'Will he be ok?'

'Sure. They'll find him. Let's get going.'

The blue world is fading fast. 'Martyn, I'm running out of energy. We need to hole up.'

'Where?'

That's a good question. I push Tampoline through the door. He stumbles on the stairs beyond. I grab his arm. 'Up.'

At the top a corridor stretches into the distance. There's no noise. The blue vanishes. The kernel in my head freezes. My leg sings. But more than that, my energy vanishes. I stagger. 'Martyn, grab him.'

MELTDOWN

Martyn steps in. He doesn't look much stronger. 'In the classroom.' I open the door next to me. The desks are gone but the blackboard signals where the teacher would have stood. I slump against the wall. I need to rest. Martyn collapses beside me. He kicks the legs from under Tampoline. He joins us. 'Craig…' I use the last of my strength to hit him on the head.

Chapter 36

Martyn is asleep next to me when I come to. Tampoline is standing next to the window.

'Shit. Get down.' My voice is loud. Panic.

He drops.

I crawl over to him. 'How long have I been out?'

'An hour.'

'And my friend?'

'Half an hour.'

'And you're still here?'

'I thought I'd stick around.' Tampoline has a grin on. A hateful thing.

'For what?' I'm tempted to slap him.

'To find out what this is all about.'

'Bullshit.'

'You want me to go?'

Sirens are bouncing off the walls. I sneak a look out the window. 'There's a shit storm going down out there.'

'Kidnapping a presidential hopeful. I should say. What do you hope to gain by this?'

'To see your face when I kill you.'

'I don't believe you.'

'Why?'

'I'd be dead by now.'

'Are you sure?'

'No.'

MELTDOWN

I check my thigh. The wound isn't as bad as I thought. The blood has stopped. The burn will be worse than the wound. But it hurts like a cigarette to the eye. Every time I hit an event I'm a waste of space after. And it's getting worse. I try and clear my head. We're far from safe. I have to assume that they will turn every building upside down. As soon as they find the limo we are dead in the water. How in the hell do we get away? A blind man. Walking wounded. A man out for the count. Some escape plan. If it was night we might stand a chance but that's hours away. I don't think it'll take long to figure out that the limo wasn't seen leaving the area. At least we couldn't have been seen entering the school. They would be here by now.

'So what now?' Tampoline seems more than calm.

I don't answer. I let my head roam away from the problem. I think of a mountain top covered in grass. Deep, luscious green. Soft velvet. I'm lying on it. In it. Beneath it. A warm wind. Hot sun. Birds and a distant tractor. I'm naked. No clouds above. A man approaches. One of the men we exchanged clothes with in the lane. Ripped clothing. A bum. An anonymous man. He lies down next to me.

Home run. I scramble to Martyn. A slap. Another. He responds. I leave him. 'Take off your clothes.'

Tampoline is tapping his fingers on the floor. 'Me?'

'You.'

'Fancy me, do you?'

I don't answer. I simply stand up and slap him in the face. He gets the message. When he's down to his Calvin

Kleins I grab the clothes. His paunch hangs out over his legs. I take his pants and start ripping them. The blackboard is still thick with chalk. I run the ripped pants across it. I repeat the exercise with his jacket.

'What are you doing?'

'Improving your wardrobe.'

Martyn stirs. 'Martyn, I need you to rip your clothes.'

'Why?'

'Just do it.' I vanish downstairs and grab some plastic bags. I empty them and take them back upstairs. 'The latest in water proof, cheap jackets.'

I take Tampoline's clothes and spread them on the floor. I unzip myself and let rip. Spraying them liberally. I halt. Trying to hold some back. I shake off the excess from the clothes and throw them at Tampoline. 'Put them on.'

He smells the urine and feels the damp. 'No way.'

'Yes way.'

He throws them to one side. I crawl over. 'Look, one way or another you are putting them on. I'm not up for any more of this macho crap. I don't need a gun. I don't even need to threaten you. You didn't leave. You chose to stay. I can spend the rest of our time together going Dirty Harry on your ass or we can get along. I'm not going to kill you. You're right. I could. I probably should. But I'm not going to. I'm tired and I'm only here because of your shit. My wife's dead. My life's a crock and you're at the center of it all. So we can drag you out of here naked or in my piss. I don't care. Work with me and we all come out of this on top. I just want my life back. So does Martyn. It's simple. We work this out. You do what I say. You want your brother? I can give him to you. You want out of this alive, I can do that to. You want out of this the hero, I can even do that. Think of the ratings boost. The tambourine man – kidnap victim – a born survivor.'

I push the clothes towards him. 'I'm on your side. Why? Because it's the only way out. You are my 'get out of jail free' card. Alternatively I tie you up and go on the run. You don't get your brother. You might look the hero. Then again, maybe I'll blog how you cried like a baby and pissed yourself. The internet is a wonderful thing. A few well posed photographs. A Facebook phenomenon. A twitter trauma. www.thetambourinemanexposed.com. All so easy.'

I place his hand on the wet clothes. 'So play along and we all might walk away.'

'Nice speech.'

'Thanks. Not bad for on the spur of the moment.'

'And how am I supposed to react?'

'What do you think?'

He fumbles around and picks up the clothes.

'Do I have to piss on my own clothes?' Martyn is down to his boxers.

'Up to you. We're entering a new world. The smell of piss is a strong repellant to the shoe shine people.'

'And we just walk out?'

'Not just. But everyone out there...' A police car wails by the window. '...everyone out there's looking for two men in coveralls and a presidential nominee.'

'And every eye on the planet is looking here. The place will be locked down for miles.'

'And exactly who are they looking for?'

'Us.'

'Who's us?'

'I've lost you.'

'Ok, so they know we are in coveralls. They may even have our faces, although I doubt it. I didn't see any CCTV. Did you?'

'I could have missed it.'

'Maybe. Even so, Jesse and Kent will have given us up by now. Especially Kent.'

'Well that seals it.'

'You still don't get it.'

'Get what?'

'They don't want us. They want him.'

'But we took him.'

'And?'

'Craig, what are you on about?'

'Who is the most important person in all this? The Senator over there. Not us. We may be America's most wanted but this all spins on his axis. They want him back. And they want him back unharmed. This is embarrassing. The first presidential related kidnapping since when. Ever? We've stirred up a hornet hurricane. Every law enforcement body in the US will be involved. Every TV station, website, social media channel will be alive with our guest. We will be the main news but unless they have a picture, and I doubt they have, it'll be Tampoline that will be the face of this.'

'Kent will lead them to my mum.'

'It's already done.'

'They'll have a photo of me.'

'Good point. How old?'

'A few years.'

'How many years back?'

'Twenty maybe.'

'A kid. And I can assure you they have none of me.'

'They know who you are.' Tampoline is still in his shorts.

'You do, and the agents that chased me down do. But I don't think they'll be going to the papers soon. You covered me up. Buried me deep. I can bet my last cent on it. You wanted me. You didn't want to share me. I'm not in a frame on your desk. No, unless I missed a camera at the building. We have a window of opportunity. And everyone looking for us is in the same boat. Sure they have a description but it's you they can easily spot. A blind man with a limp. That's who they'll focus on. They may want us but they need you.'

'And how does that help us?' Martyn still has a quiz face on.

'What else are they looking for?'

'I don't know.'

'Three men. A lot of people were around. Someone saw us jump the car. So everyone's looking for three men. A tall bald man, a medium sized skinny man that used to look like this kid and the Senator. What if we lose the blind man, the bald man and the skinny man?'

'How?'

'I've got a few ideas.'

'And how do we get away from here?'

'Because they won't be expecting us to be here. Think about it. We just kidnapped a senior politician. It has to be well planned. Doesn't it? Everyone will assume so. They'll be working on the premise that this was a professional job carried out in a prepared and planned manner. We would have worked out the escape route. We must have spent time on this. Covered every angle. Down to the last second on timing. Spirited the Senator away by now. The fact that no one saw the car leave just proves how clever we must be. We stole Tampoline from under their noses. We have to be serious professionals.'

'I get that. And how did we manage that?'

'Luck.'

'Looked like a hell of a lot more than luck to me. Smelled a little like the nonsense outside my mum's house.'

'Whatever you say. Anyway up, we have just pulled off one of the crimes of this century. No one will think we are hiding out locally. We would have to be insane to believe we would get away with that. Focus will be elsewhere. Sure, they will go through this place carefully, but it won't be the priority. There's no sign of break in. The doors to the garage are locked. A few minutes and we can cover the car downstairs with bags. Make it invisible if you look through the windows.'

Tampoline coughs. 'I think you might underestimate our law services.'

MELTDOWN

'Never. But in this case confusion will reign to start with. Five hours after Aaron Alexis started shooting at the Washington Naval Yard they were still trying to track down a second killer. Even though there never was one. It took seven hours to declare clear Fort Hood after Nidal Hassan went on the rampage. It was a mess when we left. These things are not easy. Conflicting reports. Poor eyewitnesses. Unclear chain of command. Sightings will already be coming in. Every black limo within ten miles will be suspect. They will start with them first. This is a large area and staying local isn't going to be up there as a plan. We don't have a lot of time but we have some. We need to use it. Martyn, keep an eye on our guest.'

I hit the corridor and start a search of the rooms. Most are empty. Dust is the norm and further down there are still old style desks in place. I root in a few of the teachers' desks and come up with scissors. I discover some Elmer's School Glue. An old teacher's donkey jacket sits on its peg. A box of crayons and I'm done. Better than shopping at Wal-Mart.

I get back to find Tampoline struggling to put on his clothes. The smell is foul. Martyn has sliced and diced.

I grab Trampoline's comb over, pull it up and cut it free. 'What the fuck?' I ignore him.

I turn to Martyn. 'Go down stairs and lift some of that shredded paper. Stuff as much down your shirt as you can. You take the donkey jacket. It's too large for you. We need to fatten you up. See if there's another jacket in the car.

Can you also lift the spare gasoline can? I saw it in the trunk. Be careful of the driver. '

While Martyn goes on a hunt I lean back on the wall. Ok so there are holes in this plan the size of the Lincoln Tunnel, but the next step will make those holes look like straws. Tampoline is still dressing.

A few minutes later and Martyn is humping a full can and carrying a black overcoat.

'Dirty that coat up and rip a pocket or two.' I check the can. Full. Now to work out where the next part all goes down. 'Watch him again.'

I spend twenty minutes recceing the school. I find an old baseball cap and push it on my head. Twice I need to duck as police cars crawl by. Once a group of men in the usual black suits cause me to duck beneath a window on the ground floor.

'The boss says they might have had a plane.' A thick New Jersey accent.

'Didn't they shut down the airports?' Lighter. Maybe mid-west.

'Rumor is that a small jet got off at 'Igor I Sikorsky Memorial'. We're checking it.'

'Where did it…' the voices fade.

The more red herrings the better. But the voices push me on. I return to the room.

'Ok I have a game plan. Risky, but we need to get the hell out of here. I need to make one last trip.'

I'm back in five. 'Drink anyone?' I hold up some vodka and an Ardbeg 18 Year old from the limo.

MELTDOWN

'Really?' Tampoline is in his clothes.
'A little drink, but then the rest goes on our clothes.'

Chapter 37

I'm standing in the main lobby of the school. I've positioned myself so I can see the main doors. They're locked. Tampoline is with Martyn a few doors down. I've soaked the last classroom in gas. In my hand are matches from the limo. The whole thing is now a gamble. I'll set fire to the room in a few minutes. But I have a few concerns.

In order: I don't want to die. I don't want Tampoline and Martyn to die. I don't want the driver to die. I need the fire to attract the right people first. I hope the right people don't get suspicious and tell the wrong people. I need them to find me first. Then find Martyn and Tampoline. But not straight away. I pray my hair doesn't fall off. I need Tampoline to play along. Strike the last one. Martyn has orders to knock him out cold as soon as he hears rescue at hand.

In order: Please don't let Martyn accidently kill Tampoline. Let them think I'm in need of hospital.

In order: There's no order to this going right.

I head for the Exxon room. The fumes waft along the school, mixing nicely with the piss and booze on my clothes. We are in for a down and out party. I was hoping that I might stumble on a few more people, the real deal, to add to the confusion. We're still three. We're still too close to the point of kidnap.

MELTDOWN

This is not a plan. More of a wish. A series of events that, even if all goes right, will still end up somewhere that I can't predict.

The gasoline begins to win the battle of the smells. I've piled in some of the paper from the garage to add fuel. I skirt round the drying liquid and take out the scissors. The windows are a series of small windows framed into one large one. Eight by eight blocks of glass. I listen for signs of life. Nothing.

I take the scissors and slam the handle into one of the panes. It shatters. I take out a few more. I listen. I'm now committed. Someone will notice fresh broken glass but I need the smoke to escape as soon as possible. There's no way back.

Back at the door I'd like to take one last deep breath. I can't. Not if I want to stay standing. I flick the book of matches open. *'Jill's Bar – Food and Good.'* A Manhattan number is picked out in gold beneath the writing. I tear one match free. Zip it over the rough. Let it catch. Touch it to the rest, and watch them all fire up. I hold the matchbook by the corner. And throw. I close the door and am moving as flame hits fuel.

There's a whumph as the unleaded ignites. I hobble away from the nonsense. I reach the front door and slump down. I can be seen if you look in. All I can do now is wait.

Smoke catches in my lungs. The fire is grabbing hold.

At first I think the siren is another in the chain from this morning. But this one doesn't fade. Seconds later a helmeted face appears at the door. He puts his hand up to shade the glare. My eyes are closed. The door rattles then there's an explosion. Axe on door – probably. A few more blows and voices.

'Get him out of here.' Strong, in charge.

In my ear. 'Wake up.' I feign unconsciousness.

'Get him out.'

I'm lifted and then dropped. 'Christ he's covered in piss.'

'I don't care if he's covered in shit. Get him out.'

'Crap, I'll need decontaminated.'

Fresh air causes me to gag. I cough and I'm on the sidewalk. I open my eyes.

'Are you ok?' A paramedic kneels next to me. Pretty.

'Ahh...' I have no intention of making sense. I cough. Not for effect. There was far more smoke than I expected.

The paramedic examines me. 'He needs hospital. Apart from smoke he has a wound on his leg that looks fresh.' She's speaking to someone out of sight. My pant leg is cut off and the wound examined. If it's recognized as a gun wound would she says nothing?

Off stage, a voice. 'Do we take him now?'

'May as well. We have five other ambulances round the corner that are doing nothing.'

'We need to tell the police.'

'This is our missing boy?' The voice is heavy with sarcasm.

'We have strict instructions.'

MELTDOWN

'He's not going anywhere that they can't visit him. Get him to the hospital and tell the police. They can interview him there.'

A stretcher is dropped from the back of the ambulance. I'm lifted on to it and into the guts of the vehicle. The door slams and we move. I have a watcher with me. He tries to strike up a conversation but I slur my way to saying nothing.

Ten minutes later the doors open on a red brick façade. A sign high up tells me this is Stamford Hospital. Underneath another sign reads 'Bennett Medical Centre'. I'm out of the ambulance and on my way to the emergency department. I wonder how Martyn and Tampoline are faring.

Half an hour later I'm in a gown, bathed, wound treated and lying in a bed. I wonder who is paying for this. A police officer appears. I keep up the slurring and he leaves. But he'll be back.

This all has an air of unreality. Given our proximity to the kidnapping we should be knee deep in law enforcement by now. Two and two doesn't equal four around here.

Another half an hour grinds away. The desire to move is huge. A nurse approaches. 'Did you have friends in the school?' I ignore the question. 'Well, they're in emergency.' I want to ask how they are but the police officer is nearby. I stay quiet. My act will not last. A connection to the kidnap can't be far away. Time to move.

The police officer moves out of sight. I slip from the bed. Clothes will have to wait. As second door sits to my right. I try the handle and it opens. An old lady is sleeping in a bed. I walk in. She doesn't stir. A hospital gown hangs on the end of the bed. I lift it and pull it on. It hardly covers my manhood. I pull a towel off a rail and wrap it round my head. This is never going to work.

I exit and head away from the police. I wait for the shout but I hit the head of a stairwell and hear nothing. I pop open a door next to me. A small meeting room. I cross and try another door. Another meeting room. Third time's the charm and I'm in an office. A coat hangs on a rail and I lift. It's too small but it'll have to do.

Down the stairs. I ride up two floors in the elevator. I keep my head down. Make the ground floor. The emergency area is quiet. I scuttle across. Two beds to my left are occupied. A doctor is examining one of the patient's hands. In the other bed a small girl is flicking at a phone despite the 'No Cell' sign above her head.

The world down here is quiet and to quote the movies, too quiet. I spot Tampoline and Martyn. Both are unattended. Something is off kilter here. Tampoline should be singing like a canary. But he sits in silence. They're still in their stinking clothes.

'Martyn. Time to move.'

Martyn jumps at the sound of my voice. 'Quiet isn't it Craig.'

'Gift horse, Martyn. Let's go.'

MELTDOWN

He gets up and we drag Tampoline up. Deep breath and head for the exit. No shouts. No yells. Too easy.

'We need a car.' I look at Martyn. There's plenty of choice in front of us. Martyn heads to the parking lot. We follow.

It takes him the longest two minutes in my life to find a car. An old Taurus. Well past its sell-by-date. He fires up the engine. I jump in, Tampoline beside me in the back seat. Wires hang from under the steering wheel. Martyn needs no bidding. Foot down, we flash from the parking lot. He stops at the exit and looks at me. 'Which way?'

'Head for the 95.'

When we enter the mid-afternoon traffic I turn to Tampoline. 'Ok, what gives?'

'In what way?' He stinks. I crack a window. 'Why are you still here? You've had more chances to escape than Steve McQueen.'

'Have I?'

'You want to be here. That much is obvious. I can think of two reasons.'

'Only two?'

'Your brother, and to rack up the notoriety of the kidnap.'

'Sounds good.'

'Except you must want your brother bad. When this story gets out there are going to be a lot of questions about why you didn't get away. Especially at the hospital. How did you magic all the cops away? The place should have been alive with them. After all, all you had to do was say the word and we were ground beef.'

'As you say, my brother is someone I need a small conversation with.'

'And that's it?'

'He clearly sent you after me.'

'You figure?'

'Craig, be serious. If he didn't send you, you would be a thousand miles away. After our last encounter are you that desperate to see me again? Why come back? It's obvious. Because you had to.'

The smugness in his voice is irritating. I want to swat him 'Ok. So we need to end this.'

'I agree. But could we do it in a civil manner. A wash and brush up wouldn't go a miss.'

'I know the very place.'

Chapter 38

Back in the day, before my foreshortened military career, before the onset of my events, before my life was a hole, I used to make a pilgrimage every fall to upstate New York and north. I would sign up for a Fall Foliage Tour. Up there with rail buffs, rubber band ballers and nose mining – it was a guilty pleasure. You sure as hell, at the age of seventeen, didn't admit to it. But it was glorious. The colors, the peace, the isolation. I loved it. I couldn't afford to do it for long but when I could I would grab my camera, binoculars and backpack.

Most people made for New England, but I had a thing for New York. I would base myself in Purchase. An upmarket golf course ridden village just over the 684 from White Plains. We are on the way there now. Maybe ten miles out.

'Martyn, when you see it, take the 287.'

Martyn nods.

'Where are we going?' Tampoline's smell may be my own urine but it's eye watering.

'To visit an old friend.'

I direct Martyn onto the 684 and into the back woods. We cruise past a sign for Old Oaks Country club. I left/right Martyn until I'm close to being lost. We zip by a small dirt road. 'Stop. Back up. Up there.'

The road is rutted and heavy with growth. The trees fold in behind us as we twist and turn. We are down to a crawl as the holes threaten to take out our shocks. I'm testing my memory in the extreme. Another dirt road flicks to the left. 'Down there.' The road is almost solid green and cratered. SUV only. Truth be told, tractor only. The underbelly of the old Taurus takes a hammering. We nearly beach out before we enter a clearing.

The center is dominated by a derelict clapperboard two story. The paint that was once blue is now peeling black. The windows hang to the building for grim death. The grey shingle roof is sliding to the ground. It hasn't changed a bit.

'Where is this place?' Martyn bumps the car next to a chronic pick up.

'I have fond memories of this place.'

'Past tense being the money. This is a wreck.'

'Always has been. See the sign over there?'

A small board is nailed to one of the veranda pillars. It's possible to make out *Just Enough.'* A smile leaks onto my lips. 'Just enough to keep it standing. Just enough to get us drunk. Just enough to keep us warm.'

Martyn has the look of the bewildered. 'What in the hell are you talking about?'

'You'll see. Stay here.'

The veranda is as rotten as I remember and it's been fifteen years since I was last here. The doorbell won't work. It never did. The old brass knocker in the shape of a

MELTDOWN

hammer is a little rustier, but still works. A lift it and knock. Dust falls from above me.

Footsteps echo from inside. Slow. Deliberate. The door handle turns and the hinges squeal in protest. A face appears. A thousand wrinkles on top of a thousand wrinkles. A wart the size of a blackcurrant on the nose. The hair is white. It had been black back then. I draw a breath. I thought her surely dead. Old eyes peer at me. Old but bright. Steel blue. Once the most attractive in the state. I lean forward. 'Mary-Anne. It's me, Craig. Craig McIntyre.'

Recognition doesn't flicker. I'm not surprised. When I was last here I had thick dark hair. I'm thirty pounds lighter than I used to be. The coat won't help. I look like a pervert waiting to strike. The old lady cocks her head. 'Speak up. I'm not so good with my ears these days.'

'Craig McIntyre. It's been a while. How are David and Karen?'

Still no recognition. 'I don't know you.'

'Mary-Anne, I spent months in this house over the years. Craig McIntyre. I used to hang out with David. We went looking at the foliage.'

A flicker. The blue sparkles. Then full effect. 'Oh my god. Craig. As I live and… Craig McIntyre. Are you serious? I mean it must be… well, years! Boy have you changed.'

'We all get older.'

'Well that's sure damn the truth. Come on in.'

'I have two friends with me.'

'Tell them they are welcome.'

I turn to Martyn. 'Bring Tampoline.'

Mary-Anne steps away from the door, vanishing into the gloom. I follow. The smell of rotting wood assails my nose. It brings back good memories.

I read once that smell is the only sense that doesn't go through extensive processing in your brain. It's either recognized or it's not. In a split second it can trigger memories in a way that the other senses can't. It bypasses analysis and pumps the images straight into the movie screen in your head. The rotting smell is a good movie.

The house is as dark as sin on a bad day. There was no electricity when I was last here and things don't seem to have changed. The clutter is deeper and wider. A rough channel allows me to navigate to the kitchen. Mary-Anne wheels through the junk with ease. I kick a few items and trip half a dozen times.

The kitchen is snapshot in my history book. It hasn't changed a single pixel. A large walk-in fireplace has flames licking the upper brickwork. The drapes are pulled tight and the dancing light hides as much as it reveals. A large wooden table, hewn from a single trunk, dominates. Six heavyweight chairs surround it. The floor is flagstone, shining from years of over use. This is the only room we ever sat in. Add in two bedrooms and a bathroom, and the rest of the house is uninhabitable. Long since left to its own devices.

A blackened coffee pot sits on a metal hot plate next to the fire. You don't find many five pint coffee pots today. Mary-Anne used to live on the stuff. She's immune to caffeine. At least that's the way it looked. Twenty plus mugs a day. Three before bed and she still slept like a baby. And the coffee was always good. The pot never empty. Sugar ok. Milk banned. There had never been a refrigerator to keep it cool.

A Belfast sink is full of dishes. One in - one out was the order of the day. The range is hidden beneath a stack of pots and pans. Not that any of them see much use. Sandwiches and alcohol was the Mary-Anne diet of choice. Slabs of fresh cut meat – cured in the woodshed - and fresh vegetables from the garden. Mary-Anne had told me that she had never stepped inside a supermarket in her life. I don't think much has changed.

She grabs the coffee pot and, with practiced ease, pours two mugs. Full, the thing weighs six pounds. She lifts it like it weights six ounces. She transfers the cups to the table and pours two more. Martyn and Tampoline stumble in.

'Mary-Anne, this is Martyn and…'

'The recently kidnapped Senator Tampoline.'

Chapter 39

Tampoline laughs. 'I may be blind but this feels like the middle of somewhere close to nowhere and this lady is onto us already.'

I ignore him. 'Mary-Anne, how do you know? Have you entered the twenty-first century? Is there a TV hiding somewhere?'

She slugs half the mug. 'TVs are a waste of space.'

'Radio?'

'Try Internet.'

'You have Internet?' The incredulity in my voice is comic.

'Craig, I adore the Internet. My one modern vice. David wired me up ten years ago. We tapped into the golf club's cable. They've never noticed. I even got a free upgrade last year.'

'Electricity?'

'A generator. So how much do you want to raffle the senator for? You do know its mug's game. Kidnapping is for Somalia and Afghanistan. Not for here. It's the money that gets you.'

Martyn said that. I look at him. 'Can we sit down and discuss this?'

She stands up. 'Where are my manners. Please gentlemen, take a seat. Coffee is on the table. Does anyone want anything stronger? Like a bath?'

MELTDOWN

The smell of the three of us is rank.

'A small brandy.' I hold out my cup. Mary-Anne disappears into the gloom at the back of the kitchen. She returns with a bottle of Hennessy XO. Not cheap. She tips in a generous measure into my mug. Martyn takes a shot as does Tampoline. Mary-Anne joins us.

For a few minutes the only sound is the crackle of wood dying. The coffee is as good as I remember, the brandy welcome. I can feel tiredness creep into my bones. The day is catching up with me. Martyn leans back and his eyes are heavy.

'You all look beat. Maybe a short nap before we chat.'

I can't disagree. Even Tampoline nods.

'Use the spare bedroom. I'll call you all in a few hours.'

The brandy kicks in and we cut through the junk jungle to the bedroom. It's cold and damp but the beds look fresh. There's a double and single crammed into a room designed for a single. The ceiling is low.

'I need to get these clothes off.' Tampoline has a point. The smell isn't getting any better.

'The bathroom is across from us. I'll see if Mary-Anne has any old clothes of David's. It'll be cold water only.'

'I don't care, I need to scrub until I bleed. Craig, do me a favor and show me the way.'

I show him and then make the trip to the kitchen. 'We're short on clothes.'

Mary-Anne is pouring another coffee. 'In my room. The large wardrobe. Anything that fits you can have. It's all David's stuff and he doesn't need it.'

'Why, did something happen to him?'

'Dear me, no. Later.'

Mary-Anne's room is as cold as ours. A four poster bed and an ancient dressing table make up two of the three pieces of furniture in the room. I open the wardrobe. On one side is Mary-Anne's stuff. A small and pathetic collection of jeans and tops. On the other is a rack of heavy knit, checked shirts and dungarees. We will look like the cast from Deliverance. I pull out an armful of clothes, drop them in our room and return. High up a box holds woolen socks and boxers. We'll need shoes but I can't see any.

Tampoline stands in the room. Naked. I hand him clothes and he struggles to get them on. From Senator to woodsman in one act.

Once we are all in period costume I hit the sack. But I don't sleep.

Two hours later the smell of bread drags me from the bed. The sun is missing from the window. Darkness has wrapped itself around the house. Tampoline and Martyn are out for the count. I struggle from the bed's warmth and cross to the window.

In the moonlight the clearing before the trees is mottled. The debris of Mary-Anne's life softened. We could be a hundred miles from the nearest neighbor – but we're not. This is expensive real estate. Only a few hundred yards beyond the clapped out shed that holds wood is a five star golf course. A few hundred yards to my right is an estate. In my day it was owned by a newspaper magnate. Mary-Anne owns the land around her. It's worth millions but she doesn't care.

I first met her when I was nineteen. A bus had dropped me off a mile or so from her house. I started walking, taking in the explosion of gold that had commandeered the trees. With no sidewalk I was forced to take to the hedges and edges as cars rolled by. Seeing the dirt road that led to Mary-Anne's place I sat down, unwrapped a sandwich, and popped a can of seltzer.

The bread was stale, the meat dry and the seltzer warm. But I didn't care. I was struggling at college. Academia and I were enemies. A new year had just kicked off and already I was behind the eight ball. Looking at foliage was my escape. A chance to ignore the fact that I wouldn't get through college. It was already written. Craig – early season drop out.

I stared at the road, focusing on nothing, when a horn wrenched me from my stupor. I turned to see a pick-up truck that had once been a forecourt vision. It was now a wrecker's dream. Dented, scraped, battered – it idled a few feet from me. The engine ran in lumps and black smoke was filling my world. An old lady had me fixed in her vision. Even back then Mary-Anne looked ancient. Good, but ancient.

I stood up and moved to one side. She pulled level with me. 'Private land, sonny. Can't you read?'

I followed her outstretched hand. A sign lay on its side. 'Private Property.'

'Sorry. I was just having lunch.'

It should have ended there. Her driving off and me chewing old meat. But she eyed me up and down. 'You look like you need a good meal.'

'Everyone says that.'

She looked at the sorry sandwich in my hand. 'That looks appetizing.'

I smiled. 'It's not the greatest.'

Something in her voice magnified the pathetic nature of my situation. At my age there should have been a thousand other ways to celebrate my youth. I drop the sandwich to my lap.

'Have you any muscles?' Mary-Anne was taking in my less than Schwarzenegger figure.

'I'm stronger than I look.'

'I tell you what. See the metal tank in the back?' The rear of the pick-up was filled by a giant cube of black. 'It took me two days to get it in there. I need to drop it at a friend's. If he's not in it'll take me the same to get it out. I'll swap you some of your labor for food.'

Now, I wasn't short on money to buy that night's meal. But I wasn't flush either. I just wanted solitude. Then again, I remember thinking, how do I decline? She didn't look she could lift a wet newspaper. How she had got the tank in was a superhuman story waiting to be told. I agreed.

Two hours later, one tank deposited. One brandy and coffee down, we were chatting.

MELTDOWN

For the rest of the week I stayed with her. Over the next few years I returned. The place was perfect. A wilderness within striking distance of my home. A few acres of no-man's land. She told me of her desire to keep it the way it was. Of the locals who had moved heaven and earth to have her evicted. Of her lawyer son who had kept them at bay. Of her daughter who had recorded every incident in her battle and had released it all to the local rag, who rejected it. What else would they do? They were financed by the local millionaire club. She talked, pride in her voice, of her daughter publishing a book. *Just Enough.*'

She did it off her own back. Self-published. A copy found its way to ABC. A breakfast crew arrived, and Mary-Anne appeared on national TV. And not a person could be found that wanted her evicted. All vanished in the glare of the TV. The book became a minor hit. A small publisher in New York picked it up. It spend one week in the top 200.

Mary-Anne held a barbeque to celebrate. She invited all the neighbors. Not one turned up.

I mist up the window with my breath. A breeze. The last gasp of the long gone storm. A car engine. An owl. I inhale the night. My mind is chilling, my brain melting onto the pan of my skull. Back to a place of normality. A place with no events. No rogue agencies. No persecution.

Martyn steps in beside me. 'Penny?'

'It used to be like this all the time.'

'Quiet.'

'Peaceful. Like standing in a warm pool.'

'Is that why we're here?'

'Probably.' I looked at Tampoline. His chest rises and falls evenly. No eye flicker. Asleep. 'This isn't going to end well.'

'Better than it would have.'

'Are you sure? Tampoline is playing us. We're on his agenda.'

'No one will find us here.'

'I wish that was true.'

'Who could know we are in this place?'

I look to the dark sky. 'We've got the might of the US intelligent services on our case. Have you any idea how many intelligence and counterintelligence agencies there are. The National Security Agency, National Geo Spatial-Intelligence Agency, the Defense Intelligence Agency, the FBI's Bureau of Intelligence and Research, the intelligence arms of the navy, army and air force. There are intelligence agencies for the Treasury, the Energy Department. There are even intelligence agencies for the Coast Guard. Add in the CIA, Tampoline's agency, the state police, local police – even the National Guard. And ever since 9/11 they now all talk to each other.

Once they know who we are, and they probably do already, our lives will be open book. Every contact, every action, every reference will be examined. Will they know about Mary-Anne? Maybe. I told people back then. It might take a little time but she'll pop up somewhere.

If they have a make on the Taurus the sky will be alive. Satellites trained on the area. Reviews of every minute of footage. Requests for as many eyes as possible.'

MELTDOWN

I rub a small circle in the condensation my breath is causing. 'Add in the media frenzy. TV, radio and the killer, the Internet. All squawking about us. There will be a reward the size of Croesus's cellar. Then we add in your old boss. The Factor will be on the case. Everybody and his second cousin will be in on this. And I haven't considered foreign countries lending a hand. Getting out of this shit storm isn't going to be easy. It may not even be possible.'

Martyn stays quiet. Another breeze moves the branches around in an old oak tree. The Taurus is invisible beneath it. The smell of bread grows. 'Come on, let's eat. Bread, butter and fresh meat. It's just about all Mary-Anne eats.'

The kitchen is a hot faucet to the rest of the house's cold shower. Mary-Anne is drawing a loaf from the oven. A slab of butter and a side of cooked ham sit on the table. Four plates are set. The coffee pot is bubbling. I sit down and Mary-Anne carves hot bread. Three wedges land on my plate. Warm to the touch. I smother them in butter. It melts. I slice some ham, layer it on and bite. The taste is exquisite. Martyn fires in.

Ten minutes of masticating and Tampoline appears. Martyn helps him to the table and Mary-Anne loads up his bread. I'm breaking bread with a bastard that killed my wife.

Mary-Anne throws another fistful of bread on my plate. 'So tell me about life since you were last here?'

I give her the shortened Cook's tour. I omit the nastiness. When I mention Lorraine's death I look at Tampoline. He munches away. In his world it was me that

killed her. An event and she died. In his world I'm the killer.
In my world it's him. 'And you?'

'Nothing to tell. Karen is married. I'm a
grandmother three times over. David is still a lawyer. Only
now his paycheck is a bit bigger. He never married. I think
he has a boyfriend but he never talks about it. I'm still here.
So's the house. Just.'

Martyn stops munching. 'Who are Karen and
David?'

'My daughter and son. And Senator, what brings
you to my home?'

'Abbott and Costello.'

'You think? I don't believe you. I did a bit of
searching on the Internet. Seems to me that there was a lot
of luck involved in your kidnapping.'

Before Tampoline can reply I put down my bread.
'You've been on the Internet?'

'I told you. I'm a free rider on the golf club's cable.'

'Shit.'

'Language.'

'Sorry, Mary-Anne. How long were you on?'

'A good few hours. There's a ton of stuff out there.'

Tampoline shakes his head. 'Not good.'

I agree. 'Not good at all.'

Mary-Anne looks confused. 'What are you on
about?'

'They'll be monitoring the web for unusual traffic
and searches.'

'Surely not. I mean everyone use the Internet. How could anyone keep track of it all?'

'Oh they can. Especially when they know what to look for. Anything with the Senator's name in it. Anything with our names. Anything to do with the kidnapping. Anything to do with kidnapping in general. Especially if it's in the right geographic area.'

'But I tap off the golf club.'

'That's good. Their first port of call will be there. But it won't take long to figure there's something not straight. We need to move. And Mary-Anne, so do you.'

'Move where?'

'With us.'

'Craig, I'm not going anywhere. I drive twice a week to meet up with a couple of friends. Once in a blue moon I pick up a package. Other than that I stay here.'

Tampoline has finished his meal. 'Craig's right. You have no choice.'

'Yes I do. It's my home.'

'Of course Mary-Anne. I can call you Mary-Anne?'

'Yes.'

'Thank you. Consider the options. Stay here and when the FBI arrive, or whoever they send, you'll be questioned and if they figure I was here you'll be arrested. Accessory after the fact. So you can come with us or you can go with the authorities.'

'Who's kidnapping who around here? Who's in control?' Her face is flushed. 'I don't get any of this.'

I know what she means. I fell like the tail is wagging the dog. 'I'm sorry Mary-Anne…'

'How can you be sorry? You knew that this might happen if you came here. I haven't seen you in an age and you bring this on my home. If you had thought about it you would never have come. I was a fool to let you in.'

She's right and I feel like cold sick on a birthday cake. 'You're right, but what's done is done.'

'No it's not. Nothing is done. All you need to do is tie me up. Let them, whoever the hell they are, find me. I'll play dumb. I'm real good at dumb.'

Martyn pushes his plate away from him. 'She's right. It could work.'

I shake my head. 'No it won't. Nothing in this whole mess will be taken on face value. Mary-Anne, you need to come with us.'

'Craig McIntyre, I will not leave this house. You can scare me all you want but I'm not going.'

'Be sensible, dear lady,' Tampoline has put on his best politician's voice. 'What is to be gained by remaining here?'

'What's to be gained by leaving? It makes me look worse. Part of the whole shooting match. As if it were planned. That's what they are saying out there. That this was meticulously planned down to the last detail. They don't know that this is a screw up. They think that this has taken a lot of resource and that just makes me more suspicious. I've no idea what game you are playing Mr Senator, but you're not the injured party in this shebang.'

MELTDOWN

My taste for the bread has gone. I push my plate away. 'I agree. Tampoline, I haven't got this figured, but there's so much in this sorry mess that doesn't add up. But now's not the time. We need to move.'

The window behind us shatters and a smoke canister rolls in. Of old I know whose signature entrance that is.

Chapter 40

'No!' Tampoline shouts.

'Mary-Anne, we need a way out.'

We all hit the floor as the smoke rolls in. She grabs my hand. 'This way.' I grab Martyn and he grabs Tampoline. We crawl from the kitchen. Around us the world is alive with noise. Voices. Orders. More breaking glass. Wood splintering. Mary-Anne leads us into the darkness. She reaches around and I hear metal clicking as lock throws. 'Inside. As quick as you can.'

The four of us scramble into a tiny space. Mary-Anne whispers. 'We're under the stairs.'

Lights seep under the door as heavy footsteps join the shouting. The place is being invaded. 'Down here.' In the half-light I see Mary-Anne lift a trapdoor.

We tumble down and the trapdoor slams shut. We are now in Tampoline's world. There's no light. We unwind our bodies. Mary-Anne whispers again. 'This will be dirty. We had heavy rain last night.' I have no idea what she's talking about.

Above us there are a thousand footsteps. Engines roar as more vehicles pour into the yard. Mary-Anne tugs at my hand. I crawl behind her. I've lost Martyn but I can hear movement from behind. The floor is stone. Ice cold. I hit my head on something. As I rub it Mary-Anne pulls at me. 'We're nearly there.'

MELTDOWN

She stops and lets go of me. I sit and rub at my head. Another click. 'In here. Where are the others?'

'Martyn?' My voice is shaking.

'Here.' I feel him move next to me. 'And Tampoline.'

'I'm also here.'

Mary-Anne moves. 'Watch the stairs. They'll be slippy.'

I wave my hands around looking for a door edge. When I find it I slide my feet forward. I feel the first step. I slide my backside onto it and begin to descend. In seconds my pants are soaked through. I hear Tampoline curse and Martyn yelp.

As we descend the noise from above abates, soaked up by distance and rock. There's a loud scratch and light floods in. Mary-Anne is holding an oil lamp. 'Watch your head.'

To prove the point I head-butt an outcrop of rock. Painful. Mary-Anne leads off. I follow. 'What is this place?'

'In the twenties the owners used to make hooch. They dug this as an escape.'

'Where does it go?'

'It used to come out about half a mile away. But part of it filled in when they build the house next door. It emerges at the edge of their land.'

'Then what?'

'Good question.'

With the invasion noise gone we tramp on. Under foot is mud and apart from Mary-Anne we are all bare footed. The tunnel bends to the left. It dead-ends in a concrete wall. Mary-Anne points up. A rusty ladder leads to a metal grill. She climbs it. 'I'll need a hand.'

I climb up beside her. We grab the grill and push. It flies up and we place it to one side. I scramble out. Next to us is a swimming pool. That explains the concrete wall. I help Mary and Tampoline out. We can hear the commotion of the raid still unfolding. Flashlights flicker in the distance. Then I hear dogs. 'Where to?'

Mary-Anne points to a beautiful three-story mansion. 'Behind the house the golf course wraps rounds. If we go left we hit the road but there's a ten-foot, broken glass topped wall down there. On the far side there's the McMutrey place. Then it's the Jackson's, then the country club.'

I look at the mansion, picked out in spotlights. 'What's beyond the golf club?'

'If we cut straight across we hit PepsiCo's head office. Then into more houses. If we go the other way we hit King St.'

'We need transport.'

'Now I might be able to help you there.' Tampoline is standing to my left.

'How?'

'We could fly out of here.'

'Forgive me for asking but why would you want that?'

'Craig, let's just say that's it's not in my interest to be freed just yet.'

Mary-Anne touches him on the shoulder. 'Is that why you shouted 'no' back in the house?'

'Did I?'

'Clear as a bell. I'd have thought yes would been the word of the moment.'

'Very well spotted.'

I shrug my shoulders. 'Tampoline, whatever it is you want with your brother has to be good. We're hardly going to give glowing references on your behavior if we're caught. Your reputation will be shot.'

'I don't think so. Now do we want out of here or not?'

'A plane?'

'If I'm not mistaken we can't be far from Westchester County Airport.'

Mary-Anne nods. 'A couple of miles as the crow flies. We can cut through the golf course. After that we would be on the road.'

'I need a phone. A payphone.'

Silence.

I turn to Mary-Anne. 'Is there still the wine and liquor store around here? It used to be on the edge of the course. It had a payphone.'

'Still there. George Carmichael owns it now.'

Martyn steps forward. 'Golf course it is.'

Holding to the property line we walk around the mansion. Martyn has taken on role of guide dog to Tampoline. Mary-Anne is on point. Occasionally we see a crack of light in the woods. Thankfully the dogs don't seem to be getting any closer.

We reach the far end of the golf course. A small fence keeps the golfers in. Beyond is darkness. We cross over.

Mary-Anne keeps us close to the edge of the course. She uses the lights from the back of the houses to give us some vision. 'Senator. Why are there no helicopters?'

Tampoline has his hand on Martyn's shoulder. 'I have no idea.'

'Don't you find that a little strange? I mean with you being so important and all.'

She has a point. A damn good point. Given the trees a helicopter would be a prerequisite if we made a run for it.

'Maybe, my dear lady, they didn't have time to source one.'

'And they got half a dozen cars, God knows how many trucks and even sniffer dogs to us double quick? I don't buy it.'

The sound of a chopper engine ends the conversation.

I shake my head. 'Mary-Anne. Next time keep your thoughts to yourself.' Mary-Anne stops and slaps me on the chest. I'd like to laugh but the helicopter has my attention. It appears above Mary-Anne's home. 'They'll have infrared on that thing. Let's pick up the pace.' Easier said than done in the half-light.

MELTDOWN

A small copse appears and Mary-Anne leads us onto a fairway. The grass is soft and lush underfoot. We are on moonlight only now.

The helicopter is still hovering over Mary-Anne's land. A search light is playing on the scene below. We are slow. Too slow. A blind man, an old woman, lack of light, lack of footwear. It's no way to run a railway. 'Mary-Anne, where is the club house?'

'Not far. To our left. See the lights?'

The soft glow of outdoor lighting edges the trees to our left. I break from the group. 'Keep going. I'll be back.' I break into a hirpling jog. I aim for the light. A concrete path appears and I take to it. The path winds through the trees. I follow it. The clubhouse unfolds before me. A magnificent stone clad building. Gravel crunches as cars glide up. The vehicles empty people at the front door. Nothing less than a Mercedes appears as I watch. I cut to my left, away from the arriving hoards. Light, dance music is carried along with the smell of cooking meat. I keep to the shadows. A glass wall keeps the cold away from a gathering of the well to do. Drink is flowing from a champagne bar. Nice.

I leave the party behind. I'm looking for the pro shop. I cross by a small pond. Ahead, a set of vehicles sit in neat rows. Let's hope security is lax. I reach the nearest one. A two seat golf buggy with space for two more where the clubs sit. Ideal. The key is in the ignition. I flick it. Nothing. I sit in, press the accelerator and it leaps forward. I smack the buggy in front. I select reverse and take it back. There's the quietest of hums as the buggy moves. Then the buggy jerks. There's a snapping sound. And then we're on the move. I roll over the charging cable that has just been ripped from the buggy. I'm guessing there's a quick release. I can't be the first to drive off without unhitching.

I circle the pond. Enter the trees. Back to the fairway. The helicopter has moved, circling out from Mary-Anne's in concentric circles. Searching.

I can't see my party. I wheel away from the chopper. Shadows appear. Three bodies. I purr up beside them. 'Did anyone order a cab? Quick, all in.'

We load up, Tampoline and Martyn in the back, Mary-Anne next to me. I get moving. 'Which way?'

Mary-Anne nudges me. 'Keep to the right of the fairway.'

I speed into the dark. 'Keep an eye on the helicopter.'

We bump up a slope. I manage to miss the flagpole on the green. The grass beneath takes a battering as we slide left. A trail for those looking for us once the sun is up. I want to be long gone by then.

Mary-Anne nudges me again. 'See the dull glow ahead? That's the highway.'

I take the heading and keep us moving. I risk a look at the chopper. Its circle is now edging the golf course. They know we're not in the house. The search will be spread quickly. After all, how far can a team with our limitations run?

MELTDOWN

I curve round a dogleg. A neat par four. This time the moon picks out the green and I avoid it. 'Is there an exit near the highway?'

Mary-Anne is watching the helicopter. 'I've no idea.'

I keep up the nighttime golf tour. I'm on the edge of controlling a vehicle with a top speed of no more than ten miles an hour. It feels like a hundred. I can't use the buggy paths. They are woven in the woods and there's no light there. I skirt another green and the glow is closer.

The course runs out. An edging of trees appears. There's a fence and then road. I slew to a halt. 'Out'

We move to the fence. I scan it for an exit. None. It's over or nothing. I grab the chain link and scan the road. Clear. I see the wine and liquor store. It sits on its own. Maybe a hundred yards away. May as well be million. The road will be alive with the hunters soon.

Mary-Anne shouts. 'There. A gate.' It's fifty feet away, hidden by a small fir tree. We hustle, exit, cross the road and walk onto the store parking lot. 'Martyn, you take Tampoline in. Tampoline, make the call and make it quick. I need to find more transport. Mary-Anne, come with me.'

Martyn and Tampoline enter the shop. I circle to the back. Mary-Anne tails me.

The wine and liquor store is a stand-alone one story. The parking lot sits out front and the rear is neat grass stretching back to the house a few hundred yards away. To the left and right is more grass. An oasis of drink in a sea of green and gray.

'Aren't we looking for a car?' Mary-Anne is scanning the grass.

'A waste of time. We're not going to the airport. It'll be covered. The whole state will be covered.'

'What are we going to do?'

'Make like the Alamo.'

Chapter 41

I knock on the back door. It opens. 'Hi Gaylord.'

'Craig.'

Gaylord stand aback to let me in. 'Gaylord, meet Mary-Anne. Mary-Anne, say hi to Gaylord Butterworth.'

'Hi.'

I shut the door behind Mary-Anne and turn to Gaylord. 'So are you ready for this?'

'How long do you think we have?'

'Not long enough.'

'You need to hold up your end of the deal.'

'Of course.'

Mary-Anne is looking a little confused. 'Craig, what's going on?'

'If I'm truly honest Mary-Anne, I'm not sure. Gaylord here wants to talk to his brother and in return we vanish.'

'Vanish? I don't want to vanish. I want to go home.'

'So do I, Mary-Anne, but it isn't going to happen. Not for a while. I give it twenty minutes before this place is searched. When they do all hell will break loose.'

'And the plan is?'

'It's kind of loose.'

Getting Gaylord here had been easy enough. The timing had been tougher. Mary-Anne's house had always been my planned bolthole. I'd thought we would have got a bit longer. I could have told Gaylord to meet us at Mary-Anne's but I don't trust him. I needed a safe house to do some thinking. I remembered the wine and liquor from years back. A call from the hotel in New York had confirmed its existence. The call to Gaylord had set up the rendezvous.

'Where's the owner?' I put an edge on my voice. I need control here.

'Enjoying a well-earned break in a local hotel. He'll be well compensated.'

'And how will Tampoline and Martyn get in? I told them to use the front door.'

'Denholm is minding shop.'

Mary-Anne sits on the edge of a desk. 'So let's get this straight. You have kidnapped a potential future President and holed us up in a building with no escape route? I take it this building isn't built on top of some old mine complex that no one knows about except us.'

'It would be nice if it was.' I think it would be very nice if it was. 'No, we're a little restricted in our options. I'm counting on the brothers to sort the shit out for us. Shall we go facilitate a family reunion?'

Gaylord nods.

The storeroom at the back is a simple affair. The walls are lined with units groaning under the weight of booze. A heavy-duty door is the only other exit. It opens onto a small office. All the furniture is pushed to one side to free up a pathway to the store. Another door opens and we three become six.

MELTDOWN

Tampoline is on the phone. He's facing the wall. Martyn is staring at Denholm. Denholm is sitting behind the counter slugging a beer. He acknowledges Gaylord as he enters. Martyn's jawline achieves new, hitherto unknown, dimensions. His mouth wants to ask a question but his brain is still processing the information. I step in beside Gaylord and scan the store.

The shop has a counter running along the back wall. Behind it is a gallery of golden liquid. Beyond the counter a second wall is lined with chillers for beer, wine and soda. The wall opposite is lined with red wine. Next to the front door is the phone. A few armchairs sit in one corner with a small table between them. The floor is wooden and the lighting subtle.

Decoration is olde worlde. A nautical theme dominates. A ship's wheel hangs from the ceiling. Brass lamps wrap the lights. An oar is mounted high on the wall above the beer. A model of a nineteenth century man-o-war sits in a glass case next to the armchairs. All in all a classy little establishment. Tampoline hears the door open and swings round. 'Who's there Martyn?'

'Good evening Constantine.'

Tampoline replaces the phone. 'Gaylord. Well what a surprise.'

'You weren't expecting me?'

'Of course, but not quite now and not quite here. Martyn informs me that this is something of a bad place to hole up.'

'Oh, I wouldn't say that. There's some fine liquor here. Very fine indeed. I found a fine bottle of Almaviva Baron Philippe de Rothschild 2001. Would you care for a glass?'

'It would seem rude not to.'

'Denholm, be a dear. The bottle is sitting on the desk in the store. I opened it earlier to let it breathe. Could you bring it through and a couple of glasses? Would anyone else care to partake?'

Mary-Anne screws up her face. 'You want to drink? Now? Are you for real?'

'My dear lady.' Gaylord moves his bulk from behind the counter and sits in one of the armchairs. He barely fits. His attire is immaculate. No change for ten grand. 'My dear lady, one always has time for a drink.'

I cross the shop and pull a six-pack of Coors Banquet from the chiller. 'Martyn?' He nods and I pass him one. Denholm reappears with a wine bottle and four glasses. Mary-Anne shrugs. 'Ok, count me in. I'd like a glass of red.'

Denholm takes the fourth glass. He gently touches Tampoline's arm. 'Seat?' He guides him to the other armchair before returning to the counter to pour the wine. I lean on the counter and Martyn perches on the other end. Gaylord struggles to stand up. 'Sorry, my dear lady, please have my seat.'

'I'll get my own.' She vanishes into the office to return with a wheeled office chair. She slides it into the main body of the shop and sits. Denholm is a good wine waiter and once everyone is charged up he retires behind the counter.

I pop my can and take a slug. Martyn does likewise.

'Well this all very cozy.' Gaylord squeezes his bulk back into the chair. Half the wine has already gone. I remember the early morning drinking at his house. I need him the good side of sober. Gaylord seems to have other ideas. 'Denholm, I think we might need a few more bottles at the ready.' Denholm sips his wine and leaves.

'Gaylord, a drink is one thing, but this is not a social event.' I take another slug.

'Craig, relax. My brother and I have a lot of catching up to do. I would suggest that you get comfortable.'

I can see out on the parking lot. The road beyond is quiet but the chopper has been joined by a second. I hold my hand up to get a better view. 'Martyn, back in the store there was a tarpaulin. Can you bring it through?'

'What for?'

'This door is the only way to see in here. When company arrives I don't want them to have a front row seat.'

He leaves as Denholm returns with two more bottles of red wine. Tampoline and Gaylord are on small chat. Not what I had expected. Rain bounces off the door. Light at first, and then it puts on its boots. In seconds the road is blurred by sheets of water.

A car sloshes by, wipers on full. Steamed up windows in the back. The silhouette of a man dragging a cigarette while driving. The red glow picking out a beard as he speeds away. A large rig follows, spray rising from it like a whale spouting. No sign of police or agency. Not yet. The helicopter is at the edge of the course. It hovers above the spot where we left the buggy. The searchlight illuminates the buggy. Another step closer to finding us.

Martyn drags in the tarpaulin. 'See if you can find the outside lights for this place. Let's make it look like we have shut up shop.'

I heave the tarp up and use a hook above the door to support it. It drapes down, covering the door. I pull it to one side and pin it with a case of white wine. I leave the other side free to let me peek out. A few seconds later and the lights in the shop go out. They flick back on and the parking lot darkens. Martyn is flicking switches at random. I pull the plug on the two neons on the door and let the tarp drop back. 'Martyn, can we lose more of the light inside?'

Lights flick on and off. He kills them all and we are left with the light of the chillers. It's enough to see by. 'Can you check the rear door is locked? See if you can slide something in front of it. Take Denholm with you. Move one of the units if you have to.'

Tampoline and Gaylord are lost in chat.

'Mary-Anne, would you do me a favor and see where the owner keeps his guns?'

'How do you know he will have any?' The red wine glows ruby in her hand as the chillers catch the liquid.

'It's a liquor shop. Even in the good areas they have bad guys.'

MELTDOWN

She gets up. Her movement is slow. Uncomfortable. Her years show in the half-light. She had to be well into her sixties the first time I met her. Her feisty independence was being dulled by something she could not fight. Old age was coming to get her.

She roots around and comes up with a shotgun. ''I think this might do the job.

'For starters. There'll be more.'

I crack the tarp. The rain is settling in for the night. The moon has gone, replaced by the searchlights of the two choppers. The nearest one is still hovering over the buggy. The light shimmers in the falling rain. A hard cold light. The chopper moves away, tracking towards the clubhouse. The light picks up the gate. It's swinging open.

Two steps closer.

I let the tarp fall. Mary-Anne taps on the counter. 'And these.' She has two handguns.

'Are they loaded?'

She checks. 'Yes.'

The rain picks up a more insistent rhythm on the roof. Mary-Anne brings the weapons over. 'What do you want to do with them?' I point to the wine case holding the tarp in place. 'Put them there.'

'Are you really thinking we can shoot it out with the combined forces of the US law forces?'

'No. If it comes to that we are dead meat. I just like a little insurance in case we need it in here.'

'And what will go down in here?'

In the dim light her wrinkles are smoothed out. She was once a stunning looking woman. She had showed me pictures of her younger days. She'd been a model. In the sixties she had also done a little work that required less clothes than most. She had shown me the pictures. I was embarrassed beyond belief. She had laughed hard as I blushed from my toes.

'I'm not sure what will go down, Mary-Anne. I'm not running this show. Those two are.'

'And what is it with them?'

'History. History that needs sorting.'

'And you?'

'Sorry?'

'Why are you here?'

'Where else would I be?'

'Well, I wouldn't have walked in the back door of this place for a start. I'd have been off. Putting in some distance.'

'And how far would we have got?'

'I didn't say we.'

'Like I would leave you behind.'

'I would. On your own you might just have slipped away.'

'To what? I have no money. No clothes. Nowhere to go.'

'Better than jail. Better than dying.'

'Mary-Anne, I need my life back. Tampoline and Gaylord might be able to do that.'

MELTDOWN

'Or they will hang you out to dry. Look at them. Thick as thieves.'

That was worrying me. I didn't know what I had expected but not this. Fireworks. Anger. Retribution. But not a quiet fireside chat. Gaylord is leaning in. Almost whispering in Tampoline's ear. His glass has been refilled. The conversation is intense.

I look back at Mary-Anne. 'I know, but I still have a card or two to play.'

'I hope they're good ones. I can't see how this ends well for anyone but those two and the servant. I think we're surplus to requirements.'

I wanted to tell her that I knew that she was wrong. While I could do what I did I would never be excess baggage. I had, after all, with a little help kidnapped a high ranking US politician. It had been a long time since that had happened. And that had me worried. It had been all a little too easy in the end. Too many little breaks that made the job flow. Or maybe the breaks were just the rub of the green. A few thoughts nestled in the back of my head, next to the cold kernel that could unleash my inner monster. The thoughts were half formed but like all good thoughts they would grow. I was missing something in all this.

Above the beat of the rain the pulse of the chopper snaps me back to the here and now. It slides in above us. Tampoline and Gaylord stop talking. The engine howls and the blades slap heavy wet air onto the roof. The building vibrates.

'Well the fun should start soon.' Gaylord was shouting over the noise.

'They don't know we're in here.' Mary-Anne was shaking.

'Maybe.'

The noise is deafening. The helicopter is right on top. Even with the tarp in place the searchlight are finding gaps. Steaks of white bounce off the walls. They dance and weave as the helicopter sways. Then the noise eases and the helicopter moves off.

'See.' Mary-Anne has slumped to the floor. 'They're gone.'

But the helicopter doesn't vanish. It sets up camp above the road. Waiting.

I think the ground troops might be on their way.

Chapter 42

Gaylord and Tampoline get back to chewing the fat.

'Mary-Anne. Watch the guns.' I walk over to Tampoline and

Gaylord. 'I hate to break this family reunion up but we are going to be knee deep in bad guys soon. What's the plan?

Gaylord looks up. 'Plan? Not sure we have one.'

Shit.

'So how do we get out of here?'

Tampoline smiles. 'We walk.'

Double shit.

'So what happens next?'

Gaylord sinks a half glass. 'Well you probably go to jail for a few years. My brother runs for President and I pick up a few nice contracts to tide me over until I can run for office myself.'

Life is going south. 'And I'm just going to stand back and let this happen?'

Tampoline has the smug look on. 'Yes.'

I look at Gaylord 'So you don't want me to kill your brother anymore?'

'Was that the plan? Well, well. Gaylord, you should be ashamed.'

'Terribly.'

Tampoline smiles. 'It seems that Gaylord and I may have more in common than we thought.'

Gaylord's turn to smile. 'I thought I had this all worked out. My ambitions. Constantine's ambitions. Mutually exclusive. He had me over a barrel with some of my misdemeanors. I had him on his. One of us had to go. I needed to see him and he needed to see me. But then we got talking. Why screw each other over? Why not work together?'

'Just like that?'

Tampoline's smugness is growing. 'I'm a politician, Craig. To my marrow. I can flip on any subject you like in the heartbeat of a mouse. It's how you thrive on the hill. You see the way the mop flops and you adapt. And now, thanks to your screw up, we see the light.'

'My screw up?'

'But of course. Do you really think bringing us to a rat trap like this that we were going to have many options? I had this meeting placed for somewhere a little more private. Maybe things would have shaped up in a different way. But you've put us in a corner here. What were you expecting? That you would pull your little trick and Gaylord would kill me? Or was it vice versa?'

I stood. Silent.

Gaylord adds his ten cents worth. 'When you phoned I thought you had this a bit better figured out. When I got here I realized this was hopeless. This is no Butch Cassidy and the Sundance Kid ending. This is survival of the fittest. And you, Mr McIntyre, are not the fittest.'

A light flashes deep in my head. I'm getting angry. I want to switch on the monster. 'So I become collateral damage? I don't think so. Do you think I'm going to just fade away in some supermax facility? This was a set up from the outset and that won't look good for your hero of the kidnap story.'

'Your word against mine.' Tampoline is in smug heaven.

Then the light shines in. I pause, letting my head play with an idea. 'Shit, you planned this. You knew I was coming for you. How? Not Gaylord. Why would he? He could have just phoned and you could have had a Starbucks moment. Gaylord really wanted you dead. It took me bringing you both here to see another way out. He really wanted to kill you. So how did you know I was coming?'

I turn. Martyn is staring at his shoes. 'You. Fuck, you are in on it?' My head spins. I stagger back. My stomach knots. I feel sick. 'You?' Martyn keeps his eyes down.

Tampoline laughs. I want to rip his head from its roots. I take a step towards Martyn. 'But they kicked the living crap out of you at the agency. Why would you work for them? And the house. The Factor. They tried to kill you.'

A siren cuts through the rain and chopper.

My head is buzzing. 'So Martyn, what do they have over you? Your mother? Something else? It must be big to take a kicking for show. The boy wasn't laying off.'

'Of course not.' Tampoline has caught the sound of the siren as well. 'It had to look real.'

'And of course the Factor wouldn't know that Martyn had turned.'

'Just found out myself.' Gaylord is into another glass.

I walk up to Martyn. 'The kidnapping. It was your idea. Back in the hotel it was your idea. Not mine.'

He says nothing. I look at Tampoline. The dice are tumbling. 'That's why we got to you. The guy searching the houses. Called off as he walked up the driveway. The idiot at the office reception. Martyn's old friend. He was meant to let us in. But outside. When we bundled you in the car. The guy that ran at me. Who dropped him? He had me dead to rights.'

Tampoline's face is so smug I want to boot his teeth down his throat. 'You didn't have to shoot yourself, Craig. I'd have got in the car if you'd asked.'

'No. You had to make it look real. I can figure the hospital now, the lack of police and the chances you had to run. You wanted this meet.'

'Sure. And if asked why I didn't run, well, I'm blind. How do I know what's going on around me?'

'That's bollocks.'

'But it helps. Add in that I wanted you to take me to the man behind my kidnapping. That I kept myself in the firing line to meet the mastermind. Think how that will play out in the media. I go from being a kidnap escapee to an All

American hero. After the TT I already piss gold. Now I'm shitting diamonds.'

'But you're not going to hand over your brother.'

Gaylord laughs. 'Of course not. After all, I'm a kidnap victim as well.'

I rub my face. 'And I'm in the frame for that.'

'Of course.'

'Clever. And Martyn?'

'Oh, he'll be a hero in an hour or so. Once the authorities turn up he'll be the one that rescues us.'

'And that will wipe out his part in the kidnap?'

'What part in the kidnapping? We had you marked from day 1 and placed Martyn with you. All part of the plan. He's been our inside man all along. After all, I knew I would need inside help to get out of this.'

Smart. Very smart. I'm to be left holding every baby in the room. 'And Mary-Anne?'

Gaylord looks at her. 'Her call. If she plays along she comes out as a victim and goes home. If she doesn't, well, I can't be held responsible for the fug of war.'

Mary-Anne picks up a handgun. 'And if this old lady doesn't play ball?'

I look at her. 'Put it down, Mary-Anne. This is your moment to do the sensible thing. I'm screwed, but you can get out of this.'

'And you go down.'

'Maybe.'

'There's no maybe about it, Mr McIntrye.' Gaylord is slurring. 'You go down.'

'And what if I don't go quietly?'

'Linda and Charlie.' Tampoline drops the words like depth charges.

'You're a bastard.'

The sirens are close.

'Technically incorrect, but it's all part of the game as a politician. Cover all the angles and then cover them again.'

'No choice?'

'None.'

'So we sit here until rescue arrives.'

'And the rest. We have to make it look real. A good few hours of negotiation. Wait for the media to arrive. Walk out in the full glare. Watch my ratings climb. Stage management is everything.'

I cross to the guns and pick one up. I place it against my thigh. 'Tampoline I'm holding a gun against my leg. You know what happens if I pull the trigger?'

'Sure. I might kill Gaylord. Gaylord might kill me. Maybe Denholm gets involved. Could be Martyn joins in. We all have history. But it isn't going to happen.'

I bury the gun a little deeper. 'Why not?'

'It just isn't.'

I hold the gun steady.

Tampoline leans back. 'Go ahead. Pull the trigger.'

Mary-Anne is standing next to me. 'What good will shooting yourself do?'

'It'll cause chaos.' Martyn speaks.

I look at him. 'I take it Tampoline told you about me?'

MELTDOWN

'No. He didn't have to. I've seen it first-hand. Twice. Once at my Ma's house and once outside the office.'

'Saw what?'

'That you can manipulate people. Drive them to do the unthinkable. Mine rage from within and watch them implode.'

'And you believe in that crap?'

'More than you know Craig.'

The sirens are multiple. It sounds like the second chopper has arrived. They are putting all their eggs in one basket assuming we are here.

'Well if you know what I do, then why won't I shoot?'

'As the guy said, go ahead. See what good it does.' Tampoline relaxes into the armchair.

This was my plan all along. To get Gaylord and Tampoline in a room. To let the beast out. I look up at the CCTV camera in the corner. Merrily recording away. The evidence that I did not harm them. That whatever went down was between them. But then what? I have no escape plan. I have one, maybe two dead bodies on my hand. If I'm lucky, both Gaylord and Tampoline are out of my life. But I still spend time behind bars. A lifetime. Mary-Anne was right. I should have never walked in the back door. This had gone tits up before then. I was never in control. I finger the trigger. Well if I'm going to go down, why not take a few with me. It won't change what's coming down the line.

'I expected more.' Tampoline was now ten out of ten for smugness. 'I mean the whole kidnap was amateur.

Without my help you would have been dead before you reached the building. And although I admire the ingenuity of the school fire, you have to question the efficacy of the whole thing.'

'Would you have done any better? Look at the oil story. That was a doozy.'

'It did its job. I needed you motivated and confused. The latter was easy. Even I know that a deal with Iran is not a deal breaker. And as to spiking the SPR, it would have been in the public domain in hours. I thought you might have realized that.'

'What would I know about the Strategic Petroleum Reserve?' My voice is high.

'What do you know about any of this? What do you know about your own life? You have a gift that could be turned to your advantage. There's money to be made. Good money.'

The noise of sirens has been added to. More cars. People. Probably. The rain is keeping the noises indistinct.

'I don't want *good money*. I want a life.'

Gaylord reaches for another bottle of red. 'Everybody wants money. It's what makes the world spin. I can think of no end of uses for your talent.'

'You wouldn't say that if it was hardwired into you.'

'Oh but I would. Think of all the time I could save. Eliminating competition. A gun for hire. I could be a wealthy and powerful man.'

'And a basket case. It's not a free ride. Every time it kicks in I'm left a shell and it's getting worse. It strips me bare. What's the good of causing chaos if you're still around when it calms down?'

Mary-Anne points to my gun. 'I have no idea what you're talking about, but can you please put the gun down?'

I'd forgotten I had it in my hand. The barrel is still pressed to my thigh. I pull it away. Then I put it back. 'Look, this is a no win for me. So if I fire a bullet and let the beast out, how am I worse off? Maybe one or both of you will die.'

'And you think I haven't got that ripple figured?' Tampoline stands. 'Do you think I let you loose with no backstop? Give me credit. Pull the trigger. It won't help. The guys outside will just ramp it all up. They still have to figure if we are in here. And when you do shoot yourself it'll just advertise we are here.'

'And? You know what goes down if I do.'

'I do, and we've had a year to work on it. You'd be amazed what we've discovered in the last year. You opened a whole new world to us.'

The phone rings. Tampoline puts his hand up. 'Leave it. It'll be them. Let them sweat a bit first. As I was saying, a whole new world. You were, no are, living proof that man can influence man with just the mind. Single handedly you prove that ESP, telekinesis, mind control – even mind reading - are all now possibilities.'

'Except I can't do any of that stuff.'

'But you don't need to. When Columbus stumbled on some islands he didn't need to see the rest of America to know it was there. You are the ground zero of a new breed of human.'

'Sure, a genetic freak.'

'No. A genetic experiment.'

'A what?'

'You think your little party trick is natural?'

'What else.'

'Martyn, do me a favour. Slug the old woman.'

I step between her and Martyn. 'Like hell he will.'

'Do I have to? It rips the crap out of me.' Martyn looks less than happy.

'Just show Craig here why his bullets are no threat. Just a small one. Nothing major. Just drop her for a few seconds.'

I push Mary-Anne back and level the gun at Martyn. 'No one else is going to hurt Mary-Anne while I'm here.'

'Martyn, do it.' Tampoline's voice is strong.

'I'm telling you Martyn, you're not getting near her. What in the hell will that prove, Tampoline? Mary-Anne is in her eighties. What would hitting her do for this conversation?'

Tampoline is agitated. 'Martyn, now! Or I'll see to it that your mother meets with a live wire.'

I take a bead on Martyn. 'Take one step and I will shoot.'

Martyn doesn't move. He simply closes his eyes. I feel woozy. As if I've been deep asleep and just woken. I stagger and there's a thump from behind me. I swing round to find Mary-Anne on the floor. Martyn drops to the ground with a sigh. I follow suit and check on Mary-Anne. Her eyes are closed. Her chest is moving. Tiny bird breaths. 'Mary-Anne?' She doesn't respond.

Tampoline laughs. I level the gun on him. 'Just in case you don't know, I now have the gun pointing at your head. So laugh away.'

Tampoline ignores me. 'Well done Martyn. How do you feel?'

'The usual.'

'It'll pass.'

'Clue me in Martyn.' I keep the gun on Tampoline. 'What's going on?'

Martyn's voice is shaky. 'You're not the only one with a party trick.'

'You did that to Mary-Anne? You knocked her out?'

'Yes.'

My face must be a picture.

'Well it seems that you're not quite as unique as you think.' Gaylord is on his feet. Unsteady. 'How?' The question is from me to Tampoline.

'A combination of natural talent and a deep brain implant in just the right place. All courtesy of Mr McIntyre.'

'Me?'

'You pointed the way. We just followed the path. You were our first success. Only we didn't know it at the time. The only one that worked.'

My head takes a spin. A solid 360. Someone moves the shining wooden floor beneath me. *First success.* The rhythm of the rain. The helicopter chopping the air. The building presence outside. All fade into background noise. A counterpoint to the rushing in my head. *First success.*

Iraq. Fresh out of the wrapper. No time to learn the ropes. You either got it or you got dead. A head shot. My helmet saving me. Then darkness. Only not quite. Hospital. White. Gowns. People moving in slow motion. Then back on the street. No return to home. Back in the dust. Patrols. Then more death. Three of us trapped. I wake to find the others dead. Shipped home. Broken. Hatch Roll. A place to recover. A place for nightmares. Visits from suits.

The sequence speeds through. Unconnected. Pulsing. Nothing new. Yet something scrapes at the corner. *First success.*

Mary-Anne is still down. Martyn is down and energy leaks from me. Questions bubble up. *First success.* Man-made? Not natural? Me?

Tampoline is still talking. 'Crude. Very crude. No implants. Just manipulation of brain matter. A hundred times it failed. Even you were a failure. Then you weren't.'

I lie against the tarp. Cool. Rough. Man-made? Natural? *First success.* I want to sleep. Ease away. Take the dark route. Let this all go away. I can't process the failure of the kidnap. I can't mix it with *first success.* I can't blend it with Martyn and what he's done to Mary-Anne. Any of the three would tax me. Tax anyone. Man-made. Martyn. Failure.

The phone rings again. Tampoline is talking. I can see his mouth moving. I can hear a buzz. Words, but my head is full. There's no space to take in anything else. The

gas tank is brimmed. My wires are shorting. Man-made –
am I? Martyn – is he? Kidnap – gone south?

I slide further. Prone. Legs pointing into the shop.
Head on the tarp. The phone rings. Another buzz to join
Tampoline's mouth. Gaylord. Fat Gaylord is watching me.
Small eyes. Small thoughts?

I look to the ceiling. Drift my eyes over the ocean of
white to the oar. Dark. Stained. A used item. The shaft
worn into grooves from hands. Callouses pulling at the
timber. Setting up a beat. One to match the rain. One to
counterpoint the helicopter. A solid thump as oar hits water.
A deep pull. Then release. Scythe through the air. Down.
Back in. Two men on an oar that big. Muscles pumping.
Blood flowing. Smooth. Drawing the boat through the
water. Thoughts never more than a stroke ahead. Lose
yourself in the tempo. Oar. Rain. Helicopter. Then man
made. Martyn. Failure. Mixed. A young DJ on the deck. A
three turntable job. Unusual. Hard to work. But it's his job
to keep people moving. Dancing to his tune. Difficult, but
not impossible.

I breathe. Three decks. Three problems. Make them
work for me. Work with them. Coalesce the beat. Bring it
together. I am what I am. Martyn is what he is. We are
where we are.

But what am I? Trash it. For later. And Martyn?
What is he? The same as me? Trash it. For later. The
kidnap. The main tune. The others are in the mix. I sit up.
Shake my head. Stand up. Shake my head.

Mary-Anne moans. Her eyes are open. I walk to Tampoline. Hitting a blind man isn't done. I still slug him so hard I think I've snapped a knuckle. He crashes onto the table. Gaylord, unsteady on his feet, gets the second punch. He goes down. Denholm moves and so do I.   Over the counter. I raise my hand and he cowers. I kick him to the floor. A solid foot in the stomach.

Chapter 43

Back to Mary-Anne and I help her up. I look at Martyn and he's back on his feet. Time to get my shit in order. 'Ok, we need to take control. For the moment let's use what we have and question it later.' Martyn, I need those two tied up and gagged. If they resist feel free to pull your trick.'

Martyn doesn't move. I walk over and stand next to him. I put out a hand. 'Look, do you really think that this ends well for you? They chased me across America. Killed my wife. They tried to kill me. They will do the same with you. Maybe not soon, but at some point. And don't bring your mother into this. Nothing you do will help her. When your time is up they will kill her as well. Let's see if we can sort out this shit first and worry about the other stuff later.'

'How do we get out of this?'

'As I said, use what we have. You and I are worth an army if we play it right. Gaylord was spot on. I shouldn't be running from this. I should be using it. Controlling it. Winning with it. And so should you.'

Martyn looks at Tampoline. He's trying to stand up. I tap Martyn on the shoulder. 'Martyn, you are either in or out. There's no halfway house. The two minute warning went one hundred and nineteen seconds ago. In or out. We need to act and I'll do it with or without you.'

Gaylord moans. 'McIntrye, you'll pay for that.'

GORDON BROWN

I stroll over and crack the top of his skull with a balled up fist. He falls back. 'Gaylord, I was going to pay regardless. Think on it. Whether you now live or die makes no difference to me. I'm a cruise missile locked onto one target. I don't need you or Tampoline. Either I get out of this or I don't. And by the way, thanks for the idea.'

'What idea?'

'Butch Cassidy and the Sundance Kid. I loved that film. Well, Martyn, in or out. Do obey your master or are you with me on the run again?'

'In.' Martyn lets a breath go as he speaks.

'Good man. Bag 'em and tag 'em. And Denholm as well.'

Denholm looks at his boss and back at me. He says nothing. Martyn vanishes and returns with a couple of rolls of duct tape. Ideal.

The phone rings. 'Mary-Anne, I want you to answer it.'

'And say what?' Her words are fuzzy.

'Tell them you are on your own. Sleeping. Then hang up.'

'What will that achieve?'

My head is clearing. The DJ ramping it up. Not top form yet. Maybe 100 BPM. At 140 the world will be dancing to my tune. Use what we have. 'They don't know who is in here. They are grasping at straws. A blind man and an old lady just outran them. They can't come storming in here. They don't know the situation. They should have sent someone on their own to buy a bottle of JD. Then strap on some listening equipment. But they've come mob handed. Desperate to save the man. Not thinking. This could be a busted flush.'

'The helicopter. Hasn't it got infra-red?'

'Probably, but I doubt it can see deep inside. Maybe it caught us at the door. So what? They need to know what's going down. The longer we keep them in the dark the longer we have to think.'

She picks up the pay phone.

'Yes? I was sleeping. What in the hell do you want? I'm not coming out. The shop's closed. Now fuck off.'

She slams the phone down.

'Good girl. That'll throw them.'

I help Martyn truss up the three Stooges. Backs against the chillers. All three are gagged with their hands and feet bound. The glow from the glass frames them. If anyone comes through the front door it's the first thing they'll see.

The rain finds a new, more insistent, pattern. I stay away from the tarp. I want to see the lie of the land but they'll have eyes on the door. Any movement will be noticed.

Mary-Anne sits in one of the armchairs. 'Ok, so what now?'

'We take a little breather. A little down-time.'

'And then?'

'We escape.'

I lift a pen and a piece of paper and write.

Chapter 44

Marry-Anne is still rubbing her head. 'Craig, what happened to me? One moment I'm standing next to you and the next I'm on the floor.'

I sit next to her. 'You're in the presence of a new generation of human beings.'

'Sorry?'

'Superheroes. Meet Rage Man and The Stunner.'

She looks at me with those gorgeous eyes. Blank, but gorgeous. I explain as best I can. Then turn to Martyn. 'And your story. You had me fooled.'

'I had no choice. They caught me trying to break into a secure facility four months ago. It was on Gaylord's instruction. After a week of endless questioning they had me sign a waiver. I had no idea what I was signing. Waterboarding will do that to you.

Then they run tests and more tests. Next thing I'm prepped for an operation. I wake up with a head bandage. Then I enter hell. They tell me that I can do things that I know that I can't. They run more tests. Then one day, I don't know how, one of the suits collapses in front of me. I feel like I've been hit by a truck. Everyone else seems pleased. A month later and I can do it at will. Each time it canes me. And if I do more than one at a time I'm a bigger mess.'

I shake my head. 'Then they set you free after letting me see you take a kicking. With instructions to stick to me. What were you supposed to do? Knock me out if things didn't go Tampoline's way.'

'Something like that. I was Tampoline's insurance policy.'

I look at the gagged senator. 'Clever man. You know what I can do so you fix me up with a safety switch. I go off on one and down I go. Martyn to the rescue. That also explains how we got away at the office. It was you', I flip back to Martyn, 'that knocked out the agency guy outside the office.' He nods.

'Well just look at the two of us. Genuine super powers. A bit ragged at the edges. Kind of fucks us over if we use them. But all the same I love the irony. Here we have the senator and his brother flipping on us. Teaming up in their moment of need. And now Martyn and I are doing the same. Only we are one scary duo. Think on the sheer mayhem we could cause together. Gaylord, you said this is the survival of the fittest. You said I'm not up there. You are so wrong. How dumb was your brother to put Martyn and me together.'

Tampoline is struggling at his bonds. I watch him wriggle. 'You think *I'm* stupid? Tampoline, did it never occur to you what might happen if Martyn and I got friendly? Where was your scenario planning? Surely this must have figured somewhere. But I guess not. You're an arrogant bastard. You in control. Us the puppets. It never crossed your mind to think one plus one might equal three.

You so want that presidential nomination. Look at what you have in front of you. McIntyre and Wheeler. The dynamic duo. Ok, a bit dysfunctional, but then again name me a superhero duo that aren't. So what did you do to me? Back in Iraq. In the hospital.'

I laugh. I'm expecting a gagged man to talk. 'Don't worry, I'm sure it was all ethical and above board. And are there others? Now that's a good question. What can they do? Interesting. What *are* we capable of when the leash is cut? And how do you control us? You can't threaten us all. That just doesn't wash. Are you sure you should have opened this door?'

The rain is easing. The helicopter is gone. Probably on the ground. The nonsense outside sounds like a party winding up. The phone rings. 'Leave it.' Mary-Anne withdraws her hand.

'So what's the next step?' Martyn is looking at the tarp.

'We need transport.'

'Well that should be easy. Plenty of patrol cars to choose from. Maybe we could ask for a helicopter.'

'I'm serious. Look, these things never work out because the people outside wear down the people inside. We can't allow that. So we take the initiative. What are the rules in your world when you knock someone out?'

'Not much. I need to see them. Be in close proximity.'

'How far?'

MELTDOWN

'In the tests they ran up to a few hundred yards. Beyond that, zip.'

'I need you to take someone out?'

'Who.'

'I'll tell you in a minute. Can you kill the chillers for a moment?'

'Sure.' He scuttles into the back shop. Seconds later the chillers die. We are in total darkness. I drop to my knees and crawl to the tarp. I can't see it. So I feel for it. When I reach it I work to the free edge. I pull back. Slowly. A few inches at a time. A crack appears and I place my eye to it. The scene outside is a melee. Cars are strewn across the road and the parking lot. Patrol, paramedic and plain cars in a random pattern. Guns are pointing in our direction. Lots of them.

I pull half an inch of tarp to one side. Next to the entrance to the lot there's a group of men. All are in slicks. The rain has eased but it's still falling freely. The focus is round a man in a heavy raincoat. The black tie suggests agency. He's pointing and gesticulating. Giving orders. I drop the tarp.

'Martyn, put the chillers on.' They fire back up. When Martyn returns I call him over. 'Ok. As we stand there's the parking lot entrance to our left. Maybe twenty yards away. A group of men are standing there. We need to be quick. I want you to pick out the guy in the black raincoat and drop him. I need him out for a bit. Can you do that?'

'Sure.'

'Mary-Anne, you're on chiller duty. When I shout, turn them off.'

'Where are the switches?'

'Martyn?'

'On the back wall next to the door. It's the top four switches.'

She vanishes.

'Now to make a call.'

I pick up the receiver. No dial tone. No surprise there. 'Hello.' There's a click. 'Hello? Who is that?' The voice sounds calm. A negotiator? A senior player?

'Who I am makes no odds. Here's how this works. I am giving you two minutes. One hundred a twenty seconds to roll a patrol car up to the front door. Drivers door in line with the front door. The driver exits. Engine running. We come out. We get in the car. We drive off. Any deviation and the Senator is dead meat.'

'How do we know you have the Senator?'

'The clock has started.'

'We need proof the Senator is ok.'

'I make it one hundred and ten seconds.'

'Put the Senator on and we can talk further.' Calm. Easy. To make me feel good?

'One hundred seconds.' I hang up. The phone rings back. I ignore it. 'Are you ready, Martyn?'

'As I can be.'

'Mary-Anne, are you ok back there?'

'Yes.' Her voice is faint.

The phone rings again. I pick it up. 'Yes.'

MELTDOWN

'We need to talk to the Senator.'

'One minute.' I hang up.

'I don't hear a car.' Martyn is lying next to the tarp.

The phone rings again.

'Of course not. They think my threat is empty. I can't kill the senator. That way the game is over. And the rest of us are dispensable. They think they are holding all the cards. Thirty seconds. Mary-Anne, kill the chillers.' They die. 'Martyn, get a bead on the main man. But move the tarp it slowly. They have it lit up like Times Square at New Year. Twenty seconds.'

The phone rings.

Martyn pulls the tarp back. Small movements. I see a stream of light. 'Can you see him? Ten seconds.'

Silence. Then 'Got him.'

'Five, four three, two...'

The phone rings.

'..one.'

Martyn slumps to the floor. The tarp slides back. 'Mary-Anne, put on the chillers.' Light returns. I rush over to Martyn. He's awake but looks stunned. 'How are you doing?'

'Same as usual. It knocks the stuffing out of you.'

'Anything I can do?'

'No. It'll pass.'

The phone rings. 'How long before you can go again?'

He sighs. 'Half an hour. Tops.'

I stand up and grab the phone. The voice on the other end starts. 'Look…'

I cut him off. 'Ok, so your main man is down. If the car isn't here in twenty minutes then we take down another.'

'We need to talk.'

'No we don't. Send the car. Your boy in the raincoat will be ok. The next one won't.' I hang up. 'I'm an idiot. I should have asked how long you need between hits before I phoned. They'll wonder why the rush and now why the gap. Anyway it's done. Martyn, you have twenty minutes. I reckon they're going to need another hit before they react.'

Outside there's the sound of commotion. What order had been established as they had settled their sights on the building had been disrupted by the dropping of the raincoat man. I'd loved to have seen what was going on. They'd find no bullet wounds. Then the confusion would set in. How had we done it? Of course Tampoline's agency may be out there, but I'm betting Martyn is a need-to-know secret.

I didn't think they would send the car. They will wait out the twenty. No raid though. It's too fluid. They have no intel on what is going on inside. I walk to the back. Mary Anne is standing next to the switches. A small window is the only other breach in the walls. The drapes are tight shut. I grab the corner and ease it back. An eye is sitting level with mine.

Shit.

Chapter 45

I drop the drape and sprint to the phone. 'Get the men at the back of the shop the fuck out of here now. Do I make myself clear? They vanish or we get serious.'

'Look, we need to talk.'

'Now! They leave right now or the Senator is going to have to do with one hand.' I hang up and run back to Mary-Anne. There's shuffling and then silence. I ease the drapes. Pitch black. Let's hope they have gone.

'Mary-Anne, come on through.'

'Craig, what are you doing?'

'The best I can.'

Back in the shop I check on Martyn. 'How are you doing mate?'

'Getting there. Can I have a beer?'

'Sure.' I take one from the six pack and crack it for him.'

'I have one on the counter.'

'This one is on me.'

'Do you think they'll send a car?'

'Not without some additional pressure.'

'And how do we do that?'

'We'll leave through the front door. We have fifteen minutes and then we are going for a walk. Time to get our guests up and about. I'm going to have some fun with the duct tape.'

GORDON BROWN

I cut the tape from their feet. Once I have all three on their feet I line them up and tape their hands together. A neat daisy chain. 'Ok team, here's the play. I open the door with the three of you wrapped round me. Facing out. We take it nice and easy and head for the nearest patrol car. After that you're free to go. Martyn, this is all about timing. Mary-Anne, you're the quarterback on this one.'

I push the three duct tape triplets to the chiller and check my watch. Twelve minutes. The phone rings. I pick it up. 'Twelve minutes. Car, or we are good to go again.' I hang up.

A bullhorn sounds. 'We do not want anyone to come to harm. This is Police Chief Frank Wayne. Please exit the building…'

I pick up the phone. 'Frank stops with the bullhorn or I start slicing and dicing. I mean right fucking now.' I hang up.

Frank stops speaking.

'Right, this is the gig. I use the three musketeers as cover to get a car. If I make it then I'm going to drive it into the door. The frame is wood. It should cave in easy enough. Then I'm going to stab myself. That way leads to hell. I need you both in the car. Then Martyn, drop as many people as you can. Pick on the ones that aren't occupied with killing each other. I'll get a few minutes in the blue world. Don't ask how it works. But I'll get some grace before I collapse. Mary-Anne, you're driving. We get one shot at this. Head north. Flat out.'

MELTDOWN

Martyn seems reluctant. 'Craig a lot of people could die out there.'

'No one is going to die. When you've lined up everyone to stun add me to the list. As soon as I'm down the nonsense will stop. It's all about timing. Me out with the three. Up to the car. In the car. Into the door. Stab myself. All of you in the car. Martyn drops me. I'm gone. Mary-Anne, you will be driving two dead weights. Are you in or out?'

'Do I have a choice?'

'Of course. Tell them I coerced you into coming. They don't want you. It's the senator and then Martyn and me.'

'And I walk?'

'No way of knowing. I've no right to ask. You've been nothing but an angel to me and now I bring this on you.'

She runs her hands across her face. When I was young I once asked if wrinkles hurt. I was told no. They were wrong.

'I'm in. Hey, even if I go to jail, at my age life could mean a week.'

'Mary-Anne, you'll be here well after I leave this world.'

'If your human shield doesn't work that could be in the next ten minutes.'

I smile. 'Martyn, are you up to this?'

'I need more time.'

'We don't have more time. We have...' I check my watch, 'six minutes. You only need to drop me.'

The phone rings. I lift it. 'Six minutes.'

'We need...' I cut the connection.

'What if the patrol car has no key?' Martyn is sitting up. It's something.

'I'm screwed. I don't have all the answers. You should know that by now. This is a one-time only sale. When it's gone it's gone.'

'We could try and bargain our way out.'

'Not going to happen. Even now they will be planning a hundred ways to get us out. We ARE America's most wanted. Five minutes.'

I walk up to my shield. 'I've got a gun with me. In my pocket. If any of you try and run I've nothing to lose by shooting you. They will drop me like a hot coal once they can. Play along and you all walk free. Do you understand?'

They all nod.

'Martyn, Mary-Anne, stay out of sight. Don't give the snipers a shot at you. Martyn, kill the chillers and come back.' He does so and we are back in black.

I grab the three. 'Are we all ready to go?'

My heartbeat is in the hundreds. The kernel is cooking. 'Shit, the knife. Martyn, there was one in the back room. On the wall.' He stumbles in the dark. The phone rings. I ignore it. I can't see it to pick it up anyway. We must be down to two minutes. Martyn is banging around in the dark. I hear him return and he bumps into me. 'Here' He hands me a fish gutter. I palm it. It's going into my bullet wound. I blank the thought. I try and avoid thinking about the pain.

'One minute.' I hustle the three to the door. They shuffle along. Gaylord is soaked in sweat. Denholm smells of sun struck aftershave and Tampoline is breathing heavily. I place them in front of me. I grab the tarp.

'Showtime everyone.'

Chapter 46

I know what Gaylord and Tampoline are thinking. I don't need super human powers. They know the plan. And it isn't the bullets they're worried about. No one is going to shoot while they're tied to me. It's after I let them go. Once I stick the knife in myself. Once I let the beast rip. They will be tied to each other. Nowhere to hide. The gags will stop them shouting, pleading for the police, agency, anyone to shoot me.

I can feel them shivering. I place the gun at Tampoline's hips. Pressure. 'I promise I will pull the trigger. Remember I have nothing to lose. So just play dumb.'

I reach up for the tarp. And pull. It falls to the floor. Light floods in. I'm dazzled. I reach for the door and push. I keep the three in front and force them through. I step out into the parking lot and pull them round me. It means Denholm has to walk backwards. I keep my head low. No headshot on display. All focus is on us. I scan for a car. The nearest is facing away from me. I need one facing this way. I will have seconds once I let everyone go. I need to be pointing at the door.

I crab walk forward. I keep the three bodies wrapped tight. The bullhorn cuts in. 'Stop there.' I keep the quartet on the move.

MELTDOWN

Man made. Martyn. Failure. Three decks. Tampoline. Butterworth. Denholm. Me the DJ. Me calling the tunes. Me the MC.

'If you don't stop we will shoot.'

No you won't. I know you won't and you know you won't. Lying doesn't help. Keep on moving. The rain is down to drizzle. Spotlights are lighting us like Springsteen on his last song. There's no talk. Except the bullhorn.

I spot a car. Ten paces. Tampoline stumbles and I catch him. I hear rifles cock and I duck. Tampoline regains his balance. 'Keep walking.' I hiss the words. I concentrate on the car. Nothing but the car. Not left. Not right. Just the car. Aim for the driver's door. A police officer is using the door as a shield.

At five paces he gets the gig. 'Move.' My words are loud. The bullhorn tries to convince me to stop. The officer looks for instructions. I show him the gun. He moves.

'You can't get away.' Bullhorn. Bullshit?

We'll see.

I round the door, guiding the three. A suit moves in and I fire the gun in the air. He freezes. I grab the door. I look in. Keys. I let go of the breath I didn't know I was holding. I force the three to my side. I'm vulnerable to a bullet through the window. I pull Gaylord to the ground. I keep him level with me. Any bullet hitting me will hit him. I slide into the seat. Check for park. Turn the key. Plant my foot. The car slams forward. The triplets fall to the ground. I aim for the door. I hope Martyn and Mary-Anne are clear.

The car hits the door square. The frame shatters and my world is glass and noise. The car screams into the shop. I stand on the brakes. The driver door is still part open. 'In the car. Right now.' I'm screaming. I throw myself into the passenger seat.

Mary-Anne climbs in the driver's door. Martyn in the back. 'Time for part two.' I don't hesitate. I don't think. I just plunge the knife into the bullet wound in my leg as the bullets start to fly.

I shriek. My head explodes. The kernel cracks. 'Mary–Anne, take over.' I slump into the well. Blood streams. 'Mary- Anne, drive.'

The car leaps backwards. The light returns. We're accelerating.

Martyn is shouting. 'When?'

'What's happening?'

'Looks like a frat party on steroids.'

'Then go for it. Don't forget me but make me last. Let Mary-Anne get clear before you do me.'

I vomit then my lights go out.

Chapter 47

There's no blue world when I come round. My leg is numb and I'm sitting in a pond of blood. The car is still moving. I look up. Mary-Anne is fixed on our future. I whisper. 'We need to dump the car. Too hot.'

She shakes her head. 'I know what I'm doing.'

There's no light outside. No street light. 'Where are we?'

'Clarence Fahnestock Memorial State Park. Middle of nowhere in the middle of somewhere.'

'Choppers?'

'Lost them.'

'These police cars have trackers.'

'Did.'

'It can't be that easy.'

'Who said it was? We've been on the go for four hours to travel forty miles.'

'Four hours? How did you get away?'

'I phoned a friend or two. Jimmy owns a garage. He's good. No tracker and a paint job. All in less than sixty minutes.'

'The tracker?'

'In a dump truck heading south. They'll have found it by now.'

'You're kidding?'

'No she isn't.' Martyn's voice comes from the back. 'Welcome back stranger.'

'You sound fresh.'

'All a front. But you should have seen our star here. I woke up in a garage with an old man running around like a whippet. All he kept saying was '*We need to do this now.*' Next thing he's under the hood and then he's at his bench and then out on the street. A perfect throw and a bunch of electrics lands in a moving truck.'

Mary-Anne laughs. 'Jim is older than I am but he can still move if he needs to.'

Martyn chips back in. 'Boy did he move. He masked every inch of the car like a dog with its tail on fire. Then I hear hissing. Then I can't breathe for the smell of paint. I swear he re-sprayed the entire car in under an hour.'

'All the time waiting for the police to break in.' Mary-Anne is still fixed on the dark ahead. 'The truck must have taken the interstate because Jim had us on our way before they could back track to his garage.'

'What will happen to him?'

'He had started masking and spraying another car. If they turn up he'll play dumb. There's nothing to connect him to us.'

I'm impressed as hell. 'And where are we again?

'Clarence Fahnestock Memorial State Park.'

'And where are we going?'

'I'm going to sleep once you're fit to drive. This car might be a different color but it's still a patrol car. One look inside will give it away. That's your problem. I've done my bit for the party.'

And some.

'Martyn, what did you see when we backed out of the shop?'

'Fun and games. Nothing clear. Just a lot of people dancing with their neighbors.'

'Tampoline?'

'He was trying to run away from Butterworth. Butterworth was trying to kick him or worse. Denholm was on the floor. All looked a bit of a mess. So what next?'

'Mary-Anne gets her sleep and then she goes home.'

The road swings sharply to the right. Mary-Anne gets some squeal from the tires. 'I just go home?'

'You just go home.'

'No repercussions?'

'No.'

'I don't think so.'

'I do. Look, Tampoline is likely to come out of this a hero. The man who survived a kidnapping. Assuming his brother didn't kill him. He will want to max on the publicity. How he survived brutal captors. Rescued his brother. The works. The last thing he wants is an eighty-four-year-old in the mix. Think of the questions that would raise. He will want you as a victim, not an accomplice. Another body he saved. You are gold dust from a PR point of view. The icing on the cake. I'd get a PR manager on the books if I were you. Get him to phone Tampoline. He'll be desperate to talk to you. And this could be worth a bit of cash.'

Mary-Anne gave me a look of disdain. 'I don't want money.'

'All the better. Do a few interviews and back to the house.'

She doesn't look convinced. Neither am I, but it sounds plausible.

'And us?' Martyn sounds like he expects an answer.

'We keep on the move. We stay below the radar. But we ring the changes. We have the upper hand in some ways. Look what we can do together.'

'Yeah. Cool. We're so good we needed an octogenarian to dig us out a hole.'

'True, but tell me how many people would have made it out of there?'

'Tampoline will come looking for us.'

'Maybe. '

The car falls quiet. We crack on through the dark and I expect a helicopter at any moment. But if Tampoline is on the ball there will be no chopper. No public hunt. He'll create a wild goose chase and then come after us in his own time.

'Mary-Anne, we need to ditch the car. But we need to ditch it good and proper. My DNA is all over the thing and your friend Jim will be in for a world of pain if they tie him to the re-spray.'

'We can torch it.'

'Harder than you think.'

MELTDOWN

Martyn coughs. 'Empty the fuel tank into something. A gas can. Bucket. Spread the gas on the back seat. Don't overdo it. Spread some on the front floors. Again, don't overdo it. Soak the trunk. Let it seep into the corners. Open the front windows. Open the barrier between the front seat and the back. Trail some gas between the back and the front. Ensure the car is in a place that can't be seen. Use hard ground. Ensure we have a path or road that we can use. We don't want to leave footprints. Save some gas. Light a roll of paper. Open the back door and throw it in. Stand well back. Let it burn out. Return and check. Repeat if necessary.'

Mary-Anne laughs. 'Done this before?'

'A few times.'

Chapter 48

The patrol car will be found in the morning. If we're lucky it'll be a few days. Without shoes the walk is tough, but Mary-Anne knows the area. 'I come here once in a while to free my head.'

She'll report to the nearest police station. We'll be long gone. Martyn needs to get us some cash. Then a change of clothes. Then we vanish.

Then some R and R.

I pull a pen from my pocket. I throw it in a nearby trash can. No-one is ever going to link the ink in the pen to the ink on the note I placed in Tampoline's pocket as we walked out.

'Dear Constantine

I hope this finds you well. To be honest, no I don't. Just being polite. I really hope that Gaylord kicked the living shit out of you. Or maybe you were the attacker and your brother the victim. Either way I don't care. What I do care about is my freedom, my health and the health of my friends.

I know you'd love to get your hands on us. Use us. But I know you don't want us in front of a court. We might not be credible witnesses but we could sling some dirt. We could dirty up your campaign. Not good news for a future president.

And, after all is said and done, the truth lies in our abilities and that's not something for the public domain. You wouldn't allow it. You can't allow it. I'm fairly sure that you'll do all you can to put the others off our scent. No doubt your goons will come after us. But you don't want the others to get us first. So I only need to worry about you.

Whatever it takes we'll be ghosts to everyone but you.

So let's make a deal. I'm not naïve enough to think that you'll stop looking for Martyn and me. I wouldn't expect anything less. So I'm going to take to the keyboard and write it all down. Everything we've been through. The whole nine yards. Then I'm going to upload it to the web. I know a great site that loves this stuff. And there it'll sit. Unpublished. In my account. Waiting. An insurance policy. In return I want you to leave Linda, Charlie, Martyn's mother and Mary-Anne alone.

It's that simple. I don't care how you spin the story. I don't care how you paint us. But I'll be watching. Finger on the publish button.

And if that doesn't work – well, maybe McIntyre and Wheeler will roll up at one of your future press events and… Well, just and.

Yours,
Craig.